THE

Bantams of Sheffield

BY

Guy Balguy

The Bantams of Sheffield

First published in 1891

This edition published 2016 by 1889 books

1889 books 2nd edition

www.1889books.co.uk

ISBN: 978-0-9935762-1-8

INTRODUCTION

The Bantams of Sheffield, published in 1891 is the second oldest novel set in Sheffield, so far as is known. It has some unique features which make it of interest to modern readers.

In his preface, Guy Balguy (real name George Henry Addy) talks of the compromises he had to weigh up when trying to write what is essentially a Victorian romantic novel about Sheffield, which he describes as a "busy, work-a-day town."

He is also mindful of not wanting to make over-use of dialect – an acknowledgment that its use is not quite the done thing – but despite that it is the modest use of Sheffield dialect that makes *The Bantams* unique. The first novel set in Sheffield, Charles Reade's *Put Yourself in his Place*, does include a smattering of dialect words, but for the most part all the characters use standard English – though there is perhaps a nod to northern English in some of the less standard speech patterns. Reade's knowledge of Sheffield probably arose from one visit and what he had read in the newspapers.

The author of *The Bantams*, however, was a Sheffielder. He appears to have composed the rather fancy pen name from names he liked. (One of his sons had Balguy as a middle name and he named his youngest son Guy.)

George Henry Addy was born in 1853 in Jordanthorpe Lane to parents James and Sarah. His father was a "coal master" and employed 36 men and 8 boys, presumably in a small private mine. George was one of 6 children. By the age of 18 he was a "steel merchants clerk." Then in his twenties appears to have moved south with his wife, Harriet: in 1891 he was working as a collier's agent/coal dealer in Hendon. By 1891 he was living in Cannon Place, Hampstead and was clearly quite well off. He died in 1919. His one other novel was *The Maids of Dulverton* (1889).

The Bantams was published at an interesting time – a very much "end of the millennium" era when people felt change was coming with the approach of the twentieth century. There was growing unease politically, and a shift in European balances of power, starting to be felt. The monarch was ageing. There was an inevitable social change in the air as pressure grew for universal suffrage and old ideas were being swept aside. In literature too, there was a new dawning with the likes of Hardy coming to the end of his reign as the last of the Victorian giants. There was a new vogue for science fiction and gothic works: Wells, Verne, Stoker, Marsh, Wilde, and even Conan Doyle. Writers such as Gissing, Zangwill, Morrison, Moore, the young Somerset Maugham and Pett Ridge were challenging the ideas that reality had to be given a sugar coating as they produced gritty stories depicting working class characters, warts and all. The English novel was in transition, almost as if not quite sure of itself, before a new confidence emerged with the likes of Bennett, Forster, Wolfe, Lawrence, Joyce etc.

In a way Balguy stuck to the conventions of the earlier romantic novel, but, even then, some late 19th century influence comes through.

Some readers will find his overly romantic style, at times, a little trying, but some of his prose is hard to fault: the last scene in Attercliffe and the pulling down of the blinds, the opening scene in Llandudno, or the description of Froggatt Edge, for example.

He uses lots of exclamation marks in his writing. Modern creative writing "experts" tell you not to use them – except very sparingly ("you must let the words speak for themselves") – but I found myself enjoying his free use of them: a novel not being rejected back then by sheer pedantry

Balguy has retained place names – refusing the urge to make his novel more "accessible" by not siting it in an unfashionable place, the stigma of which would potentially put off readers as much as the use of dialect. It is nice to read of someone catching a bus to Broomhill a hundred and twenty five years ago to go for a walk in the Botanical Gardens!

These sensitivities, over tying a work to town not graced by the literati, still exists today – the Metropolitan bias in novels is possibly stronger than ever; and anyone writing about anywhere in Northern England is automatically pigeon-holed and sub-categorised as a Northern writer: anyone ever heard of anyone being referred to as a Southern writer? Novelists are discouraged from use of dialect – the most you are supposed to do is hint at it, but heaven forefend that you actually *use* any real dialect (*"Ey up me duck, shall we take the whippet for a nice blow up on the moors."*)

Balguy's decisions not to compromise too much have to be applauded. Others have tried representing regional accents in novels with limited success. Old Etonian, Henry Green, was feted for his experimental style in representing working people and their speech – but can anyone argue that the effect was other than somewhat condescending? Why feel the need to represent the way people speak other than *how* they speak?

This was certainly how I felt when writing The Evergreen in red and white. How could I truly breathe life into my characters if I denied them their own voice? If I had dubbed them into standard English? In the end I toned it down an awful lot, but some people are still put off by it.

It wasn't really until Doherty, then Sillitoe, came along that northern characters were given a true voice.

It is not just Sheffield accents that feature in The Bantams. There is a fair smattering of Irish voices. This is as would be expected in Sheffield in the nineteenth century – there was a large Irish community in the town, as in many industrial towns, following mass migration from the island. There were parts of Sheffield where it was unusual to hear a Yorkshire accent until well into the twentieth century.

Balguy draws some of his minor characters wonderfully: the Stallybrasses, and Mrs Mottram for example – most Sheffielders will recognise them even today.

This may not be the greatest work of literature you'll ever read, but it is still very readable; and it is much better than many of examples of contemporary fiction that grace supermarket and bookshops shelves. Original copies are very rare. Just by making it available to readers again is, for me, job done – that satisfaction being the reward for the hours I have poured into digitising and formatting this work. If others get pleasure from it too, that will be vindication.

So let's celebrate this novel – the first one where a real attempt has been made to represent Sheffield people.

STEVEN KAY, 2016

THE
BANTAMS OF
SHEFFIELD

PREFACE

It were no easy matter to clothe the busy work-a-day town of
Sheffield in the lofty and idealistic garb of romance, while it
were an easy one to descend to a realism that might be painful
to the "gentle reader" whom it is hoped is yet to be found,
even in the very heart of Hallamshire.

The *via media* is the way whereon the writer of these few
pages has endeavoured to plod, not unmindful of the lofty
idealism of the chivalrous champion of romance who, in the
days gone by, did well to immortalise the valley of the Don;
and at the same time not unmindful of that realism of today,
whereby many writers make their characters stand out as
portrait's true to Nature in her kindlier moods.

The author has, as far as is possible, abstained from using
the wealth of the dialect of the town and its vicinage which he
loves so well, but has found it impossible to leave out the
manner of speech of some of the middle classes prevalent not
many years ago.

He would not have it thought, whatever may be herein
written to the contrary, that he, in writing these pages, wished
to slight the town that gives the title to his story.

GUY BALGUY

PART I

CHAPTER I

As Kenneth Millwood, getting quite away from the smoke of Sheffield, passed by the trellised gateway of the old weather-beaten cottage known as St Osyth's, he fondly gazed, as was his wont, towards the little window that was level with the grass plot, and as he did so he could feel his heart beat somewhat quicker, although he could see no one at the window; but he heard the rich, sweet, and melodious voice of the girl he longed to see. She was singing that simple and restful little song, "Children's Voices." He paused a little, looked about him shyly, and then walked homeward.

At dinner, as he sat between his mother and father, he was more than usually uncommunicative; indeed, he seemed to be altogether absent-minded, and ate his food in quite a mechanical manner. His mother could not but observe his mental abstraction, and to rouse him from his reverie asked, 'Busy to-night, dear?'

'No, thank you; I would rather not—I have got a headache.'

'Whatever are you dreaming about, boy? I simply asked if you would be busy to-night.'

'Beg pardon, mother dear; I thought you asked whether I was going to the Spelling Bee to-night.'

His mother and father exchanged glances. The latter helped himself to another glass of Madeira, and asked for another omelette, which he pronounced 'lovely,' and then observed to his wife—

'Kenneth's headaches coincide remarkably with our weekly gatherings at the chapel.'

Kenneth ventured no reply, although his mother's look towards him plainly said, ' 'Tis remarkable, dear, is it not?'

The conversation flagged. The Rev. Theodore Millwood helped himself to another glass of Madeira, and to another omelette—the last omelette!—which he called 'beautiful.' After a while the Rev. Theodore finished his dinner, and then produced a big golden toothpick from his waistcoat pocket, which he used in a manner the reverse of polite.

Suddenly turning towards Kenneth, he said—

'I am very pained to think, Kenneth, that you purposely absent yourself from all our gatherings. It seems to me that you are gradually 'drifting away' from the good old moorings. Yes, 'drifting away,' as the Bible says.'

Kenneth shrugged his shoulders somewhat and sighed, but ventured no reply.

'We pray for you, don't we, darling?' said the minister, casting a sanctimonious glance towards his wife, and putting the tips of his forefingers together —such sleek, sausage-like digits!— 'yet ofttimes we grieve,' continued he, 'to think that our prayers are unanswered as yet, and that a son of ours—'

'I am not *your* son, sir,' said Kenneth, as he got up from the table and strode out of the room, apparently with his "dandher up," as the Irish say.

He went straight to his bedroom, and threw himself on the bed, and then thoughts—such thoughts!—multitudinously crowded upon him, and buried him in their depths, while a scalding tear burned his face.

Immediately after Kenneth had left the dining-room Mr Millwood opened his big grey eyes a little wider, digged both his thumbs deep into the armholes of his waistcoat, and casting a wild questioning glance at Mrs Millwood, said—

'Matilda!'

'Theodore!' she replied, uplifting her head, and putting on an air of effrontery, as if her sincerity were being doubted.

'Have you ever breathed to him anything concerning his paternity?'

'Not a syllable, dear.'

'But he *knows*,' said Theodore, rolling his eyeballs in a sort of kaleidoscopic maze. Then his beetling eyebrows fell. Uneasy thoughts seemed to darken his face, while 'Confound the fellow!' was written on his every feature.

'Matilda,' said he again, with a stern and almost monosyllabic articulation, 'something must be done; our peace is at stake; the lad means mischief. Did you not see the contemptuous curl of his lip as he strode off? As I said before, he is 'drifting away.' But, my darling, who has told him this secret? You must question him, love. You must worm it out of him.'

'*Worm*, indeed!' said Mrs Millwood. 'Rubbish, Theodore, rubbish! Don't you think my boy will tell me when I ask him straightforwardly?'

'Of course,' said Theodore dubiously; 'but a little strategy sometimes —'

'Makes a muddle of it, dear,' she added good-naturedly. 'You men don't understand how these little matters are managed. Really now, Theodore, can't you see what's the matter with the boy?'

'For the life of me, no,' said Theodore.

'Were you never in love?' asked she, lowering her voice to a dovelike sweetness.

'Certainly,' said he, as though it were a highly disputable point. 'But what has this got to do with Kenneth, pray?'

'He, yes, *he*—is in love, dear.'

'Fiddlesticks!'

'Theodore! Do you doubt me?'

'N-n-n-o, dear,' said he, shaking his head, lifting up his hands, and opening out his fingers, as though he were wiping his hands of all knowledge of such a carnal matter as love. 'But of whom do you suspect the boy is enamoured?'

'Cathie,' she said, with a significant nod.

'What! the parlour-maid?'

Mrs Millwood again nodded knowingly, as she twirled her thumbs.

'Why, she's Irish!' said Theodore, with an incredible air. Another nod.

'A Catholic too. Good heavens!'

The oracle nodded.

'Rather a pretty little minx?'

One more nod, and a little pursing of the lips.

'A most awkward predicament, dear. How came you to know it?'

'Intuitively,' she replied, trying to assume the charming *naiveté* of a schoolgirl of sweet seventeen. 'Are you blind, Theodore? Have you not seen the sly glances, the blushes, the tell-tale eyes, the unmistakable pensiveness, the absent-mindedness, and, above all, that supine indifference to the most delicate cuisine —'

'Ah, that's a clencher!' interjaculated Theodore, 'that ever was placed before mortal man. Why, darling, the thing's as plain as a pikestaff. You're right, Matilda. We must get rid of Cathie,' said the minister.

Then, suddenly looking at the clock, he exclaimed — 'My dear, look at the time; we shall be late for the meeting.'

In less than two minutes they were off, arm in arm, towards the lecture-room.

Kenneth, upstairs, hearing them go, peeped through the Venetian blinds, and as he saw them going out of the garden, he soliloquised: '*She* loves me still, but as for *him*, never!' He shook his head and repeated, 'Never!'

'Whatever made her marry him passeth all understanding. Twice to soup—thrice to fish—thrice to lamb—three omelettes—ugh! Good heavens! he may well be so corpulent. No, he—never—married—for love! Love! wheugh! I know his secret now; but I am independent, and shall never need any of his gold—the vile trash.' Kenneth's thoughts suddenly veered round, and in a very short time he was faring St Osyth-wards. He left his headache behind him. His pulse beat quicker as he drew near that enchanted ground. Fondly he looked towards the beloved room. She was there, sitting at her davenport by the open window, and dressed in loose attire—some soft shade of silk. She looked like an Attic goddess uprisen from the past. Her wild dishevelled hair fell over and wellnigh hid from view the sweet, warm curve of her fair neck. Her right hand was supporting her head, while a quill pen was lovingly clasped 'twixt her long white fingers, and her arm rose bare from her long loose sleeve.

She saw him not. She was thinking, dreamily thinking, and gazing at nothing. What was she dreaming about? Ah! at that moment Kenneth would have given all he possessed to have known that her thoughts were as arrows winged with love, singing through immensity to find a hero worthy of her heroine's heart.

How he loved her! and yet they had never spoken to each other—never had whispered one little word together, nor touched each others' hands; but he had met her often in the pleasant by-ways of Ecclesall Woods, and their eyes had spoken. What a quenchless, fiery, flaming brand is youth's first love! How deeply hidden from all vulgar eyes! Only twenty-one, yet thus he went by, sighing and consuming away like a roaring furnace. Slowly he passed the hallowed spot; unheeded his longing, wistful gaze. Towards the loveliest and loneliest part of Ecclesall Wood he went, listlessly strolling about, till tired out, he laid him down amongst the bracken, near where the trailing brambles and the long, lank swordgrass commingle, and where the pensile birch was fitfully quivering in the sun's mellowing rays. There he lay flat on the bracken, supporting his head with his right hand, dreamily thinking, gazing at nothing too, unconsciously imitating his beloved nameless one.

The air was still, and the mellow light of the setting sun was enkindling as with shimmering gold each tender blade and airy spray. Alas! be it said, the splendour of departing day was unbeholden of him. But hark! he hears a rustling, a stirring amongst the grass, a footstep. She comes, she passes by, she sees him not. She stands motionless, wrapt, as it were, in deep poetic thought. Thud, thud, thud—how his heart beats! She glides along. She disappears amongst the silvery tangle of the birches. He buries his head in the bracken earthwards, and utters a sigh that surely is heard in the remotest Antipodes.

Poor Kenneth! He was hard hit. As he lifted up his head he could see her receding in the distance, thridding her way through the woody by-ways towards St Osyth's. He saw her fair form disappear over the brow of the hill, and then he got up and sauntered along the shady path. He lingered about the woods until dusk came on, and afterwards night; until one by one the starry sentinels began to peep from the deep silence of infinite space.

Then he turned homeward—not straight homeward. He must needs deviate a little—just to see if he could catch one more glimpse of her, or hear once more her entrancing voice. more her entrancing voice. So he passed along by the pathway whereon her airy feet had trod, and once more fondly gazed towards the windows of St Osyth's.

Yes, she had returned to her beloved alcove. How cosy the room looked! There was a rich harmony of colour about the blinds and the curtains. The lamp-shades cast a sweet mellow light through the open lattice; and indeed, to Kenneth's imagination, the room seemed to be quite lit and warm with love. What would he have given that minute to be inside! He paused a little, then stood listening on the path behind the brick wall, that was lichened and grey with age. There was nobody there. He felt like a guilty eavesdropper at the court of love, and yet he felt chained to the spot. How charming he thought was her voice! What a grand undertone of feeling in it!

What poetry! At that moment he did not hear footsteps behind him. Had he done so he would have moved on. As it was, a tall, lithe young fellow, dressed in flannels and with noiseless tennis shoes on, got close up to him unaware, and startled him considerably, especially when he turned round and saw Bryan Wolverton's face.

'Murther alive! you here?' exclaimed Bryan, putting on a little of his native Irish brogue.

Kenneth was confused and almost speechless, but muttered something about music having a strange "fascination by moonlight."

'What nonsense you talk, sowl,' said Bryan; 'it's not the moonlight lends fascination at all—divil a bit, Kenneth; 'tis a pretty girl that gives the fascination and the witchery; but come along with me, boy, and it's meself will show you the charmer,' continued he, as he proceeded to open the gate of St Osyth's, and seized Kenneth by the arm.

'Don't be an idiot, man,' said Kenneth, drawing back. 'I have no wish to make a fool of myself *there*. I am known in these parts, and moreover, a perfect lady lives in that cottage.'

'It's an obsthinate animal you are,' said Bryan, 'but if yer won't be led, it's coairce you I will.'

Kenneth began to move on homeward, but Bryan grasped hold of his arm.

'You hear that sweet girl singing?' says he.

'Yes.'

'She's my sister. She's living here with her aunt, and I've just come up from town to see her; and you're going in with me, or it's slauthered ye'll be in a minnit,' said he, literally dragging Kenneth through the gateway.

'Bryan, is that you?' said the voice of one, running down the garden path to greet him.

'Sure, it's meself, love, and it's an eavesdropper I've caught. Mr Kenneth Millwood — my sister Connie,' said Bryan, introducing them to each other, and still holding Kenneth by his arm, as the latter awkwardly and confusedly raised his hat, blushing to the very roots of his hair.

Bryan kissed Connie, while Kenneth stood amazed.

'Pardon my brother's want of ceremony, Mr Millwood, *please*. He has become quite a wild Irish-man since he has been home to Connemara,' said Miss Wolverton.

They went inside the house, through the old passage to the "beloved room," where Kenneth was introduced to Aunt Dorothy, with whom Connie was living. Kenneth stammered forth apologies about such a late and unceremonious visit.

'Pray don't apologise, Mr Millwood; I am delighted to see a friend of Bryan's. Besides, I think we have seen each other before.' Connie said this with a sweet air of unconcern, looking with her soft pitying eyes at poor Kenneth's deeply-blushing face.

'Yes, I live near here,' he said, 'and have often met you in the delightful woods hereabouts, and have often seen you as I pass this very window.'

'This is your nearest way from Ecclesall to town, maybe?' she asked, with a sweet Irish accent.

'Well—er—not exactly, but I prefer this way,' said he, looking painfully guilty.

'Exactly,' said Bryan, with a mischievous smile, as he seated himself at the piano and began to sing "Father O'Flynn."

After he had done "Father O'Flynn" ample justice, he turned round on the music-stool, and, facing Connie and Kenneth, began—

'It's nothing short of a miracle, Millwood, that I should have dropped upon you by chance, listening to Connie's singing. Why didn't you ever tell me you lived up here?'

'Well, because I don't want everyone in Sheffield to know my quiet sylvan retreat.'

'But why?'

'Because they would be dropping in to see me, and wouldn't find over-much hospitality at Patmos Lodge, where our people live.'

'What! are you ashamed of the old folk, eh?'

'Well, this is a painful subject,' said Kenneth, suddenly looking rather unhappy.

'Is it? I beg pardon, old man. Play the young man a tune, Connie; he's getting melancholic.'

She did not require any more asking. She immediately began to sing "Auld Marie," and sang it with such exquisite taste and pathos that at the end even Bryan shouted 'Bravo!' and Kenneth, in thanking her, spoke straight from his heart and said, 'I never heard anything half so sweet in my life, Miss Wolverton. The whole thing is a delightful poem.'

'You are right, Mr Millwood,' she said; 'the song creates such a pleasant crowd of thoughts—such a sweet melancholy. One can almost hear childhood and old age lisping the same sad song, as the withered leaves of perished hopes, are whirled away.'

'Connie! Connie, acushla! it's fairly bewildhered I'll be if you talk like that. But tell me, my jewil, how are you getting on with the novel you are writing?'

'I have lost the hero, and I am in a terrible fix,' she said. 'Murther! 'said Bryan, 'that's awkward, anyway. Have you looked in the Preface, or the Addenda, or the Advertisements?'

'He's not there,' she said, laughing. 'I've lost his ethereal essence, I mean. He has fallen earthward. He has told his future mother-in-law an abominable lie, and for the life of me I cannot see any possible or honourable way of retraction.'

'If that's all he's done, absolve him, love, absolve him. What do you say, Kenneth?'

'I should suggest a death-bed repentance,' said Kenneth.

'But that's out of the question, Mr Millwood; he is not *going* to die,' she said, with a sweet smile.

'Let him grant her an annuity, then; surely that would rehabilitate him in her good graces and in his former ethereal sphere,' said Bryan.

'The Three per Cents. go a long way,' added Kenneth dryly.

'Well, yes, perhaps you are right,' she said, 'although, mark me, this is not my ideal of what is right. It is but a poor makeshift, only worthy of this poor mundane travesty of ours; but to change the subject, do not you sing, Mr Millwood?'

'A little sometimes,' he said, 'but nothing new; only one or two old English songs, which I fear have a certain barrel-organ and metallic ring about them.'

'Sing us "Tommy mak room-for-yer-runcle," then,' said Bryan.

But Kenneth caught sight of a song that he knew, and asked Miss Wolverton to play the accompaniment. It was Ben Johnson's old song, "Drink to me only with thine eyes." He sang it with considerable tenderness of feeling, and was not a little flattered when Connie told him, with sweet frankness, that she was quite delighted with his singing.

They sang many more songs, and chatted about music generally, and then the conversation drifted on to painting, Connie showed her last attempt in water-colours. It was criticised rather severely by her brother Bryan, who was an artist by profession; but Kenneth pointed out beauties that were invisible but to the eyes of hope, and spoke highly of the exquisitely tender light she had produced by her delicate pencilling and subtle colouring. Connie was pleased to have one of her first attempts so lovingly criticised.

Kenneth had been so charmed and overcome by Miss Wolverton's conversation, singing, and playing, and indeed so delighted was he at this happy introduction to such a sweet girl, that he had forgotten how the time was passing. When he looked at his watch, and found that it was half-past eleven, he was horrified. He said he must be off, as he had no latch-key, and his people at home might possibly lock him out.

So, after thanking Miss Wolverton for the charming evening he had spent there, he set off homeward, but not before she had told him how glad she would be to see him again with Bryan. The latter, who was going in another direction, stayed a few minutes longer to arrange about a picnic to Wharncliffe Crags.

Kenneth's apprehensions as to his being locked out were not ill-founded, for, much to his disgust and annoyance, every light was out at Patmos Lodge, the house where his mother and Mr Millwood lived.

He rang the bell and knocked thrice, but no one came. He could hear no one stirring, so he turned round and left the house, and determined, if need be, to spend the night in Ecclesall Woods. Had he known that, after the third knock, Cathie stole quietly downstairs to let him in—against all orders, too—he would not have uttered a half-smothered malediction against all the indwellers of that house, save one, his mother, whom he pitied and loved from the bottom of his heart.

Mr and Mrs Millwood had heard Kenneth's knocking, and the former had steeled the latter's wavering heart—for, in truth, her heart was not encased in the lifeless ashes of the faith that he had long ago sacrificed on the altar of expediency. She still loved the boy, with all his faults, and was secretly glad when she heard some one go downstairs to let him in.

Theodore heard too. He peeped out of his bedroom door to see who had dared to disobey his mandate.

Alas he saw Cathie on the stairs. It was enough. As the huge man crawled into bed again, he said, 'Matilda, your intuition was right.'

'Why, dear?' she asked. 'Because *she* has dared to let him in.'

But they were wrong. Kenneth had strode off towards Nether Edge, an outlying suburb of Sheffield.

Their suspicions had no more foundation than 'the baseless fabric of a vision.'

CHAPTER II

That night Kenneth found rest, not in Ecclesall Wood, but in the rooms of the junior partner of the firm to which he had been apprenticed, and with which he was still supposed to be learning the business of a Sheffield manufacturer. Kenneth, finding himself locked out, made for the apartments of this junior partner, who rejoiced in the name of Dandelow Bantam, of the house of Bantam, Underwedge & Shout, Otterclough Forge, Sheffield. This gentleman had apartments at Nether Edge, hard by Bannercross, so Kenneth had not a long distance to walk from Patmos Lodge in the Abbeydale Road, where he had been locked out. Fortunately Mr Bantam was just going to rest, after returning from Mrs Humphrey Shout's party.

After Kenneth had gone to bed he found that he could not sleep at all till near day-dawn, so many thoughts took possession of his mind. The feeling of disgust at being locked out of home exercised him but a little, whereas the thought of having had such an unlooked-for introduction to Miss Wolverton thrilled him with an excitement sufficiently delightful to keep the drowsy wings of sleep at bay.

The Rev. Theodore and his spouse were likewise unable to slumber and snore as was their wont. The latter's heart was indeed more than touched by pity for Kenneth—a pity all the keener to bear because she had no one with whom to share it. The former, on the contrary, was never over-harassed by pity, therefore it was not this that kept him wakeful and restless in his bed; but what weighed upon him with so heavy a load was the thought that some one had told Kenneth of his right parentage, and that what he—the Rev. Theodore—had been so careful to conceal, should have been revealed to Kenneth from some unknown source.

The more he tried to unravel the mystery the more intricate became the tangled skein. As he tossed about on his bed, Matilda quietly asked—

'Restless, darling?'

'That omelette!' he replied in a husky voice between a guttural grunt and a groan.

'What, dear?'

'It's that omelette worries me, that's all,' said he.

'Nothing else, darling?' she asked, hoping that perhaps his conscience was smiting him also.

'Don't worry, Matilda, don't worry,' said he of the cloth, rolling nearly all the bedclothes round his unwieldy bulk, and leaving her but the fringe thereof.

After a short space the omelette or his conscience ceased to worry him, for a heavy snoring proclaimed that the Rev. Mr Millwood had entered the domain, and was denizen of, the land of Nod.

On the morrow following, Kenneth Millwood and Dandelow Bantam sat at breakfast in a cosy little room overlooking the stretch of fields towards Ecclesall. After a while the latter, who was a plain, middle-sized man, with sandy hair and a nose somewhat *retroussé*; and who, by-the-bye, had an undisguised preference for the good old Sheffield vernacular, observed—

'So you werr over at St Osyth's last night, eh, young man?'

'Yes,' replied Kenneth.

'An' what d'ye think of Connie?' asked Dandy, who was quietly eating a plateful of oatmeal porridge.

Kenneth put on a look of surprise and annoyance at the curt matter-of-fact way in which the name of that goddess of his imagination was mentioned.

'What! Do *you* know Miss Wolverton?' he asked.

'Of course I do. I kno' ivveribody in Sheffild; an' what's more, ivveribody kno's me. Why, we're related some'oworruther, I think; but she's no catch.'

'What do you mean?'

'Why, she's wuth nowt.'

'Beg pardon, I didn't quite catch the expression.'

'Wuth nowt,' I said, which is plainer Inglish nor sayin' she's afflicted with an unfortunate impecuniosity.'

'I understand,' said Kenneth. 'But you surely would not, in the case of a lady, measure worth merely by the monetary standard.'

'Why not? That's exactly what ivveribody else does—beggar or banker, saint or priest. I mean to marry for munny—there! I b'lieve in t' Poit Loriet, who sez, "Doant thou marry for munny, but goa wheer munny is." '

'But you surely wouldn't fall into a pit because most fools do. You will live to change your mind about this. Gold is not real wealth; it is but the token or counter thereof, and is no more real wealth than is a collier's cast-iron "motty." Yes, Dandy, you will change your mind some day, if I am not very much mistaken.'

'I never shall,' said Dandy; 'never! You see, I've been brought up "to horder, regulation pattern," as we say in Sheffild; and in matters of this sort my muther and father have been very careful over my eddication.'

'And what about your brothers and sisters?' asked Kenneth. 'Why, they're all cast i' t' same mould, but they haven't gotten t' straightforrardness to confess it, more's the pity.'

'May I ask how Miss Wolverton is related to your family?'

'Well, to be plane, I believe her great-grandmother was a Shout.'

'Beg pardon, I didn't quite catch the name,' said Kenneth. 'A Shout, I said; and the Shouts are related to the Underwedges, and the Underwedges to the Bantams, and if I'm not much mistaken, we s'll soon be a bit closer related, for Barbara Shout has accepted this child. She's my feeanzy,' as they calls it.' Dandelow said this with a broad grin, chuckling to himself the while, as though he was about to make the best

of the bargain. 'But,' he continued more meditatively, 'it's a
pity she isn't a bit younger, although that's better nor bein'
owre young and flighty, like Connie Wolverton.'

'What do you mean by flighty, Mr Bantam?' asked
Kenneth, feeling rather annoyed.

'Well, I'll tell yer. At the last Freemasons' ball —not that
I'm a Freemason, not I—no sich rubbidge for me—'

'No, but you accept their hospitality?' interrupted Kenneth.

'Yes, of course; just as you're acceptin' mine, and not agoin'
to pay for it. But as I was sayin', at the last Freemasons' ball
Connie was reckoned t' belle, although, mind yer, our lasses
had spent ten times more apiece on their get-up. 'Owever, she
was reckoned t' belle, and that's enough. Well, d'ye kno, she
danced a walse with me, and we danced it through. She
danced as light as a feather, and looked so nice and becomin'-
like, that, as we sat down together, I felt a bit gone, and I axed
her a plane question.'

'Yes, I understand—a plain question,' said Kenneth, rather
impatient with Dandy's prosiness.

'Certinly; I axed her 'ow she'd like to become Mrs
Dandelow Bantam.'

Kenneth burst into a loud laugh at this piece of
information.

'Whatyer laffin' at?' said Dandy, looking wild as an irate
bull.

'I think it was such an odd conceit on your part, Mr
Bantam; and the idea teems with such a delightful incongruity,
that I cannot but laugh.'

'Them as laffs last laffs best,' said Dandy, looking very
cross; 'but what d'ye think she did? Why, the hussy cracked
out laffin' like an 'iena—yes, yes, that's it—exactly as you're
doin' now; and then she, scuttled across the ballroom, and left
me gorpin alone like a bloomin' scarecrow. *A'! I waz mad!* But
I jumped up, and as ill-luck would have it, I tilted up agen a
chap as was handin' round a dish of iced goozeberry fool.

Well, some'oworruther, that iced goozeberry fool got into my neck'ole, and at that minnit the M. W. M. of all the stirrin's comes up to me and slaps me on the back, and sez to me, as if he had a plom in his mouth, "Well, Dandy, my booy, and how are you enjoying yourself?" "Middlin'," sez I, gaspin' for breath, and givin' him a masonic wink. *A'! I waz mad!* 'Owever, I soon made tracks 'ome, and the next time they catch Dandelow Bantam at a Freemasons' ball, they can hang him.'

'It certainly was a most unfortunate and unromantic piece of wooing,' said Kenneth, who was still shaking with laughter, much to Dandy's annoyance.

'Yes,' continued Dandy; 'and the next time I meets Miss 'igh and mighty in the street, she has the impidence to *move* to me.'

'To what?'

'*Move*, I said; dang it, can't you understand Inglish? She *bowed*, man—ducked 'er 'ead.'

'Certainly, I was forgetting —'

'And she crosses over the street by Cole's corner, tryin' to look angillic, but I gave her a cold stony glare, enough to freeze the noze off a brass monkey. Yes, I cut her dead, as if I'd niver clapt eyes on her afore.'

'And perhaps you are now glad that she gave no affirmative to your artless question?'

'Glad, man! glad? Glad isn't the word! Why, I orter be turnin' thanksgivin's out of me 'olesale this minnit.'

'Yes, you had a narrow escape,' observed Kenneth dryly.

'Rather!' said Dandy. 'Why, she hasn't a brass fardin'—and spends all her time in painting and poetry and sich rubbidge. But come along, we'd better be off to the works; it's half-past eight and I've got to get a big horder off for Rotterdam; and if I'm late old Shout'll be mixin' big D's with his bad grammar.'

So off they go towards Otterclough Forge, whilst Dandy chatters nineteen to the dozen, and Kenneth is thinking of Connie Wolverton, while the song "Drink to me only with thine eyes" seems to dither in his brain. On their way to the Forge, it is arranged between them to join at apartments, Kenneth having sworn that he would never be locked out of home twice, albeit his conscience pricked him not a little when he thought how his mother might be pained, but he, as a good son, resolved to write to her every week.

Otterclough Forge is situate on the banks of that one-time silver-footed river, the Don, wherein now no more the lusty trout, "staying his wavy body 'gainst the stream," keeps a sharp look-out in the gentle swirls that roll, eddying and glimmering as wine, into the deeper pools of the river. The trout has long since ceased to leap in the rippling waters. The mayfly no longer flutters thereon, and the otter is as extinct as the dodo. The water now crawls lazily along as though it had long been engulfed in Stygian depths, "of blackest midnight born." Imagination can but dimly conjure up the time when, in the delightful days of romance, a Locksley with his buckram band held sway hereabouts in the merry greenwoods; when a Gurth or a Wamba, or even a Rowena, found pleasaunce by the babbling stream. King Coal, in his kingdom of grim unloveliness, now reigns supreme, and—

> *Here the live gleam of the sun comes never,*
> *   Nor the splendour of night when bright stars burn,*
> *For the smoke from the stythies of Vulcan doth sever*
> *   The light from our eyesight wherever we turn;*
> *And Atlas and Cyclops are wild with endeavour*
> *   To worship King Coal as he shouts in his glee,*
> *Here's a health to King Soot and his kingdom for ever,*
> *   Here's a health to my fiddlers three.*

Otterclough Forge is no mousehole of a place, for the works cover twelve acres or more, whereon are two blast furnaces, an old converting furnace, and a score or so of puddling furnaces, with rolling-mills, steam-hammers, workshops, warehouses, and commodious offices.

It was said in Sheffield that they manufactured everything at Otterclough Forge, from a "graven imidge to a bastard file."

It was largely owing to the perseverance and foresight of the senior partner, Stanislaus Bantam, Esq., J.P., that the concern had grown to be such a big one. He was still the mainstay of the business, and he could have bought all the other partners out twice over had he wished to do so.

In appearance he was a rosy-cheeked, bright-eyed Ribstone pippin of a man, for a fresh rosiness still lingered about his complexion, which was further set off by white curly locks, and by a pair of well-trimmed mutton-chop whiskers as white as snow. His upper lip and chin were close shaven, and his mouth was decidedly a pleasing one. His eyes, though lacking the lustre of bygone days, were still softly clear and blue. His face was indeed chubby, yet very pleasant. His collars were of an inimitable pattern and size, and the old man's neckties were always made of the finest silk, and were loosely fastened in a big old-fashioned bow. He wore the finest black cloth and had only lately given up the old swallow-tailed cut. His appearance and style marked him out as being a man a cut above your Brummagem-brass-button-and-tin-trumpet-manufacturer.

Mrs Bantam had, unfortunately, not risen *pari passu* with her husband. She was his inferior in everything save loquacity. Here she had the best of it.

Mr Bantam had most unwisely let her have her own way with regard to the education of her somewhat numerous progeny, six sons and five daughters. Her ideas as to the mental and physical wants of her children did not extend beyond the Decalogue, the three R's, and "plenty o' pudden."

The sons had been educated at Mr Dandelow's Commercial Academy, and so delighted had Mrs Bantam been with the "suaviter-in-modo-et-fortiter-in-re" style of this learned pedagogue, that she had asked him to stand as godfather to her youngest son, whom she accordingly afflicted with the name of Dandelow.

The daughters were educated at Miss Sophia Larkin's Select Seminary. " 'Igh schools" were not invented then; more's the pity. Both boys and girls "favoured" their mother, *i.e.*, they bore a strong resemblance to her, and she was very plain. But the youngest daughter "took after" the father; and when seventeen years old she was one of the most promising young ladies in the whole of Hallamshire. Unfortunately for her, she had been afflicted with the name of Lobelia, her mother having "fancied" it in preference to Violet, as being prettier and more out of the common.

The boys, with their usual perversity, had long ago contracted the name of Lobelia into that most infelicitous abbreviate, "Lob."

Yet Lob Bantam was the favourite at the home of the Bantams, known as Sicklebrook Hail, and she was the favourite at school, albeit she was a source of terror to the stately Miss Sophia Larkin, as she was to the meek young curate who once a week taught the young ladies Divinity, and who invariably trembled ere he entered the class-room lest the sly, sweet, questioning glances from those eyes, which "blikkened" as the speedwell's, should cause him to forget both text and context, chapter and book. When Lobelia left school it was decided by the house of Bantam, in council assembled, that "Lob" was neither the pleasantest nor most euphonious diminutive of that somewhat infelicitous name of Lobelia. The boys (they were always called the boys by Mrs Bantam, regardless of age) unanimously voted for christening her "Belle." The girls, who were far-seeing enough to know that "Belle" might be taken in a comparative sense, raised strenuous objections; but "the boys" carried their point, and henceforth Lob Bantam became Belle Bantam; and, to the everlasting credit of the sons of the innumerable house of Bantam, be it said that whenever Belle Bantam's name was mentioned, nothing but love for her possessed them, a love which, strange to say, rose one peg higher than their love for "makin' munny," —not that they purblindly loved the counters of the game too much, for, as Mr Dandelow Bantam once pithily said, 'It's not the munny as gives joy, it's the scrattin' for it.' But we must go back to the forge.

Stanilaus Bantam, Esq., the senior partner and father of the firm, was seated at the head of a green baize-covered table in the little back room, known by the names of Council Chamber, Sweating Room, Inner Sanctuary, etc.

Captain Underwedge, of the Hallamshire Yeomanry, also a senior partner of the firm, sat on his right. He was a massive man, of an iron, Bismarckian visage, which was not much relieved by an eyeglass and a bristly moustache.

Mr Humphrey Shout, the third senior partner, sat on the left. He was a little, bloated, podgy Man with a harsh, rasping voice, and apparently an entire absence of neck. Belle Bantam, in her juvenile endeavour to be facetious, had once said that Mr Shout's crest was "a cheeky pig, animated or rampant on a field of lard, wherein cuffs and collars had surmounted corduroys."

The three senior partners were holding a private consultation together touching a matter which had mightily exercised the mind of Mr Shout.

He had clipped a paragraph out of the *Sheffield Daily Standard*, which stated, amongst other matters: "PATENTS— Letters of protection applied for by Mr Kenneth Millwood of Sheffield, for dephosphorisation of metal, and otherwise treating fluxed metal from blast furnaces." Mr Shout read this twice, the last time with a very loud angry voice, and then, throwing the paragraph down, he made the contemptuous ejaculation—

'Kenneth Millwood indeed!'

'What, our Kenneth?' asked Captain Underwedge.

Mr Shout gave a sapient nod, which caused his chins to shake.

'What's the joke?' said Mr Bantam, looking blandly and unconcernedly over his spectacles, first at one, then at the other.

'Joke, indeed!' exclaims Mr Shout. 'I call it no joke. Here's a young chap, just loosed from his indentures, experimentin' with our property, at our cost, under our very noses, and then applyin' for protection right over our 'eads. What do you think, Captain, eh?'

'Well, 'Umphery, my opinion is, that all such suspicious characters as this should be drummed out of our regiment, quick march.'

'And drummed into the enemy's,' observed Mr Bantam quietly.

'Drummed to the de—'

' 'Sh, 'sh, 'Umphrey, we mustn't be hard on him, said Mr Bantam. 'Now, how do you know that he has been experimenting at our expense?'

'Why, do you think he's got a blast-furnace in his bedroom?' said Mr Shout. 'Moreover, Mike Callaghan and Billy Benskin have been helping him in his experiments, and I've had 'em watched pretty closish.'

'Well,' said Mr Bantam, 'let's send for Kenneth to explain.'

'Let's pay him off, more likely,' said the gallant Captain.

'No, no, no,' said Bantam; 'I'd rather hear what he has to say. He's a pushin' smart lad; and I shouldn't wonder if he's got on the right track. He's as sharp as a razor, that he is. Why, do you know, when he went for his holiday this last summer, there was neither a Bantam, nor a Shout, nor a Hunderwedge could do his work; and one day we had to send for Billy Benskin, the ingine-tenter, to calculate the ingot weights for an order in millimetres from France. Why, bless yer, our lads have neither grit nor wits about 'em compared to him.'

Mr Shout and the Captain here exchanged sundry awkward and significant glances.

'But send for the lad,' continued Mr Bantam; 'that's the fairest way. I never convict on 'earsay hevidence.'

Accordingly Kenneth Millwood was sent for, and in the space of a few minutes he entered the private office, dressed in his overalls, which at the beginning of the week had been white, but now were black and grimy. In his left hand he held two short pieces of bar iron: one was bent, and showed a tough fibrous fracture; the other broken, showing a bright, brittle, and very close-grained fracture.

Taking off his cap, he salutes his masters politely with a "Good-morning, sirs," whilst his clear ear dark eyes lighten forth a kindly welcome from his handsome face—handsome, in spite of certain dirty smears on his close-shaven chin and his noble forehead.

'What about this paragraph in the paper, young man, eh?' asked Mr Shout, suppressing his emotion.

'Ay, lad, what about this grand invention of yours?' added the gallant Captain, putting on his eyeglass, and giving his fierce moustache an extra angry twirl.

Kenneth began fearlessly to explain the nature of his experiments, concluding his observations by saying—

'But here are the results of my work—these fractured bars. Please look at them, sirs,' said Kenneth, with a feeling of pride in his heart.

Mr Bantam wiped his spectacles with his red silk pocket-handkerchief, and then took up the bars separately and examined them carefully, with a benignant expression on his face.

'Never been puddled?' he asks, gazing kindly over his spectacles at Kenneth.

'No, sir,' said Kenneth, feeling quite excited at the notice taken by the senior partner.

Mr Bantam then handed the specimens to his partners, who examined the bars with an air of cold indifference, which made Kenneth feel very anxious as to what they would say.

'Has it cost you much to conduct your experiments?' asked Mr Shout, as he rubbed one of his chins, while a wicked twinkle shone in his eye as he caught that of the Captain.

'Yes, sir. I have been over two years studying metallurgy, and have made five experiments at the blast-furnaces here.'

'When?' sneered the Captain, readjusting his eye-glass.

'Always during the night-shifts,' said Kenneth.

'Pray, why during the night-shifts? Were you afraid of being found out?'

'No, not exactly, sir. My reason for working during the night-shifts was to avoid any interruption to the more pressing business of the day. Also I must confess that I did not wish anybody about the works to know the nature of my investigations.

'Do you attach any commercial value to what you have found out?' asked Mr Bantam.

'I do, sir,' said Kenneth, his eyes brightening up; 'if the process should develop, as I think it must, it will revolutionise the iron and steel trades.'

'Fiddlesticks!' said the Captain; 'how can it revolutionise a trade like ours?'

'Sir,' said Kenneth gravely, 'it is no secret that the drift of modern enquiry into this matter all tends in one direction. Even now, at Essen and at Middlesboro, similar investigations are being made, and success has been partially achieved; and it is generally acknowledged that complete success will revolutionise the trade.'

'Bah!' said the Captain, 'these would-be revolutions are but the whims of hare-brained 'prentice lads, who wish to become Bessemers in a jiffey.'

'That may be, sir,' said Kenneth, warming up; 'but Bessemer had to have a beginning, and then to fight against

tremendous odds. Why, it seems but yesterday when no
Bessemer-bloom was allowed to pass over *our* weighbridge
unless it was covered with tarpaulin and entered as "Hoop L"
or "Dannemora Billets."

Mr Shout looked very annoyed at this, and said, 'Sir, don't
you think it would have looked nicer on your part if you had
consulted us before gettin' this protection order in your own
name, as I think we are justly entitled to the benefits derivable
from your patent, especially as you used our whole plant and
machinery to further your ends? This we know for certain, for
your operations have been watched, sir. And if the invention
has any monetary value—which I very much question—ought
not we, Messrs Bantam, Underwedge & Shout, to be first
participants in that value, and ought not the patent rights to
have been applied for by us, who are the firm?'

'Certainly,' said Kenneth, 'I admit that you should have the
first benefits, if any should accrue from these experiments; but
with regard to the patent rights, I must confess that I was
then, and am now, very ambitious to have my name associated
with them.'

'Oh!' sneered the Captain, 'your name indeed! Ah! very
ambitious indeed! Pray, sir, may I ask at what price you would
sell these precious patent rights to your obedient, humble
servants, Messrs Bantam, Underwedge & Shout?'

'I would not sell them, sir,' said Kenneth, who felt put on
his mettle.

'Not at any price?' asked Mr Bantam.

'No, sir,' he replied clearly and without hesitation.

Hereupon the three senior partners cast knowing glances at
each other, and then Mr Bantam politely told Kenneth that he
might retire.

Afterwards they had a long and a warm discussion, Mr
Bantam taking up cudgels for Kenneth. The other two were
bitter in denouncing him as a traitor in their camp.

As Kenneth went back into the workshops his heart sank within him. He had gone into his masters' private office elated with the feelings of a boyish hope, for he had been asked to bring with him some specimens of his patent. He was proud of his invention, and had thought to receive his masters' congratulations and encouragement; but when he went back to his work, serious misgivings came over him. His honest pride was stung with the sneers of Captain Underwedge and Mr Shout; and the more he thought of their conduct, the more he felt the smart of their unkind criticisms and ungentlemanly behaviour. His ambitious dream of fame, and his still sweeter one of love, seemed suddenly to vanish and dark, ominous clouds lowered over his hopeful plans.

Kenneth was but twenty-one years old, and his kind open nature had not been hardened as yet by the unmannerly rebuffs of a world that sneers at and ridicules everything short of downright success. He felt that his hopes had received a terrible check, and unconsciously he began to entertain feelings of animosity against Captain Underwedge and Mr Shout, who had lately shown him such scant courtesy.

When he went home that night with Mr Dandelow Bantam he could do nothing but talk about their studied insults.

'You seem rather upset, old man,' ventured Dandy, after they had had tea together.

'Indeed I am,' said Kenneth. 'At this moment I honestly hate and detest such men as Underwedge and Shout, and were it not for you and your father, I would leave the Forge to-morrow.'

About a fortnight afterwards Kenneth, Mike, and Benskin arranged to conduct another experiment at the Forge during the night-shift.

'We had better do it in the mould-shop this time,' said Kenneth.

'Why?' asked Benskin. 'Because I have reason to believe our experiments have been watched by spies put on for the purpose,' said Kenneth.

'By the hole o' me coat!' exclaimed Mike, 'if I catches 'em morodin' an' spyin' about here, I'll let daylight into 'em pretty smart .'

'Why do you think we have been watched, sir?' asked Billy Benskin.

'From certain remarks made by Mr Shout and Captain Underwedge when they questioned me about my patent two weeks ago,' said Kenneth.

'That may account for their giving us notice to leave,' said Benskin, looking at Mike.

'Troth an' it may,' added Mike.

'I am exceedingly sorry for both of you, if such should be the case,' said Kenneth; 'but you may rely upon my doing the best I can for you if you really have to leave the Forge. I fear it is my fault; and indeed, now I think of it, you must be right in your conjecture, and I feel downright sorry for you. I am to blame and I ought to suffer, not you.'

'Divil a bit, Masther Kinnith. Faix, yer'd fairly bewildher us out of our sinses wid yer kind-heartidness; but let me catch sighth of the bhoys that come spyin' an' ferretin' out your saycret, an' I'll make scarecrows of them, widout benefit of clargy, that I will.

CHAPTER III

Everybody in Sheffield knows Diggles'. Not to know Diggles' discovers a sort of idle, unrevolving, vegetative mind, incurious or supine as to local institutions or traditions. To be explicit, Jerry Diggles is mine host of "The Stannidge Pole," a cosy little hostelry, situated not many miles from the parish church.

Jerry, or to be more polite, Jeremiah Diggles, was the landlord of this establishment, and had, so says local tradition, a world-wide reputation, not altogether for the excellence of his liquors, but chiefly from the fact that at one time he bad been the M. F. H. of the Wincobank Hunt. But Nimrod had had to forego the whip, the spurs, and the scarlet, because the doctors had long ago pronounced Jerry too gouty and rheumatiky to indulge in the fatigue and excitement of the chase. Indeed, he was forbidden to "join the glad throng that goes laughing along," and with pious tears he had handed over the whip to his son George, and had settled down at "The Stannidge Pole," where his cheery rubicund face did in some measure illumine the dull leaden pall which occasionally hangs over Sheffield, for his countenance was fresh and bright as the setting sun's that glints 'mong mellowing autumn leaves.

Now, although Jerry had long since ceased to tootle his horn irons Wincobank Wood to Langsett Moss, he was still thoroughly *au fait* with all the hunting gossip and sporting intelligence of the neighbourhood. His house was the favourite resort of Sheffield's good old-fashioned plutocrats, as it was of the country gentry round about Hallamshire, who often came to town on market-days, and who always put up at Diggles'. There was a very cosy little back parlour at The Stannidge Pole—a room set apart for the elite of old Jerry's patrons. Mr Shout and Captain Underwedge were numbered amongst these, while Mr Stanilaus Bantam had the post of honour reserved for him in the armchair covered with brown morocco leather by the fireplace. Mr Bantam did not however turn up on this Friday afternoon as was expected, and many were the enquiries made from Mr Shout and the Captain as to where "his lordship" was. Their inquiries were futile, as neither of the partners knew where their senior partner had gone.

They were sitting by themselves in a rather dark corner of the room, smoking their cigars, and drinking potash water slightly flavoured with a *soupcon* of the juniper-berry.

'He's evidently got the hump, 'Umphery, eh?' whispers the gallant Captain to the many-chinned one.

'Yes. Bantam can be a fool when he's a mind to,' added Shout, in a subdued, husky voice. 'But our policy is as plain as a pikestaff. Never 'eed him being "huffed" a bit. We've plenty of lads of our own to look after without lettin' a young hupstart like Kenneth Millwood into our business; and what's more, my lads simply hate him.'

'So do mine.'

'He's huppish enough in his waze, nobody more so, and yet he lowers and demeans himself by mixin' with swine like Billy Benskin, and Mike Callaghan, and every workman about the place. He's too thick with the common 'erd.' Thus spoke Mr 'Umphery Shout, while his appearance at that moment fully justified Belle Bantam's unclassic allusion to his family crest.

'Yes,' added the Captain, 'he's allus fraternizin' with the men, and some day I reck'n he'll be springin' a mine upon us.'

'Can't understand Bantam being wrapped up in him; but of course that young fool Dandelow's thick with ivveribody— Kenneth and him's lodgin' together up at Nether Edge, seemin'ly.'

'Ay, Dandy's a bit cracked,' ventured the Captain, who suddenly felt himself to be on delicate ground. 'You're right, Captain; and when he comes up to Cherry Tree a-coortin' our Barbara I kno' it. Really, I never clapt eyes on to such a sawney slormin' gommoch, but 'owever it isn't ivveribody as 'd tackle Barbara, so I says nowt. 'Owever, to go back to that young hupstart, we must get rid of him, *I* say.'

'Ay, that we must, 'Umphery; and don't yer think it would be as well to ferret out what this precious patent of his is?'

'Leave that to me, Captain. I'm on his track. 'Sh! I'm goin' to watch him myself to-night. He's goin' to experiment when they draw the furnace. Tim Sweeney and Jukes Clarkson secretly informed me so this morning, and I'm going alone, and haven't said nowt to nobody. What! eh? Will you come with me, d'ye say? All right, we'll go together. We'll spy 'em out. Waater! 'ere! Same as last, please.'

'But, 'Umphery, are you sure that the men'll be workin' to-night? There's some talk about a strike among our blast-furnace-men, don't yer kno'?'

'Strike be hanged!' exclaimed Mr Shout; 'our men isn't a-goin to strike. We've gotten too many non-unionists about our place.'

'Don't be so cocksure of that, 'Umphery. When the devil signs articles he's mighty cunnin', and some of these slow-seemin', oily-tongued chaps of ours may butter and lather us up with lies, and yet they're wakken enough to pay t' natty munny.'

'Well, I did 'earsay as "Mary Ann's"[1] been threatenin' Luke Stallybrass and his mates agen; but I'll lay long odds as "Mary Ann" nivver gets owt o' their brass. We *can* reck'n on them bein' trew to us.'

'Ay, lad; Luke's jannock[2], an' his mates too,' said the Captain. I wish we'd a few more like 'em. Let me see, isn't Mike Callaghan and Billy Benskin paid off to-morrow?'

'Ay, thank God; we can do without sich men; but, my hi! wasn't Mike vexed when I gev him t' sack, and told him that

---

[1] Mary Ann was the name used by "ratteners" – those using strong-arm tactics to enforce union membership.

[2] Decent, upright

he had better go and hoe taters, taters, thissles, an' ketlocks, an' sleep with his pigs in Ould Oireland.'

'Be careful, 'Umphery; them Irish have gotten something more than vinemous tongs. They can bite as well as bark. But how did Billy Benskin teck it?'

'Oh, he cut up a bit roughish at first; then he came back whining like an old hypocrite, but I told him to go an' meck experiments at breakin' stones for workus skilly.'[3]

' 'Umphery,' said Captain Underwedge, 'our Roberd tells me as Dandy says as Kenneth was in high dudgeon becos we snubbed him so in t' private office. The young conceited brat said he simply "hated and detested" uz.'

'Yes, we'll meck it 'ot for him, the varmint!' said Mr Shout; 'we'll meck it 'ot for him,' he repeated. 'I'll put our Tom on to his track; Tom hates him like poison.'

'So does our Roberd,' added the Captain.

Three hours after the above conversation they set off to the Forge, their heads between-whiles not having been made any clearer by the home-made Larranagas, the potash, or the flavouring. The latter did, if anything, loosen their tongues somewhat, and appeared to give them a delight in conversing, more and more in the good old Sheffield vernacular which may lack subtlety of refinement, but never the priceless millstone grit of originality.

Before leaving the hostelry they had taken the altogether unnecessary precaution of providing themselves with a flask of brandy, and had replenished their cigar-cases. Although it was in July, they argued that the night air was, or might be chilly, and that some creature comforts might therefore be desirable.

Arm in arm, they neared Otterclough Forge. It was a fine moonlit night, albeit Luna's chaste bare limbs were deflowered of their peerless splendour by the dim looming bastions of

---

[3] Workhouse gruel

smoke that shut out many a lone wanderer in the starry folds above.

They come to a private door to the works. Mr Shout opens it with his key. The door creaks on its hinges, but no one hears it, the few men who are working on the night-shift being a considerable distance off; and the noise of the blast-engine, and the sighing of the blast-furnace, were enough to drown all less sounds. Stealthily, and slowly, and unobservedly they make for the furnace, which had been blown out of blast for repairs. They can see well enough, for the ruddy glow from the mouth of the huge furnace in blast lights up nearly all the works, and the moon lends them her kindly beams. They reach the interior of the furnace, the sides of which were being re-coated with fire-bricks. A scaffolding with three landing-stages was erected in the middle of this furnace, and communication between the landings was made by means of ladders, which looked very dangerous to climb.

Mr Shout knew that from the top of this empty furnace he would be able to command an excellent view of what was going on in the other blast-furnace-shed below, so, as they slowly mount up the ladders, he observes in a whisper—

'By gum! my legs ache; but shan't we see all the stirrin's when we get to the top?'

'Ay, 'Umphery, ay; but O how my 'eart beats! I'm not used to this bloomin' hodman's job. Oh, 'ow I tremble! Oh, mercy!'

'Come along, Captain. Don't be skaddled, man—*you* as can sack a city, and trembles at mounting a lady's staircase. Here! have a drain of this. Why, man, we're at the top.'

'Thank Heaven for that!' gasps the Captain. 'But O 'Umphery, I'd give an 'undred pounds to be down agen!'

They sat down on a plank at the top of the furnace and recruited their strength by sundry applications to the flask, and then they lit up their cigars.

Mr Shout blackens his face, and insists upon the Captain doing the same, for he urges that they will be detected if they do not have them blackened— 'Because, when we peep over the parapet, the glare from the other furnace will shine on our white faces, and we shall be detected. Button yer coat up, man, an' pull yer billycock over yer face a bit more. We musn't be seen.'

After a little while Mr Shout peeps over the parapet of the furnace, and says—

'By jingo, Captain! they're beginnin' to draw her.'

'Are they?' says the gallant Captain, who was still dizzy, trembling with fear at the thought of having to descend those detestable ladders.

'She's tapped!' whispers the fearless Shout. 'The slag's flowin'! Quick! Come, Captain I don't be chickin-'earted, man.'

So the Captain gets up from the plank, and, shaking in every limb, draws near the parapet. From this coign of vantage they can see all the operations which are going on below.

'See, they're gettin' ready for work. Can you see them, Captain? What! no? Stick in yer eyeglass, man, and look; don't be afraid.'

' 'Umphery, I feel ill, so ill—so ill, so dizzy—oh, so dizzy! —an' I can feel my heart thumpin' like a tilt-'ammer. Oh, dear! I'll sit on this plank, by the side of you, while you takes observations.'

'All right, Captain. I'll report to yer what's going on in the field. Here, have another drop.'

Mr Shout every minute expected to see Kenneth, Benskin, and Mike come upon the scene, as he knew that they would experiment on the molten metal as it came direct from the furnace. He waited, and waited, and waited, and yet he could see nothing of them. He could only see a few men busy amongst the sand-moulds. These soon finished their work, and yet there was no sign of the experimenters. Mr Shout grew impatient, and said to the gallant Captain, who had been groaning all the time—

'Dang it all! there's neither a sign of Kenneth, Mike, or Benskin about the place, and the men have drawn the furnace for to-night. I wonder where they've hid themselves, the varmint!'

'Let's be off 'ome,' groans the Captain. 'Oh, deary me, I'd give a milliond pound to be out of this! O those horrid ladders! What a fool I was to risk my neck! 'Umphery,' says he, speaking in a tone of abject despair, 'lend me yer arm, my legs won't bear me.'

'Garrout, man,' says Shout; 'it's only nervousness and fright's taken hold of you. You're a nice man to be Captain of the Hallamshire Yeomanry! Why didn't yer bring yer governess with yer, man?'

After fearful trepidation on the part of the Captain, they begin to make the dangerous descent. Mr Shout wisely insists upon the Captain's going first. They reach the last landing in safety, but, much to their consternation, they find that the last and longest ladder has been removed. Captain Underwedge is in an awful fright. He almost staggers off the landing. 'What's to be done?' he groans.

'Why, there's no way left us but to climb up again and walk over the iron bridge to the other furnace, and then we can get down by the lift.'

'O murder' sighs the Captain; 'we shall be discovered by our men in this wretched plight, and with blackened faces too.'

'And tremblin' limbs,' added Shout, derisively.

However, there was no way out of it but by passing over to the other furnace, as Mr Shout suggested; so he, with due regard to his own safety, insists upon going up the ladders first, as he does not like the looks of the fearful Captain.

After they have once more made the perilous ascent Mr Shout becomes really alarmed at the Captain's nervous exhaustion, and insists upon his taking the last drop of brandy from the flask, and then he says to him—

'Come along, old man; now's the time. The men have just gone off for a snack and a drink. Let's cross over the bridge now, and we shall get down unobserved.'

'Give me your arm, then, 'Umphery,' moaned the Captain.

'All right; you can close your eyes if you feel giddy going over this beastly gangway,' says Mr Shout, looking contempt at his big, quivering, cowardly partner. They pull their soft felt hats closer over their eyes. Slowly they cross over the narrow iron bridge. They get nearer and nearer to the mouth of the fiery furnace. They feel the terrific heat as they approach the roaring cupola. The whitish-blue glare of the flames casts an unearthly light on the Captain's blackened face. Tremblingly he staggers along, clutching hold of poor Shout's arm like grim death.

One of the charging-doors of the furnace has been left open. They rush past it to avoid the scorching heat. As they hurry past the blinding glare of the flames, three men stealthily step out of a sort of recess in the outer wall of the furnace, and spring at the partners with terrific force, knocking them both against the iron door of the furnace. The Captain is stunned, and falls; but Mr Shout strikes boldly out against one of his assailants, and succeeds in felling him to the ground, where he almost rolls over into the furnace. Then there was a terrible struggle for a few seconds, and one of Mr Shout's assailants strikes him with a gavlock or small crowbar, so that he falls back into the arms of the Captain, who, having partly recovered from the blow he had had, was just getting up to defend his partner.

They both stagger and reel towards the brink of the furnace, and at that moment the man with the gavlock strikes again with all his might, and the two partners topple over into the white licking tongues of fire. A guttural groan—a whistling —a murderous, suffocating gasp—a crackling. All is still, save the sighing of the blast. The iron door clangs to. All is over! The fierce, curling flames roll up heavenward from the mouth of the furnace as before. The moon goes sailing on her way. The stars look down kindly as ever. Before long about five tons of hard coke are shot into that furnace, and the hot blast is again put on with more force than ever.

'They'll tell no tales, eh?' says one.

'Divil a bit,' says another. 'Serve 'em right.'

'It's queer pig metal we'll get to-morrer, mate.'

'Ay. Blisther steel, mebbe.'

'This 'ere gavlock's reekin' wi' blood; what s'll I do with it?'

'Chuck it afther the murtherin' bla'gards, av coorse. Divil a trace will there be then.'

The two mates then assisted their young wounded comrade down the lift, and shortly afterwards left the works.

CHAPTER IV

About six o'clock of the same morning Mr Dandelow Bantam was surprised to hear an unusual sound of voices outside his bedroom door. He jumped out of bed in a hurry, and asked—

'What the dickens is up?'

'It's Misther Kinnith, sorr, fairly onsensible. He's been murthered with the fire, an' a therrible wound on his head, sorr.'

'What's he been doin'?' asked Dandy. 'He's been experimentin', sorr; an' as he was a-pourin' out the iron like hot thracle, ivvery screed o' clothes on him seemed to catch fire at wanst, and all in a jiffey he was inveloped in flames, and he rushed madly for the door, but he fell with his head against an iron mould, and then we rowled him in the sand-pit, and put out the flames.'

'Put him to bed,' said Dandy, 'and fetch Dr Redmires at once. Bless me soul! the man's nearly dead—and covered with blood too. Kenneth, speak to me. It's Dandy.'

But Kenneth only groaned as they laid him on the bed.

Billy Benskin was not long in fetching the doctor.

When he came he made a thorough examination of Kenneth, and found that his injuries were very serious. He advised that a trained nurse should be sent for at once, and this was accordingly done.

After a while Kenneth was swathed in cotton-wool, and when the burns and the wound had been properly treated, he began to recover consciousness; and during the whole of that day he seemed to be making satisfactory progress, but towards night the nurse took his temperature, and found that it was very high, and that he had become quite feverish, whereupon the doctor was again hurriedly sent for.

When he arrived he found Kenneth was raving about Captain Underwedge and Mr Shout, and frequently spoke of Connie Wolverton, but his words were too inchoate to be intelligible. Dr Redmires gave him a sleeping draught, which he swallowed, as he muttered something about 'that detestable villain Shout.'

Afterwards, as Mr Dandelow Bantam was sitting by Kenneth's bedside, he seemed to recognise in him a familiar historical personage, for he addressed him as "Pontius Pilate."

Then he raved about his patent, and said that his head was in a flux, and that the molten metal must be poured down Captain Underwedge's throat. But in the course of half an hour or so he fell into a doze and was quiet.

When Mrs Millwood was told about the serious accident to her son her maternal instinct rose above the dead level of the lifeless muffin-and-crumpet faith so long inculcated by her husband. All at once she awoke from the delightful yet dangerous nepenthe of her deep religious drowse, and became a living stone incorporate with that living temple founded long ago by the despised, religion-rejected Nazarene. She set off to see her boy, in spite of her husband's warning that she might get wet feet as it rained so.

The Rev. Theodore would not go and see Kenneth —'No, not he.' He consoled himself with those words, so comforting to one who has a backsliding son or brother, 'Ephraim hath taken to his idols; let him alone.' Besides, had he not deserved what he had gotten? Why, had not he as good as confessed to Mr Stanislaus Bantam that he was consumed with inordinate ambition about that patent?

And yet, forsooth, the minister had certain qualms of conscience, but oh! how easy it is to soothe these when one has but the dead sea wind of a moribund faith to waft him a breeze.

In the course of the next few days Kenneth's condition was one that gave rise alternately to hope and fear. As might have been expected, there were many callers came daily to inquire after him. Conspicuous amongst these were Miss Connie Wolverton and Miss Belle Bantam.

The latter, who had often met Kenneth at Sicklebrook Hall and elsewhere, was secretly in love with him; whilst the former had seen enough of Kenneth to make her think that he was desperately in love with her.

Be it known, of course, that each wished the other to clearly understand that the object of her visit was merely philanthropic, while each secretly wished that the other's range of philanthropy might be a little more extended, albeit that was a matter which a common courtesy forbade either to mention.

About a month after the accident, these two ladies meet each other by chance at Mrs Stumperlowe's, a well-known confectioner's shop situate in the High Street, not far from where that somewhat unpretentious thoroughfare abuts upon Fargate.

'And have you heard how poor Mr Kenneth Millwood is getting on?' asks Miss Belle Bantam.

'Yes,' replied Connie; 'I met the doctor this morning, and he told me that he had ordered him to the seaside for a month.'

'How glad I am!' exclaimed Belle; 'I have felt so concerned about the poor fellow. Really I could have cried when I heard of his sufferings.

'So could I,' added Connie.

Truth was, they had both been guilty of shedding a few hallowed tears in the quiet of their respective bedrooms, for had they not once heard that poor Kenneth was dying?

'And his father has not been to see him yet. Isn't it uncharitable?' said Belle.

'It is wicked, dear, positively wicked,' added Connie. 'They say he is leaving Sheffield as he cannot agree with all the deacons of his chapel.'

'I should hardly imagine that his congregation will be moved to tears at his departure.'

'Indeed, no,' whispered Belle Bantam rather slyly, 'yet possibly there may be a few tears of pious joy.'

At that moment Mrs Shout and Mrs Underwedge appeared of the door of the shop. They were well known at Stumperlowe's. They were good customers, and therefore fit objects for Mrs Stumperlowe's sympathy.

As they entered the shop there was a subdued hush. Mrs Stumperlowe attended to them herself, while her many patrons and patronesses began to converse in low whispers anent a subject which was the then all-absorbing topic of the day in Sheffield—the great Attercliffe mystery. All sorts of conjectures were rife as to what had become of Captain Underwedge and Mr Shout, but it was generally agreed upon that there had been foul play. They were both well-to-do men of business. It was known that neither of them had much cash on his person, and therefore neither could have gone away very far. Day by day more credence was given to the theory that they had mysteriously disappeared from the neighbourhood of Otterclough Forge.

Both of them had been seen walking towards the Forge in the Attercliffe Road, late on the Friday evening when they had disappeared. They were smoking cigars, and as the man who saw them naively put it, 'he thowt they wor both a bit freshish,' which, it was understood, meant that they were not actually making indentures on the pavement with their legs, but that they were each of them rendering the other a little more support than was customary on a Friday.

This man's account was corroborated by Mr Jeremiah Diggles himself, who, although he averred that they were not even "mellow," said he distinctly saw them off his premises, and that they set off towards Attercliffe, 'walking, too,' much to his surprise, as they 'allus took a fower-wheeler when they left so late at night.'

Diligent but unavailing search was made all over the works, and indeed all round about the neighbourhood of the Forge.

The river and the engine-dams were dragged. The surface of the immense heaps of slag or ganister and ashes were thoroughly overhauled. Even the large cisterns, the boilers, and the hardening-troughs were carefully examined. The idea of their having fallen into the blast-furnace was scouted, because it was well known that the Captain never dared to go up on the lift, and it was not likely he would go up by the empty cupola under repairs.

The investigations made by the police led to no clue as to the missing partners' whereabouts. The "Force" was more than usually reticent, which made certain wiseacres nod their heads and say, 'There's summat i' t' wind yet.' The police simply gave it as their opinion that the partners went to the Forge on that Friday night, and that they never returned.

Later on it leaked out that Mr Shout had had Mr Millwood, old Mike, and Billy Benskin watched whilst at their experiments, and that he had said he would stop their "precious experimentin' with other folks' property."

Also one of the regular visitors at The Stannidge Pole, who was one of those admitted to the little back parlour where the elite congregate, said he observed the partners on that Friday night, and that they were conversing by themselves in a low tone, and that he overheard one of them say something about 'getting rid of an upstart,' and 'ferreting' out some secret.

It was also known that Mr Shout had, on that same Friday, sent a note up to his wife at Cherry Tree, telling her not to wait up for him, as he had to see some experiments at the Forge.

The Captain's gold-headed Malacca cane had been found near the private entrance to the Works. This was considered to be a very important piece of evidence.

Of course the names of all the workmen at the Forge who were working on that Friday night were taken from the timekeeper's book.

Mike Callaghan's, Benskin's, and Kenneth's were duly entered in the book as having arrived at different times, but there was no entry as to the time of their leaving the works, as they said that they had left together in a trap, which they had got to convey Kenneth home, and the timekeeper omitted to enter their names, saying that he let them out of the gates in a great hurry, as he understood it was a hospital case.

Mrs Shout and Mrs Underwedge 'had their suspicions,' and be it here said these were not very favourable towards Kenneth and his co-experimenters. Neither of these ladies kept their suspicions to themselves. In a short time their sons and daughters, and even some of Mrs Bantam's sons and daughters, began to share certain suspicions in common with the missing partners' wives. However, Mr Stanilaus Bantam and his son Dandelow (and Miss Belle Bantam of course) waxed vehement in repelling men any such idle 'tittle-tattle,' which was directed against men concerning whom nothing could be proven.

When a certain young, admirer of Miss Belle Bantam (one Thomas Shout, to wit) had, at an unlucky moment, suggested to that lady that 'things looked rather ugly against Kenneth,' she transfixed him with keen, angry eyes, and said with withering scorn—

'Trifles light as air
Are to the jealous confirmation strong
As proofs of Holy Writ!'

Thomas was staggered. He collapsed. The keen shafts of her sarcasm he could withstand, but not when linked to the imperishable bolts of that arch-thunderer of Avon.

As he went home that night he muttered something about 'the tomfoolery which boardin'-schools taught now-a-days.' Tom was downright sorry that she had not been brought up in the good old-fashioned ruts of ignorance.

Suspicion began to fasten upon Mike Callaghan. Unlike Billy Benskin, he could not control his temper. When he was interviewed in his house, in a court off Peacroft, by a certain Mr Donkin, a Sheffield detective in plain clothes, who was doing his best to clear up the "Great Attercliffe Mystery," Mike made certain answers which did not tend to allay suspicion against him, nor yet against Kenneth Millwood, for the Irish-man admitted that Kenneth had secretly sent him a sovereign for his children.

'It's my belief,' said Donkin, fishing, 'that Mr Shout and Mr Underwedge were thrown into the calcining kiln.'

'Serve the bla'guards right,' said Mike sullenly.

'You surely did not wish them harm?' said Mr Donkin.

'Why not? 'said Mike; 'they tuk the bread out o' my mouth, an' left me an' me childer to starve. Look at these poor little innocents—we'd tather-peelin's for breakfast, tather-broth for dinner, and tather-peelin's for supper. Marciful Hiv'n! it's clammin' wud hungre they are this minnit; an' faix the likes o' you expects me to pithy the man that towld me wud a murtherin' grin to go and hoe thistles, and ketlocks, and shleep wud the pigs.'

'Then didn't you see either of the partners that night?' asked Donkin, wishing to "fix" the Irishman.

'Hould hard, young man!' said Mike, smelling a rat. 'You be off, and min' yer own bisniss. Troth! it's confess to his Riverence I will, and not to a dhirty Saxon bla'guard like you.'

CHAPTER V

After Kenneth Millwood had sufficiently recovered from the effects of the wound and the burns which he had received, he was ordered by Dr Redmires to go to Filey Bay to recruit his strength.

When he first arrived there he looked very weak and pale, and at nights was a martyr to insomnia, which prevented him regaining his strength. He could hardly walk up and down the steep pathways on the cliffs; but after he had been there ten days, he rapidly began to recover his strength, and in fifteen days after his arrival he set off to walk over the sands to Speeton Cliffs.

It was a lovely day. The wind was blowing off the sea, whose long, white waves up-curled and then unrolled on the soft silken sands. The air was keen and crisp, and full charged with spray, which at times showed rainbow colours as the sun shone through it.

As Kenneth sat down to rest himself on the sand of a little rock-bound cove beneath the sheer beetling cliffs, his thoughts took quite a poetic flight. This was perhaps owing to a certain pleasing melancholy frame of mind, which was brought about by a sense of solitude and the grandeur of the scene before him; or it may have been in some measure owing to the natural inclination of his mind to the painful events of the last few months that gave birth to a poetic impulse within him. Also the glorious sheen of the ocean, that rolled so wildly and rapturously free at his feet, may have helped to fire his imagination to give shape to the following lyric, which he wrote as his Muse inspired:

DRIFTING AWAY
Where the sun-bright locks of the sea
Upcurl in the teeth of the wind,

And the spray and the foambells flee,
As the flight of a day that is kind.
Oh, there it were sweet to be dreaming
Of the daffodil days of my youth,
When my heart was fulfilled of the gleaming
Of the rainbow blushes of truth.

Where the sea's wide Appian ways
Are paved with the fire of the sun,
And uplift in the curl of her bays,
Sound the songs of her tides as they run.
Oh, there it were sweet to be anchored
Steadfast to the hopes that were dear
Ere faith waxed hollow and cankered,
Ere love waxed wan with fear.

Oh, were it not sweet to be holden
Of the dreams that once held me in thrall,
When I shaped for the gates that were golden
Nor trembled at death's footfall.
But now all the hopes that I cherished
Seem lost in the tears of regret,
For the days that are wasted and perished;
And my soul is unanchored as yet.

And seaward my dim eyes ope,
While the light in the lift grows drear,
And behind me the wings are of hope,
Ringed round by rocks that are sheer.
Lo, the landmarks of love seem shifting,
As the tide of my being doth set
To the bars where my soul is a-drifting
To leeward,—unanchored as yet.

There was a decided pessimistic tinge about what he had written, and when later on, in his rooms, he rewrote and furbished up the lines, he thought, 'Surely my Pegasus is a wayward steed; she has led me a sorry dance! Of a truth, one might think I was a very wicked ancient mariner, adrift and chartless on life's sea, and perhaps guilty of eating "the crew of the captain's gig." I will send a copy to my mother. What will the Rev. Theodore think of it? I will also show the sketch to Miss Wolverton, when she comes here with her brother Bryan to-morrow. Perhaps she may incorporate it amongst her anthology, or maybe it will provoke her to write me a sonnet on the "Desirability of an Early Repentance." O would that it were to-morrow!'

It were a matter of no surprise that Miss Wolverton, Kenneth, and Bryan spent a very happy month together at Filey. It is such a delightful place. As was to be expected, the two former fell quite in love with each other.

One day it chanced, as Bryan was busy making a sketch of Filey Bay and the famous Brig[4], Connie and Kenneth walked together over the sands towards Speeton Cliffs.

Sweet, very sweet, and so fair was she, he thought, as they walked along by the marge of the green sea. What a charm there was about her shapely little figure —so lithe and strong! It was so graceful and so well proportioned too! What poetry was there for him in her light airy step! Surely for him love walked the mazy tresses of her hair, where through the quickening wind from the sea did play and wanton as it listed. Ever and anon the breeze would blow in stronger, keener gusts. Then would she turn round to get breath, and as she did so he beheld the rosy, healthful bloom on her lovely cheeks; while through and among the tangled wefts of her hair that fluttered wildly to leeward of the wind, her eyes seemed to

---

[4] It is not clear which of Filey's numerous wrecks this refers to; though in 1851 Charles Dickens wrote an account of a wreck.

glisten with love; and as she opened her rose-sweet lips to speak to him, she artlessly revealed a row of perfect pearly teeth that were lovely to behold.

How he loved her! Almost laying on the wind against which they strove, they make for shelter to the lee of some sea-worn rocks that jut out on the sands between the loftier cliffs and the sea below. Here, "out of the wind's eye, hidden apart," they sat them down to rest awhile. Happy tryst! How sweetly her voice sounded in his ears! How blithely and artlessly she chatted away! Yes, she was very fair—*so* fair. Kenneth became quieter and quieter as they sat there, and yet his whole being yearned to say something, but he could not for the life of him begin. As he gazed under the long silken lashes of her eyes he thought he saw the lovelight in them glow warm and strong. His heart is fired as molten gold, and lo! he takes her hand in his.

Reluctantly—oh, so reluctantly—she draws it back. Kenneth is quick to observe her coyness and her sweet hesitancy, and as he again looks into her tell-tale eyes his heart is fired with hope. Love soon finds words. Love wins him empire in the gates of hope, and climbs to heaven on many an airy sleeve.

Later on, about ten o'clock in the evening, as Kenneth left Bryan's apartments, Connie went with him as far as the garden-gate. Bryan gave a little low whistle to himself, and went back to the drawing-room, and began to play on his banjo, "Drink to me only with thine eyes."

There was but one word of any real importance said at that garden-gate. There was but one hurried kiss. It was very sweet. Love's first trysts had need be sweet.

When Kenneth arrived at his rooms he found a letter awaiting him from Sheffield. He opened it at once, and began to read:

'DEAR KENNETH,—I am writing you as your true friend and well-wisher, therefore do not feel pained at what I say. When I got home last night I was shown some verses of poetry which you had written, and which one of your lady friends at Filey had copied out and sent to my daughter Belle. Now all the poetry that was ever written is, in my opinion, trash, and yours is no exception; and I think it is very indiscreet on your part to write such a dismal dirge, for if there is any sense whatever in the verses, it looks as if you were moaning by the sad sea waves like a guilty soul in pain. Are the lines about yourself? Do you not know that at this present juncture you and your co-experimenters are under a dark cloud of suspicion with regard to the mysterious disappearance of my two partners? Perhaps you are not aware that my daughter Belle, my son Dandelow, and myself are about the only persons amongst my immediate circle of friends who have unshaken faith in your innocence; and I must confess that your doleful dirge at first sight shook the foundations of my faith in you. Surely you must have studied what the newspapers say about this mystery? There was a report in last night's paper that, should the remains of my two partners be found, the police had not only a clue, but circumstantial evidence that was almost conclusive. I believe at this moment that your every movement is being watched.

'It was very indiscreet on your part to tell my son Dandy (who is not over-reticent) that you "hated and detested" my two partners.

'Mike Callaghan, your co-experimenter is wild with excitement, and has said something about "slautherin' spies," which is considered to be of a compromising nature. Also

Benskin, your other co-experimenter, is quite beside himself; and people argue that his sudden religious enthusiasm is but a cloak wherewith to hide his guilt. As a magistrate, I feel doubtful as to whether I am doing right in sending this letter to you. I should not do so did I not feel that I could rely upon your honour to destroy it as soon as it arrives.

'I should not have written you at all had it not been for my seeing those foolish verses which made me think that if you value your life you must not be reckless and incautious at a time like this. If you did but know how I have had to stick up for you, you would the better understand why I subscribe myself as

"Your sincere friend,
STANILAUS BANTAM."

Kenneth appeared to be thunderstruck when he first read the letter. He then read it over again, and laughed outright, tore it up, and threw it into the waste-paper basket.

'What tomfoolery is this?' he said, as he threw himself into an armchair and began to roll a cigarette. As the curling clouds of smoke uprose, his thoughts began to wander back to that memorable night wherein he conducted that ill-fated experiment with Mike Callaghan and Billy Benskin. He thought of everything that had happened that night. He remembered everything that was said and done up to the time when he fell, but for the life of him he could not call to mind what happened afterwards. He knew that he was stunned and rendered insensible, but did not know how.

Suddenly the thought flashed in upon him that the newspapers said the partners were "in liquor" that night.

'Might not the drunken Captain, or that drunken infuriated boor, Shout, have struck me down? And might not that headstrong Irishman, Mike, have retaliated? Might there not have been a terrible scuffle—a fatal one too?'

'These and similar ideas began to flash through Kenneth's mind. No sooner did he dismiss one train of thoughts as absurd, when another, and another, and another, each more alarming than its precursor, crowded upon him.

He began to feel quite nervous and alarmed.

'Suppose the remains were unearthed to-morrow, and that an inquest was held, and what if my co-experimenters are found guilty! What if Mike were to play me false? What if Benskin were to save his neck at my expense? Ah! what did that newspaper say about the statements of these men requiring "confirmation on certain points?" '

Such were his thoughts as he snatched up the Sheffield newspaper, which had been sent to him by his mother. His hands felt quite moist with clammy sweat as he opened it to see if there was any news bearing on the case. Yes, there it was, with a big imposing heading—"The Attercliffe Mystery." He read every word of the article eagerly. He grew terribly excited as he went on. He turned pale ashen pale. 'Good heavens! surely these innuendoes are meant for none else but me!' he said as he laid the paper down.

He began to feel uncomfortably hot. Perspiration stood in beads upon his brow, and he experienced a choking sensation about the throat. He rolled another cigarette, and then found he was too nervous to smoke it.

He got up and pulled down the long white window-blinds, and as he did so he could see that the full moon was shining brightly across the bay. It was after midnight.

He went and sat down again in the armchair opposite to the window. He could hear his heart beat, as he sat there, staring vacantly at the white window-blind of the room, foolishly imagining all kinds of impossibilities. All was still. Suddenly the faint, dim shadow of a man's figure crossed the blind, on which the level rays of the moon were shining. Kenneth started. He rushed to the window, and opened it. He could see nothing, nor hear anything, but there was a gentle murmuring breeze; and afar off he could hear, as it were, the long-drawn sigh of receding waves. But he knew that someone had passed over that garden grass-plot. Yes, he then fully realised his position. He knew that he was being watched. Then he sat as still as a mouse for some considerable time, listening. By-and-bye he heard the sound of someone striking a match in the bedroom behind the folding-doors at his back. The thought flashed across him that Mr Meiklejoy, who had taken the adjoining rooms, also came from Sheffield.

He felt absolutely certain of it. No doubt he was a detective. He thought he had better go to bed, so he lit his candle and went upstairs. His bedroom was over Mr Meiklejoy's.

He knew that it were a fond hope to think of going to sleep that night, but he got into bed, and tried to compose himself. 'What if Connie gets to know I am being watched? What if she begins to think I am implicated? Perish the thought!'

He began to wish he had not come to bed. He was so restless, and yet he felt that he dare not toss about in his bed for fear of making Meiklejoy think he was sleepless through guilt; so he lay still and listened.

He thought he heard the creaking of a door. Then he imagined he heard someone on the stairs. His heart throbbed as he listened for every sound, or imaginary sound.

How he longed for the daylight! How glad he was when the dull grey streaks of dawn began to lighten his room! Lighter and lighter it became, and the light seemed to hearten him.

Noiselessly he crept out of bed to look for a book which Connie had lent him. Ah! he had left it down-stairs. There was but one book on that dressing-table. It was the Bible. Yes, he would read that; it might console him.

He crept back into bed and began to read. It did not altogether console him, but, with a realism terrible and photographic, it made him see himself as he then was — a coward.

Kenneth felt ashamed of himself. 'What have I to fear—I that yester-eve was blessed above all men by the sweet confession of a pure heart's love? I that am guiltless, why should I tremble if the very gates of death get hold upon me?' he thought.

He began to feel more composed; and as the roseate wefts of light came stealing into his bedroom, he felt strong and fearless as one who:

"Grows straight in the strength of his spirit and lives out his life as the light?"

Later on, when he got up about six o'clock, he felt his heart was filled with thankfulness to God for giving him the promise of her love; and something like warm tears of love and joy filled his eyes as he knelt in the stillness of that room.

Then Kenneth stole downstairs as noiselessly as he could. At the foot of the stairs his feet caught something as if it had been a thin silken thread, and simultaneously something fell down with a rattling noise in Mr Meiklejoy's bedroom, the door of which was suddenly opened by that individual.

'Risin' airly, seemin'ly?' said Mr Meiklejoy.

'Yes, I'm going for a swim,' said Kenneth.

'I think I'll jist gae wi' yer, then.'

'All right, Mr Meiklejoy; come along,' said Kenneth.

When Kenneth had nearly stripped himself bare on the beach, he said to Mr Meiklejoy—

'What! aren't you going in?'

'Nae, thank'ee; I'd a guid wash in Sheffield last back-end.'

'Come along, man; another dousing won't hurt you,' said Kenneth.

'Nae, nae; I'll stop whaur I am, an' keep a tight grip o' your claes, for fear somebody should rin awa wi' 'em, mon.

'All right, Mr Meiklejoy; you can read my love-letters if you like. I'll be back presently.'

'Whaur yer goin', mon?'

'I'm off to the Dogger Bank,' said Kenneth, smiling to himself, as he leapt into the shining sea.

'Mebbe he's only tjokin,' said Mr Meiklejoy, with serious mien, as he saw Kenneth strike out seaward; 'but may the deil bail him oot if he gets tdrooned.'

CHAPTER VI

An austere-looking personage, wearing a tall and rather shabby-looking silk hat, with a very broad brim, was walking down Barker Pool in Sheffield, carrying a somewhat bulky green silk umbrella under his left arm, and a parcel of documents neatly tied up with red tape in his right hand. He held the parcel out prominently, as it were to let folk know what manner of profession was his. He held his head aloft, as he walked down the street with a long step of automatic precision. His collar was of an olden type, and its tips jutted out considerably, thereby helping to support his proudly-uplifted head. He wore a necktie of black silk, which was tied in a very large bow. He was clad in good black cloth, that had seen many years' service, and his coat was cut somewhat after the evening-dress fashion of forty years ago. He was tall and thin. He wore a pair of spectacles over his nose, which was pinched and very long, and had a certain "Bleak House" aspect about the tip. He had a sharp prominent chin, which threatened ere-long to meet with his nose, as the claws of a crab-fish do. A few straggling bristles did service for whiskers, which were a sorry crop indeed, as if the seed had missed in places. His upper lip was covered with some twenty or thirty hirsute hairs, each of which was wide apart from its neighbour. He had no eyebrows. His hair was black, and long, and straight as a rat's tail; in fact, it was a wig. His shepherd's plaid trousers were rather shabby, and hung loosely and baggily about the ankles. As he paced along he looked a very important if not sanctimonious personage, and his little, bright, ferret-like eyes glanced proudly about him to see if passers-by should mark him as "someone in pertickler."

'Who the dickens is that old poker-back?' asked a certain farmer from Norton-Lees, turning round and staring at the tall figure going down the street. 'Why, our lads calls him the

"Last of the Mohicans," replied his friend, a grazier from Hoober Stand, 'but his real name is Walt Weevil, the lawyer.'

'Lor! he looks as if he wor a-goin' to stick a writ into t' sky,' said the farmer.

'Ay, lad; mebbe he's goin to have the law agenst somebody up there, the old devilscrat. *Aw* kno' him,' said the grazier as he made for The Stannidge Pole. 'Aw kno' him,' he repeated, as they both sidled into the well-known hostelry where old Jerry Diggles "kep' open 'ouse," as he called it.

The lawyer proceeded down the High Street to his office in Castle Folds. When he arrived there he sat down in his dingy and dusty private room, and deposited his papers on the rickety table. He put the tips of his fingers together, closed and opened his eyes, sanctimoniously sighed, and then ferreted out his brown silk handkerchief from his pocket, and made a loud nasal trumpeting, so as to proclaim his arrival to the two young articled clerks in the next room, who were just then busy wrangling over the, proceeds of a certain advance which their "uncle" had made them for divers legal tomes which they had left in his custody, and amongst which was Chitty and Blackstone.

Mr Weevil pulled out his watch, and then took a pinch of snuff, and as he did so he heard a knock at the door.

'Mr Millwood, sir,' said one of the clerks, opening wide the door, and looking quite overdone with hard work.

'Ask him in at once,' said Mr Weevil.

The Rev. Theodore Millwood entered the room, and after shaking hands with the lawyer, sat down.

'Well,' said the minister, after a minute or two of complimentary vapouring; 'any more news from Otterclough Forge?'

Mr Weevil rolled his ferret-like eyes, and looked round the room nervously to see if there was anybody else within earshot.

'Yes,' he said in a low voice, and pointing towards the Police Court; 'they are on the sly young dog's trail. He's actually sending money to his accomplices, they say. Of course no arrest can be made until they find the bodies; but I am well posted up, and I am secretly informed from an unimpeachable source that the greatest suspicion attaches to Kenneth, who was badly burnt, as you are aware, and who was taken home to his lodgings by Mike Callaghan and Billy Benskin, who, by-the-bye, had bruises on them, as if they had been in a scuffle. Moreover, I hear it reported over *there*, that, besides the Captain's Malacca cane being found, there has been a cigar-case of Mr Shout's found at the bottom of the empty blast-furnace. In fact, there is almost conclusive evidence that the two partners went to the Forge on that Friday night, and that they most mysteriously disappeared.'

'But whatever motive could possess any of the three to lay hands on the partners?' asked the minister.

'Why, the theory is, that, finding their precious experiments were being observed, they were exasperated, and that some altercation took place between Mr Shout and Captain Underwedge and themselves; and as the partners were known to be rather quarrelsome when in liquor, a desperate fight ensued, in which the latter got killed; and it is now thought that the bodies may have been thrown into the calcining-kilns or even thrown into the blast-furnace.'

Mr Millwood shook his head.

'What! don't you believe it?' asked the lawyer.

'I can't,' said he in reply. 'Kenneth may be a "sly young dog," as you call him, but I know him too well, Walt; and although, as you know, there is no love lost between us, I cannot believe him capable of anything so downright wicked, although it looks very awkward against him that he should have sent moneys to both Benskin and Callaghan.'

'Then can you substitute a better theory?' asked Mr Weevil.

'Indeed, I cannot; but to change the subject, I am very much worried, Walt,—yes, worried; downright worried,' said the minister, looking painfully serious.

'What's the matter?' asked the lawyer.

'My wife seems to be drifting away from my control,' said the minister, in a lugubrious tone.

'How's that, Theodore?' asked Mr. Weevil, taking a pinch of snuff, and receiving the information with an air of absolute unconcern.

'Because I find that she is still corresponding with Kenneth, against my express orders.'

'Well, well,' said the lawyer, in an off-hand manner; 'you can hardly expect otherwise, can you?'

'No, perhaps not; but there is something worse, Walt: she has lost faith in me.'

'What of that?' said the lawyer, with a sneer; 'you have been married over twenty-one years, and 'twere strange indeed if your breastplate of righteousness and shield of faith were proof against time.

'Don't talk like that; it is profane,' said the minister, looking very seriously at his friend.

'Rubbish!' said the lawyer. 'We have known each other ever since we were boys at school, and as it is written: "Sooner shall the leopard change his spots or the Ethopian his skin," etc.'

'Don't, Walt, don't; it upsets the equipose of my conscience to talk like that.'

'All right, Theodore; I won't disturb your equanimity or serenity' said the lawyer scoffingly. 'Anything else on your mind, eh?' he asked, with dry sarcasm.

'Yes, I have something very serious,' said the minister; 'very serious,' he repeated.

'Out with it, honest man,' said the lawyer; 'confession is good for the soul—that is, if you don't happen to have sold it for gold.'

'Mr Weevil,' said the minister gravely, 'Kenneth knows that I am *not* his father.'

'Nonsense!' exclaimed the lawyer; 'you're dreaming, man!'

'But he told me so to my face,' said Mr Millwood.

'The deuce he did!' said Mr Weevil, with an air of alarm; 'who can have told him, pray?'

'I cannot find out, nor can Matilda. I have secretly read his letters to her, wherein he studiously avoids the subject, although she has asked him point-blank to say who has told him, but instead of doing so he sent her some verses from Filey Bay, where he is still staying—and if I am not very much mistaken, the lines are intended to apply to me.'

'Ay, he's a sly young dog, as I said before,' the lawyer added; 'but, Theodore, this may be serious. The young rascal may upset our plans—your plans, I beg your pardon.'

'How?'

'What if he and his mother should lay their heads together?'

'What then?' asked the minister concernedly.

'She might revoke the will which I got her to sign at your instigation.'

'Mine!' exclaimed the minister, drawing himself backward with an air of annoy.

'Yes, *yours*, Theodore, *yours*. Have you forgotten what took place in this very office over twenty-one years ago. What! yes? Let me refresh your memory, then. Your bride'—he spoke the words in a scornful, slighting manner—'yourself, and your humble friend Walt,' he said, bowing, 'had had a champagne luncheon over at the Old Black Swan and the champagne was rather heady, and we were very happy, very happy; and just walked over here to sign the— Oh! you remember, do you?'

'Remember!' exclaimed the minister, grinding his teeth; 'ay, Walt; don't remind me of it again. I sold myself for gold that day. Never more speak of it.'

'But I will speak of it, my dear Theodore,' said the lawyer, with an unctuous familiarity which was positively nauseating to Mr Millwood. 'Yes, I will speak of it. I will beg of you, my dear Millwood, to fulfil and carry out the provisions of that unholy compact whereby Kenneth was disinherited, and whereby your poor, humble, and non-reverend school-fellow Walt Weevil was to share your unhallowed gains.'

'What do you mean?' asked the minister, with vexation and surprise.

'Why, didn't you once promise to go shares with me over the unearned increment, if there should be any, from dear Matilda's property?'

'I can't remember,' said the minister. 'When was it?'

'You know well enough, Theodore. It was after that picnic to Roche Abbey, which I arranged entirely to bring you and Matilda together. Don't you remember saying after dinner that night that you would go shares in the unearned increment, but not in the then personalty, and I said "Amen" to it, and clenched the bargain.'

'Oh, well,' said the flabby minister, waving his flabby hand; 'that was merely a piece of post-prandial jocularity—a mere joke.'

'Ay, that may be,' said Mr Weevil, as his bright ferret-like eyes began to glisten, and at the same time he began to roll and rub his hands together, and shrug his shoulders knowingly, as though he could weave or squirm his way through any mesh of the law; 'but the unearned daily from your wife's property is no joke. It is getting quite serious. It alarms you, doesn't it? Why, let me see,' he continued, counting on his fingers, 'you must be worth fifty thousand pounds, Theodore— and all from your wife's property, and she is completely hoodwinked, poor woman.'

' 'Sh!' said the minister, looking alarmed, and pointing with his thumb over his shoulder to the door of Mr Weevil's clerks' office.

'You needn't be alarmed,' said the lawyer; 'they are busy at Blackstone and Chitty for the final—the brainless idiots! But to keep to my text, I am going to ask you to share and share alike, as you yourself promised.'

'How?' said the minister, who opened his eyes wider, and looked surprised and annoyed.

'I will explain,' said Mr Weevil, with an irritating smile. 'In the first place, I want three thousand pounds to pay off that mortgage on my house and land in Endcliffe Vale; and in the second, I want you to alter your will and make direct bequests for half of your real and personal estate to whomsoever you choose, and then make *me* residuary legatee.'

'A pretty request!' said the minister; 'are you mad?'

'No, Theodore; but I am just beginning to think that I have been, to let you off so long. I am in downright earnest, and I am glad you have come in to see me to-day; we'll settle the whole thing.'

'Nonsense!' said the minister, picking up his hat and gloves, and assuming a feigned smile, as though the lawyer were joking.

'But I mean every word I say, and you shall not leave this office, Theodore, without acceding to my most modest requests. I simply demand fair play,' said Mr Weevil, in an easy bland manner, but looking absolutely in earnest.

'Fair play? fiddlesticks!' exclaimed the minister rather angrily, and getting up to go.

'Fair play's a jewel,' laughed the lawyer. 'Sit down old man, and don't get your "dander up." '

'Walt,' said the minister sternly, 'you are making an ass of me!'

'Better than making a wolf in sheep's clothing a demon in saint's attire,' grinned the lawyer.

'Weevil, you exasperate me beyond all words. Do you mean to insult me?'

'Keep quiet, Theodore, keep quiet,' said the lawyer, as he rivetted his sparkling eyes on to the minister. 'Sit down and be calm,' he added, with a vexing air of nonchalance.

Mr Millwood put on his hat, snatched up his umbrella, and made for the door, but the wily lawyer, anticipating his exit, leaned his back up against the door, and with a smile ineffably bland said—

'Don't hurry, dear Theodore, don't hurry. See—here is a *billet-doux* from your wife,' said he, holding out a letter. 'She has faith in *me*, Milly, my boy, if she hasn't in *you*. She is coming to see me this afternoon. Shall I peach, eh?'

'Good heavens! what do you mean?' asked the minister eagerly. 'Tell tales and tarradiddles, and ask her to revoke, of course,' added the lawyer, taking a pinch of snuff.

The minister looked thunderstruck. Beads of perspiration stood out on his brow, and his flabby hands turned clammy.

'What! are *you* going to play me false—*you*?' he asked.

'That depends,' laughed the lawyer.

'What do you mean, sir?' demanded the minister.

'Whether you play *me* false or no?

'Yes, *you*, Theodore; are *you* immaculate? Don't you remember *we* once kept rabbits together at school, Theodore. We were partners—we shared and shared alike; and we always raffled off the prick-eared bucks and the barren does. We made many an honest penny by swindling, didn't we? We were loyal partners then, Theodore. How we gloated over our ill-gotten gains! How we wheedled all the pocket-money from the new boys! What happy rascals we were! But now all is changed. Enveloped in your cloth, you turn inconsistent, and won't share the booty. Theodore!' —he spoke sternly— 'I won't have it! Knuckle down! Shoot fair, and no fullocks, as we used to say when lads. We'll kale and kale, and share and share alike to-day *now*, or I'll know the reason why.'

The Rev. Theodore Millwood saw that Mr Weevil was thoroughly in earnest, and he felt himself in the humiliating position of one driven to bay, and strengthless as a man in the clutches of a burglar in a nightmare dream. He utterly collapsed, and sank back into an old arm-chair. His flabby hands fell powerlessly and limp on his knees. For a second or two he gazed aloft as a dying martyr, showing the whites of his bilious eyes. Mr Weevil noticed the minister's distressed look with a certain feeling of joy, and asked softly, yet in a tone that bespoke a thinly-veiled scepticism—

'Going to pray, Theodore?'

Mr Millwood did not speak. He pulled his hand-kerchief out of his pocket, and in doing so dragged with it a little parcel of peppermint lozenges, which fell upon the floor. He then mopped his forehead, for he was beginning to perspire very freely. Mr Weevil picked up the lozenges, and put one into his mouth, and then turning to his old friend, asked irritatingly, 'Have a lozenge, Theodore?'

The minister was speechless. He could only utter a deep sigh.

The lawyer's heart rejoiced as he went and sat by the side of the defeated champion of the faith. He knew that he had him in his power. He waited silently, as a fisherman does when a pike has taken the deadly gorge-bait, and then he pulled his chair close up to Theodore's, and holding out his hand, said in a low and serious voice—

'Is it jannock or *no* jannock, Theodore?'

The minister reluctantly reached forth his flabby digits.

'You agree then?' asked the lawyer, whose ferret-like eyes pierced his friend's lack-lustre ones through and through. 'I yield, Weevil, I yield,' sighed the minister, bowing his head.

'Good old partner!' exclaimed the lawyer, clapping Mr Millwood on the back. 'I knew you would have to come to; but, my word! how you sweat! Never mind, old boy, never mind. 'Tis easier for a camel—'

' 'Sh, 'sh! Walt,' said the minister, who appeared to be shocked at the idea of the lawyer's quoting from Holy Writ.

'All right, my dear Theodore,' said Mr Weevil. 'I won't shock you any more, but I'll tell you a secret instead; one that'll gladden the soul within you my boy.'

A faint sickly smile stole over Theodore's face as he feebly asked—

'What secret? What is it?'

'Why,' said the lawyer, taking another pinch of snuff and looking very roguish; 'over at the Old King's Head they've got in a parcel of the best Pommery that ever was deep delved for fat abbot or holy friar.'

'Thank Heaven for that!' said the minister, with a sigh of relief; 'let's away and broach it.' Their spirits rose within them, and they waxed quite polite and cheerful as they literally bowed each other out of the office, old Weevil insisting that Theodore should go first.

'The Church first, the Law after,' he said, with a sly wink, as they walked down the narrow passage.

When they got into the open street they went arm in arm together up Snig Hill and over to Change Alley, where they found that sunburnt mirth and jollity gradually stole over them as they quaffed the bubbling beads of the vintage from the sunny south.

In about four or five hours' time the exhilarating effects of the best champagne pass away. Not infrequently a mental depression, greater than the brief exaltation of spirits, sets in.

So it was with both Mr Millwood and Mr Weevil, the former as he faced the dismal frowns of poor Matilda at Patmos Lodge, and the latter as he sat in his house in Endcliffe Vale, thinking how foolish he had been to let his quondam schoolfellow off so easily.

'The sly old hypocrite!' he thought; 'deserves to be bound to some golden calf and melted, the miser!'

Mr Millwood also similarly ruminated to himself as he faced his wife's implacable brow. 'Sly old ferret, that Weevil! soulless sceptic! miserable scribe! Would that I were out of his clutches! But perhaps I shall outlive him, the unprincipled rogue! Ah me!' he sighed; ' 'tis hard to break the chains that bound us in our youth! Yet Weevil is surely right; we were once consistent rogues at Old Campo Lane School;[5] and alas! it seems as if we must be consistent to the end of the chapter. Terrible is the reproductiveness and persistence of the type when it is evil! Theodore, thy name still sits on thee with an ill grace! When wilt thou repent?'

'What are you thinking of, Theodore?' asked Matilda, startling him from his reverie.

'Nothing, Matilda, nothing; only —'

'Only what?'

'That you do not seem to look up to me with such respect as you once did.'

'That is your fault. You shouldn't have locked my boy out.'

'And you shouldn't have suspected that he was a love with a vulgar Irish parlour-maid,' he said sharply.

'I confess my fault, and heartily do I repent me for having lost such a priceless treasure,' she replied.

'Repent, indeed!'

'Yes, repent; why do you sneer at such a word?'

'I was not sneering, Matilda; I was thinking that repentance oft comes when it is too late, when we have lost the greatest of treasures.'

'What is that, pray?'

'The faith that earneth wages in the gates of love,' he replied, with a sigh.

'Do you impute that I have lost this faith, Theodore?'

'No, Matilda; I was not thinking of *you*. I was thinking something about that trial sermon which I preached long years ago. It was about "The Great Consolation Scramble." '

'Yes, I remember it. You loved me *then*, Theodore.'

'But I love you better *now*,' he replied.

She would not believe it. It was impossible, absurd.

Yet it was true. When he began his ministry he loved her gold, but had not manliness to confess it. Now he began to

---

[5] There were charity schools for boys and girls on Campo Lane

love her with a selfish sort of love. He felt himself getting older and weaker, and in need of a helpmeet and companion; so when Theodore told her he loved her "better now," he was but speaking the bare, unvarnished truth.

Little did he think that his wife, who was ten years younger than he, would before many months leave him for that bourne where faith may yet be paid its wages in the gates of an ever-enduring love. Soon would he have to plod alone up the steep ascent of years, with Walt Weevil for a guide.

PART II

CHAPTER VII

THREE YEARS AFTER – A TRANSITION.

'Sheffield's a werry nice place when you gets to Froggatt Edge,' once said a tramp from the sunny south, with a merry twinkle in his eye. He had previously spent a few unhappy days somewhere in the heart of Hallamshire, and was not sorry to be once more "on tramp."

The tramp was generally right in his observations, and had he only chronicled them, he would doubtless have added delightful store to our topographical knowledge.

Froggatt Edge truly is a charming spot, some ten or twelve miles south-west of Sheffield, on the Derbyshire moors, in the district of the High Peak. Fortunately it is not yet a residential suburb of that grim and mighty town, which contains from 300,000 to 400,000 souls; but rumour has it that ere long the iron horse will be heard thundering in the valley below. It may then become a fashionable suburb, and the purple heath-clad moors and the ageless rock-ribbed hills may become dotted with prim little villas, and with the more pretentious abodes of manufacturing princes; or alas! it may be that, instead of our beholding the mellowing afterglow of the sunset over the rugged and weather-beaten escarpments that have been handed down to us as a priceless memorial for ever, we may behold, swinging in the air, some gibbering ghost of an advertisement of "Yorkshire Polony" in the sky.

But a truce to such infelicitous forebodings. Froggatt Edge has still a peculiar glory of its own for us—a loveliness that time has not ravished—a quiet charm as sweet and as dear to us as "the shoots of the woodland when April is warm."

Shall time or death rob us ever of our love for the beautiful which there first shed its hallowed light upon us?

Hard by a copse of stunted mountain oaks an artist sits, lovingly absorbed in his work. His bright, keen eyes seem to glow with love for the splendour of the scene before him. He heeds not the "kabback! kabback!" of the cock-grouse that calls to his mate among the wiry bilberry bushes, and the ling, and the soft hair of the mountain grass.

His whole heart is bent upon adding one more loving touch to his canvas, for lo! a living gleam as of molten gold has enkindled the tops of the pines on the hills, and he longs to fix those mellow glinting rays of light ere they fade and perish for ever.

The valleys are ringed round with woods, and crowned with dark heath-clad moors. Far below the silvery, winding Derwent lapses and relapses along with gentle shh,' shh'—a sound unheard, save, it may be, to some naiad-loved wanderer with his rod, who, as the shadows lengthen o'er stilly reach or rippling shallow, hopes to lure from their pebbly haunts the wily grayling or the lusty trout.

On his right are the woody slopes of Longshawe, while afar up the valley, abrupt and broken, rise the hills as natural ramparts to shelter the peaceful hamlets of Hathersage and of Hope, while still further, with heads uplift, are the twin sisters, Win Hill and Lose Hill, their tops "bathed in the rays of the great setting flame."

Much nearer, and on his left, sleeps the little hamlet by Grindleford Bridge, whilst beyond, the white limestone road winds along towards the delightful village of Eyam, round which romance well might weave many an airy weft.

The shadows deepen. The night-jar flutters from the leafy copse, and then glides back as though scared at the face of man.

The artist lays him on the grass. He lights his pipe. His task is done. Then night comes on apace, and soon gets empire o'er declining day.

Hesperus climbs up the lift, with many a twinkling wanderer in his wake. The liquid air seems so elastic of sound, he can almost hear the crickets chirping in the inn below.

Hark! he hears voices. He looks round. He sees two folk coming towards him. They are walking arm in arm on the narrow by-way, that is broken with moss-grown boulders, and fringed with bracken, lady-ferns, and ling. Softly they thrid along o'er the springy mossy turf.

They pause. They kiss.

'Lovers, forsooth!' says Bryan Wolverton to himself.

Nearer and nearer they come. Suddenly he thinks he recognises the voices of Connie and Kenneth Millwood. He listens again. He is certain of it. He pulls his large slouch hat a little closer over his eyes. He hugs him closer 'mong the heathery tufts. They come quite close to him. They see him. They start as though surprised, and then pass on, not having recognised him. Before they have gone a few more paces, he jumps bolt upright, and says, with a strong Irish brogue—

'God save you, kindly gentlefolk, but shure it's meself as 'ud like to be afther dhrinkin' yer health and the childer's wid a blessin'.'

Connie turned round startled, and said—

'Surely there is no mistaking that voice, Ken. It is—it must be—it is none but Bryan's.'

'Faix, ye're right, for wanst,' says Bryan, opening his arms. 'Come hidder, Connie, aroon.'

'Jewel!' says she, leaving Kenneth's arm and rushing to Bryan and kissing him.

In a few minutes the happy trio were chatting volubly and blithely as ever, as though two years had not separated nor wide seas divided them.

'And when did you come back from Italy?' asked Connie, her eyes beaming with love—for she loved Bryan more than anyone in the world, excepting her Kenneth, of course.

'Not long ago, dear,' he replied. 'Faix I'm supposed to be studying the Italian frescoes this minute.'

'Pray why didn't you let us know you were coming? 'said Kenneth.

'Because I thought I would surprise you.'

'And of course you found we had gone away?'

'Exactly; but—er—yes—my—er—friend, Miss Belle Bantam, told me that you had gone away into Derbyshire for a second honeymoon.'

'Belle Bantam!' exclaims Connie, 'why, have you seen her lately? I thought she had taken the veil, or something of that sort. One never sees or hears of her in Sheffield now.'

Bryan whistles a low whistle to himself. Connie notices it, and gives him a keen, questioning glance. Bryan replies to her glance by a merry twinkle that flashes from the dark dreamy depths of his eyes.

'O you quiet one!' she exclaims, as though she had divined his secret; and then she leaned on Kenneth's arm and said to him, 'Ken, dear, I do believe Bryan's engaged.' As she said this she fixed her lustrous eyes on her brother's face to see if he would wince under their pitiless fire.

But Bryan came off scathless, for a calm imperturbability settled on his handsome manly visage as he stroked his long, shaggy beard.

But no woman is repulsed at the first brush of the fight. Oh no! Connie returns to the attack, reinforced with the *ingens telum* of a pretty woman's sweet suasiveness.

'And, Bryan, dear, where did you last see Miss Bantam?' she asks, smiling so sweetly.

'Why, dear, not long ago; let me see—why, I can scarcely remember—but when I came back from Italy she met me at the Sheffield station,' said he, with a quiet smile.

'By appointment, of course, dear?' says Connie, assuming such an idle, artless, and incurious manner of expression.

'Ah yes; we had arranged to meet,' he says.

'Alone?'

'Of course,' he said, smiling.

'Now, Bryan, dear, do not tantalise us any more. Are you engaged to her or not? Do tell us, there's a darling. We can both keep a secret if necessary, can't we, Ken?'

'N—n—no, darling, no; at least I can't—not from *you* anyhow,' said Kenneth, looking proud of his dear little woman's strategy.

'Of course you can't, you good old hubby. Good husbands should never keep secrets from their wives; but do tell us, Bryan, that's a good *bouchaleen dhas*[6]—do tell us all.'

'Well,' says Bryan, whispering into Connie's ear, 'she's as good as engaged to me; but mind you must ask no more questions, for all is involved in secrecy, and I am at this minute under the darkly romantic clouds of mystery.'

'O Bryan, Bryan, dearest, for old love's sake, how can you let us bide in such darkness? Pray enlighten us a little, there's a good soul. Come, aroon; confession is sweet.'

'Connie, acushla, a thruce to yer swate prattle; but faix, alanna, I will tell you all after supper, where there are no eaves-droppers. By-the-bye, I suppose you are staying at 'The Chequers'?'

'No, dear; at the cottage by the bridge. Do come and sup with us. I do so long to—'

'Vix the mortial spirit out av me, eh?' put in Bryan parenthetically.

'— have a chat about old times, love,' she said.

'Well, I'll come along with you, but I'll just leave my picture at the inn first.'

---

[6] beautiful boy

After supper was over, and long after the dear little fellow, Bryan junior, had been hushed to sleep, Kenneth, Connie, and her brother sat down in the cosy little parlour of the cottage by the bridge.

'How strange that you should have heard nothing about the affairs of poor Mr Bantam!' said Bryan after a while.

'We have not heard a syllable, dear; only that he died very suddenly some ten months ago.'

'What about his affairs?' asked Kenneth.

'Why, the sons and the daughters cannot agree about the will. The trustees are, already at loggerheads. Poor Mrs Bantam is almost driven crazy with the lawyers; and the upshot is the whole estate has been thrown into Chancery. But how strange you should have heard nothing about it!'

'Oh, not at all, Bryan. Kenneth knows simply nothing,' says Connie, looking kindly at her husband. 'He is so much engrossed with his patents, and so overweeningly fond of little Bryan, that he thinks about nothing or no one else.'

'Excepting yourself, dear,' says Kenneth; 'besides, darling, you have the newspapers.'

'Yes,' says Connie, 'but they have been so full of political abuse of late, that I have hardly dared to look at them.'

'And family squabbles have such little interest for me,' says Kenneth, 'that I suppose none thought it worth while telling me of them.'

'Then I suppose the daughters are wards of Chancery?' says Connie.

'Indeed they are, much to my sorrow and discomfort,' says Bryan.

'And so actually Belle Bantam has become a rich ward in Chancery, a charming young heiress, the prettiest girl in Hallamshire. And I? Why, I shall never be famous. Shall I, Ken?' She said this to him very kindly, as though she loved him beyond all measure of fame or of words.'

'Belle and I may possibly become *too* famous before long,' added Bryan, with a sly laugh.

'Surely you are not intending to elope with her and defy the Court. Only imagine what the *Sheffield Daily Standard* will say about it! Why, Mr Strongitharm, the editor, will write leaders for a week about that gay young Lothario, Bryan Wolverton and his—'

'Whist! woman, whist! A thruce to yer honest prattle, and pray don't mintion the name av me at all, for it's thravelling incognito I am, under the name of Phelim O'Connor, while Bryan Wolverton is supposed to be studying the Italian frescoes this minnit.'

'How absurd of you, Bryan!' exclaims Connie.

'Faix, 'tis throe as a barrer full o' Bibles; and it's a saycret I'll tell you,' says he, whispering in Connie's ear. 'I'm married to Belle Bantam and the therriblest news is the Coort knows it, and has been on me thrack this three weeks. Do you think my incognito is complete?' says he, stroking his long, shaggy beard.

'Well, Misther Phelim O'Connor, you simply astound me— and as for your incognito, it is *not* complete. The beard, the whiskers, the moustache, the bronzed complexion may be Esau's or Phelim's, but the voice, the eyes, and the "plisent banther" are all Bryan's to a T.'

'A mighty precious scrape to be in,' observed Kenneth. 'I always thought you would distinguish yourself, old man. Belle Bantam indeed! What a delightful romance, to be sure! Well, I must confess that had it not been for my dear little woman here, I should have been equally inclined for such a peerless, swift-footed Diana.'

'Ay,' says Bryan, 'now you mention it, she told me plainly she loved Kenneth to distraction—afore she clap eyes on Phelim, av coorse.'

A few minutes later on Bryan, *alias* Phelim O'Connor, sets off towards "The Chequers." As he goes up the road and gets near to his well-beloved inn, he meets old Sammy Tooley, the ostler of the establishment.

'Is that you, Mester O'Connor?'

'Troth an' it is, wuss luck,' says Phelim.

'Well,' says Sammy, 'there's tew chaps fro' Shevvild inside the bar, been axin' me all about yerself, sir.'

'Murther!' says Phelim; 'is it me characther they're afther? What did you tell them, Sammy, eh?'

'I told 'em nobbutt summat 'at's nowt,' says Sammy, with a cunning leer.

'Eh? what?' asks Phelim anxiously.

'Why, sir, I told 'em you wor only Irish, an' hadn't so much as a meg in yer pocket.'

'Faix, an' yer spoke thruth for wanst, Sammy, though it's fairly rotten wid gowld I am this minnit.'

'Ay, ay,' says Sammy, with a sly wink; 'yer kno', I thowt there was a ugly sorter bumbaillie look about them there chaps fro' Shevvild.'

'Sammy, there's a power o' wisdom in yer remarks. I'd go bail yer'd go straight for the eye of a needle in a botthle of hay or a bushel av milk. Here, Sammy,' says he, giving him half-a-crown, 'here's a bad shillin' for you. Sew it up in yer throwser's legs, sowl; or let the missus have a grip of it afore it melths in yer ugly mouth.'

Sammy winked and blinked, and, rejoicing to think that he was being so liberally treated for doing so little, hobbled away. But Sammy had been well schooled by Phelim. Sammy knew his book.

Phelim boldly walks into the bar parlour. He rightly guesses that the two "chaps fro' Shevvild" are detectives; but he determines, and fully relies on being able, to conceal his identity as heretofore. He literally throws himself into an easy-chair, digs his hands into his trousers' pockets, stretches out his long legs wide apart, throws his big slouch hat on the table, lolls back in his chair, fixing his eyes upon the two newcomers until they almost wince and look positively uneasy.

The silence becomes painful. None, as it were, dares to begin. But suddenly Phelim resolves to startle them with a broadside of his native brogue, and thereby conceal his identity.

'Has aither o' you gints got sich a thing as a plug o' Limerick consaled upon his person?' says he, producing a dirty black clay pipe from the band of his hat seemingly.

'Eh?' says the taller of the visitors.

Phelim repeated the question.

'No,' says the shorter one; 'but here's some good owd judge,' handing his pouch to Phelim, who immediately began to fill his *dhudeen*, and after lighting up, remarked—

'Thank'ee, sirr. Shure 'tis the blast av a pipes the mischief's own thing at sthrentenin' the inthellec' agin advarsity.'

'Ye're right,' says the taller one. 'Ye're a bit of a hartist, seemingly?' pointing to one of Phelim's canvasses which was reared in the corner of the room.

'Och! 'tis flatther me yer would!' exclaims he.

'But it's a pretty bit o' work,' says the shorter one, eyeing the picture carefully.

'It's stunnin'!' says the bigger one, pursing his lips as though he were a connoisseur.

'Troth, it's my mastherpiece, anyway; but faix, yer'd see the idaya of the artist to better advantage if yer'd put the picthure right side up,' says Phelim, turning the picture round.

'Ah, it lukes better now,' says the tall stranger. 'An' what might yer be axin' for it, sir?'

'A gowlden guinea—and chape at the price,' says Phelim.

'A lot o' mooney that,' ventures the short one.

'Garrout wid yer! Faix, the matayrials cost a power o' money.'

One of the advantages of being an admirer of the Fine Arts is that they soon make the whole world kin, or at any rate they help to thaw that unfathomable icy coldness in which an Englishman's heart can at times be enveloped; and so it happened that ere long their hearts began to unfreeze, and indeed, before half an hour had passed, the two strangers had revealed themselves to Phelim O'Connor as Mr Meiklejoy and Mr Donkin from the heart of Hallamshire, Sheffield.

'I reck'n yer don't kno' a clever young hartist of the name of Bryan Wolverton?' asks Mr Meiklejoy.

'Divil a bit! says Phelim; 'but I've got sich a misforthunate memory widin me. What's the likes av him?'

'Here's his photo,' says Meiklejoy, handing it to Phelim, who looked at it in an offhand, indifferent manner, as he took a good *shough* of his pipe, while his thoughts travelled at the lightning speed of millions of miles per second. It was a photograph of himself, taken about four years ago by Sully of Sheffield. He was a beardless youth then, with but the faintest suspicion of a moustache, which had been made the most of. There was a certain primness or smartness about the style of the photograph altogether at variance with Phelim's then purposely uncouth style, albeit he had somewhat of an artistic appearance.

Both Mr Meiklejoy and Mr Donkin surveyed Phelim's face very keenly as he looked at the photograph, but he evinced no sign of recognition, and quailed not in the slightest.

'Be jabers, 'tis a smart-lookin' chap he is, anyway,' says Phelim, handing back the photograph.

'You don't 'appen to kno him then?' says Meiklejoy.

'Troth and I don't; but I wanst knew a chap as like him as tew pays in the Irish Consthabulary.'

A baffled look of surprise stole over the faces of both Meiklejoy and Donkin, a look which lapsed into one of sheer vacuity, for both of them had thought that Phelim might be the man they wanted, but they were evidently off the right scent.

'We want this Mr Wolverton in Sheffield,' says Mr Donkin.

'What for?' says Phelim, blowing a cloud of smoke across the parlour.

'Becos he's run away with a young lady agenst the horder of the Court.'

'The dhirty bla'guard!' exclaims Phelim; 'faix, he orter be coairced wid buckshot.'

The conversation flagged somewhat. Had Meiklejoy and Donkin known that Mr Bryan Wolverton was bred and born in Ireland, their suspicious would have been aroused, but they had had no information on this point.

'Has aither o' you gintlemen got sich a thing as a deck o' cards upon him, for faix 'tis a bit av a shuffle at nap I'd like to be havin' this minnit?'

Oddly enough, the representatives of the law had no cards in their pockets. Nor was there a pack to be found in the house.

'Murther!' says Phelim; 'tis slain wid idleness I'll be widout me nap; but let's thry sperit-rappin', bhoys, eh? What! No? Why for shure? All tomfoolery, did yer say? Faix, 'tis thrue as gospel, and it's meself'll prove it. You'll try? All right! Come on wid yer, honest men. Here's a table—'

But the landlord here comes into the room, and tells them they had better order what they want in the way of drink, as he was off to bed. Phelim accordingly orders a bottle of "Ould Bushmills."

After mine host had locked up the bar and retired to rest, a delightful spiritualistic seance began in that little cosy parlour.

'Is aither av you a medium?' asks Phelim, as they seat themselves close to a small round table, with their fingers touching, and making as it were an enchanted ring on the table.

'Divil a bit, did you say, eh? Never mind, bhoys; sit still and be aisy, for shure 'tis a mighty sthrong medium I am.'

An incredulous sort of smile lit up the faces of Meiklejoy and Donkin, yet they waited patiently for fully a quarter of an hour. Then they began scoffing and laughing.

Suddenly the table moved. 'Pace wid honner, yer scoffin' bla'guards; they're comin'. Hould hard!' says Phelim.

As the table moved again the detectives began to take a keener interest in the proceedings. 'Hark! did you hear that?' says Phelim, as a distinct tapping was heard.

They nodded, and Meiklejoy's face grew a little paler.

'Whose sperit shall I ax for?' says the medium.

'Anybody's,' says Meiklejoy, looking rather scared.

'Julius Caesar's, if you like,' suggests the more sceptical Donkin.

'All right, bhoys; be still,' says Phelim. 'Is the sperit of Djoolius Saiser present?' he asks, and repeats the question three times. At the third time two loud raps are heard.

'*Slauntha* Djoolius,' says Phelim.

'*Slauntha* agen,' taps Julius.

Both the detectives look startled.

'He's present;' whispers Phelim; 'would aither o' you like to ax him a question?'

No, they wouldn't.

'What! no? Don't be skeered; faix, I'll ax him one myself, as it isn't often as Djooly gets a call.'

'Are you there, Djoolius?'

Two tremendous raps.

'Wouldn't yer like to be conquerin' the Great Britthans, eh, Djooly?'

A loud rap, signifying—'*No.*'

'What! crossing the Alps, wid the snow up to yer fethlocks, is it yer'd like to be afther, eh?'

A louder rap—'*No.*'

'Maybe 'tis dividin' Gaul intho three parts, an' slautherin' the inhabithants, to pacify the misforthunate counthry, ye'd like to be afther?'

'Two tremendous raps—'*Yes.*'

Both Meiklejoy and Donkin begin to look rather pale and excited, for Phelim had kept his keen bright eyes flashing from one to the other of them alternately, while he also turns ashen pale, and beads of perspiration stand out on his forehead. Suddenly he rivets his luminous eyes on to Meiklejoy's, and in a second or two he has him under his influence.

'Do as I do,' says he; 'and let's sing to Djoolius "Should auld acquentance be forgot." Now then, all together, bhoys.'

Meiklejoy and Phelim sing lustily, in exact rhythm and harmony. Donkin only sings lackadaisically and out of tune, not having succumbed to the mesmeric influence.

But Phelim's eyes are rivetted upon his keener than ever; and in an instant he seems to become electrified, for he begins to sing as lustily as his confrère, and in perfect time.

They are both safely mesmerised.

'Now, bhoys, for a lark!' says Phelim, rejoicingly. 'You see this botthle av Ould Bushmills?'

They nodded.

'Well, take it smart to the Masther Cutler of Sheffield, with my compliments, for, faix, it's fairly murthered he is wid dhry-rot in the throath. Let him have a good sthrong pull of it, and tell him there isn't so much as a headache in the whole botthle. Now, bhoys, quick march; off yer go, an' min' the sthep!'

Away they set off towards Sheffield, marching in time, holding the bottle well to the "forra'd."

'Bhoys! Hoy! Sthop!' shouts Phelim.

They turn round and listen.

'Don't go and broach the "Bushmills" on the way, and have a care not to slive intho Dore Moor Inn nor any other dhramshops on yer way. Away wid yer, honest men, away!'

In a few minutes they are both lost to sight on the road that leads towards Fox House, on the way to Sheffield.

Phelim chuckles to himself; and soliloquizes—

'By the tarn o' war! they'll have greasy fethlocks afore they gets to Shevvild—tearin' off at that rate! Murther! won't the masther cuthler bisniss luke up afther this?'

He then goes round to old Sammy Tooley's cottage, and is not long in inducing that most pliable of ostlers to put the detectives' horse in their trap, "widout so much as makin' the noise of a pinfall." '

'Here's a bit o' yallow gowld for yer, Sammy,' says Phelim, mounting into the trap; 'an' if the young lassie should come this way to-night—for a moonlight walk, yer kno', Sammy— tell her I'll meet her by the bridge in Longshawe Wood. And Sammy, if those "two chaps fro' Shevvild" come pottherin' about here afther me afore cockcrow, tell 'em they may as well dhrink my health with the "Ould Bushmills." Adoo, Sammy!'

CHAPTER VIII

When Bryan Wolverton (*alias* Phelim O'Connor) came to the little bridge which crosses over a babbling steam —a tributary of the Derwent—he fastened the horse to the gate, which opened into a sort of bridle-path, which wound along by the banks of the water towards Longshawe Woods, and towards a little woodland cottage of a certain waterkeeper and fisherman, a cottage well known to many rodsters as "old Neddy Guest's."

From the gateway to the cottage was a distance of about three-quarters of a mile, up a pathway which led through the charming sylvan scenery so lovely hereabouts.

Often in his more youthful days had Bryan, eager-hearted as a boy, wended up this pleasant by-way of the world towards old Neddy's, for Neddy was the cunningest handicraftsman at dressing a trout-fly for miles around; and moreover it was Neddy that knew which flies were "taking," and which were not; and often would he make young Bryan's heart big with hope as he told him where there were a few "silver-bellied whoppers feedin' reit mad after t' march-browns."

Delightful days those, never to be forgotten, never to return. But was there not something else that thrilled his heart, as he bounded along by that babbling brook? What? Did not another pleasing vision of bye-gone days uprise before him, and fill his soul with the sweet, tender, budding hopes of his love's first dream?

Was it not here, amongst those dew-bespangled braes, where the speedwell blikkened brightly, and where the soft hair of the grass oft tempted him to rest awhile—was it not here 'mid pale-green aisles of light and shade, that his young poetic idea had first learned to shoot and body forth some blue-eyed Daphne of the woods, with whom to wander at will in the hazel groves and brambly wildernesses? Nay, had he not here, flushed with love's wild, deathless dream, kissed her o'er and o'er again, till the roses of her lips had fired his very heart?

Now was he treading heavenly trysting-ground, and he was glad, and thanked God in his heart to be once more on those dewy ways on love's sweet quest.

The moon seems tangled in the swinging tracery of the pensile birch, where through she casts a myriad twinkling shafts of light on to the singing stream that swirls and swerves below.

Bryan is struck with the marvellous beauty of the scene before him, and he pauses in his haste to mark the steely light of the moonbeams glinting, in a sort of delirious dance, on the restless waters of the brook that shimmers along.

Then away he hastens up the pathway, round the bend.

But what's that? He starts! Afraid? Not he. An apparition! No! 'Tis but a woman in white approaching him. She glides on nearer and nearer to him. She sees his face by the silvery light of the moon. Yes, it is he. There is no mistaking Bryan's features, long wavy beard, and tall manly form.

'Phelim!' she exclaims, as she approaches within a few paces of him.

'Acushla machree!' says he, rushing towards her, clasping her gentle waist, and kissing the sweet bloom of her lips; and then, as his hand wantoned through the wavy wealth of her hair, he asks, 'But what are you doing here, darling—after midnight too?'

'Hush, dear, hush! do not speak so loudly; there may be eavesdroppers in these woods, for my hiding-place at Old Neddy's is found out. Whom do you think I have seen to-day?'

'Misther Meiklejoy and Misther Donkey,' he said, with a confident smile.

'No, love; but I have seen that hateful man, Tom Shout, and my own brother Dandelow with him. Bryan, I know their business.'

'What is it, sweet wifie?' kissing her.

'They have come to horsewhip you,' she said; 'and so I stole out at this late hour to warn you of your danger.'

'Horsewhip me, bedad! Faix, what'll Phelim be doing the while? But, dearest, are you not dreaming, and wandering in your sleep?'

'No, Bryan; they came over from Sheffield to-day, and from my bedroom window I overheard what they said to old Neddy; and I am pained to say that Neddy told them a shocking untruth about me.'

'Heaven shrive his soul!' says Bryan, whose conscience smote him for having himself been guilty of something approaching to a lamentable lapse in this direction.

'Yes; and they threatened that they would horse-whip you within an inch of your life for running away with me. Tom Shout was most furious in his rage, and made use of quite ungentlemanly epithets against you, which I dare not mention.'

'Oh, you need not attempt it, sweet; there's little differ betune the good old Sheffield Saxon and the rale ould Limerick *blasthogue*;[7] but, darling, I also have had the unhappy experience of being interviewed by two detectives from Sheffield; and had I not fondly lured them on to spirit-rapping and then mesmerised them, and sent them on a fool's errand to the Masther Cuthler of Sheffield, I at this moment should have been a prisoner.'

Bryan's young wife, after he had explained to her his wonderfully successful piece of strategy, was heartily amused, and laughed outright, although she severely reprimanded him for still indulging in spirit-rapping, and also for his questionable dissembling with Meiklejoy and Donkin. But he was forgiven at the price of a kiss.

'Bryan, dear,' she says lovingly, looking up into his manly face, 'from what my brother Dandelow said, I am sure he thinks we are not married.'

---

[7] flattery, delusive talk

'Why *should* he think so, darling?' kissing her; 'we didn't send the bellman round, did we?'

'No, love; but Dandy ought to be told that we *are* married. He, I know, is really a kind-hearted brother; though he takes pride in being somewhat rough and uncouth in his manners. Yet I am sure there is no harm in him. He always loved me so; and I loved him. I have hope of Dandy, but he now believes we are a couple of unmarried runaways, no better than we should be.'

'What did he say, Belle, dear?'

'He told old Neddy that you were responsible for causing me to run away from my guardians—"unaxed and unparsoned," as he put it.'

'Perhaps I had better drop him a line, and explain everything. As you say, Dandy can wish us no harm, not if he knows the truth.'

'Why not tell everybody, dear? It is painful to act as a couple of dissembling sinners, wandering about as gipsies. Only think what pain it caused me, and must have caused poor old Neddy, for him to swear that he and his wife were the sole inmates of his cottage, when I was in the room above, and heard what was said.'

'Sweetest,' says he, kissing her again, 'mine is, as you know, a most aggravated case of contempt of the Court of Chancery. Not only was I forewarned and threatened, but I was forbidden your house. Yet you know how I disobeyed. Then you were sent away to Italy with a guardian duly appointed by the Court—Mrs Shacklewell. Well, you know what has happened; and as I have told you before, I have reason to think the Court will make me purge my contempt with a vengeance.'

'But, Bryan, love, I will cast all the blame upon myself, and plead for you as woman never pleaded before. Was it not I who told you to take me away from the espionage of that unkind chaperon?'

'Ah!' sighed Bryan; 'but was it not I that lifted the representative of the law over that hedge when we were in such delightful seclusion at St Margaret's Bay?'

'Yes, dear, yes. I knew you were too hasty; but O how I will plead for you! It was so aggravating of that horrid man to burst upon our privacy in that garden unawares; and the idea of his taking hold of you by the collar—the rude man!—as if you were a—' she paused for a word.

'A dhirty Saxon bla'guard,' adds Bryan, completing the sentence for her.

'Surely they wouldn't imprison you darling?'

'Well, I suppose I should be let off cheaply if I only get six months for the contempt, and six months for assault and battery. Now, if you like, dear, I'll give myself up. I'll surrender. What do you say?'

She pauses awhile, reflecting what to do for the best, then she says gently—

'Bryan, dear; what could you *really* make by painting, do you think? Enough to live on? No. Couldn't you, darling, if you tried hard?' asks she, looking up into his eyes and clasping his hand.

'Belle, my sweet,' says he, gazing lovingly under the long dark lashes of her unfathomable eyes, that shone so kindly into his; 'Belle, my total income from painting last year reached the colossal sum of twenty-three pounds two shillings and ninepence; and, dearest, were it not for a small income of £200, from money which my Aunt Kathleen left me, as you know, I should often have been reduced to beggary during the last two years.'

'Two hundred and twenty-three pounds two shillings and ninepence!' she exclaimed.

'Sterling!' he added dryly.

'Why, darling, this is truly a princely income!'

'Yes, love; why shouldn't we lease a German Schloss on some *Heim-weh-fluh*, where, rapt in bliss, we might dream, close-kissed, in the vine-sheltered crannies of the rock? An excellent idea!'

'Bryan, dear, don't jest at such a time as this. Could we not indeed flee the country, and live on your splendid income for a while, until this bother blows over? My poor father married on thirty shillings a week.'

'Ay, sweet, that may be. He—God rest him!—was brought up in the good old-fashioned school of hard work and thrift. But I? Ah! how was I brought up?'

'Not on the stubbles of idleness and unthrift, that I *do know*,' says she.

Bryan nodded. 'Yes I was.'

'How can you say so? Why, darling, you often used to write to me, and say that you were so absorbed in your work that you hadn't time to write to me more than six pages at a time.'

'True, Belle, but I was only then engaged upon pleasant work—call it pleasure if you will. There was no fruition—no increase—nothing but leaves!'

'But some day, dear, your name may be far famed as Nasmyth's or Constable's.'

'Some day,' he sighed.

'Bryan, for shame! You have no faith. Do you know, dear, that I once overheard Sir Newton Canklow of Rotherham speak very highly of your picture at the Exhibition of the Sheffield School of Art.'

'What! Old Canklow, the brewer? What did he say, may I ask?'

'He said that your picture would be "worth money" some day,' she replied.

'And is that why *you* bought it, eh, sweet?' asks he, kissing once more those rose-soft lips.

'No, dear,' she said; 'I measured not your work by money. The mere counters of wealth are as nothing to me. Some things are priceless—as your love.'

'Sweetest and kindest of critics! Surely you have not been taught such doctrines in Sheffield?'

'Yes, I have. I learnt them from Mr Kenneth Millwood.'

'What! old Ken? How very odd! Do you know he is staying within two miles of this place?'

'No, darling; you can't mean it!' she exclaimed.

'It's true as gospel,' says he.

'Really?'

'Yes, dear. He is staying with Connie down at the cottage near Grindleford Bridge.'

'Then let us go and see them at once. Do you know that I really loved Kenneth before I met you, darling?'

'Most likely,' said he dryly; 'but as for going down to see them—do you know what time it is?'

'No, dear, but I suppose it is getting late.'

'It is after one o'clock; and that's a pretty hour to call on young married folk. Why, sweet, they're long since asleep, close clasped in Morpheus' gentle chains.'

'Bryan, dear,' she said, after a pause, 'let us decide what to do—whether to flee from here at day-break, or run the risk of being separated for a while by the law.'

'Sit down, darling,' said he, pointing to a lichened stone, 'and let us take sweet counsel together. How soft is your cheek!' stroking her face. 'There never was a wifie like you, Belle.'

'Bryan, darling!'

'Love!'

How chaste and fair the moon sailed aloft, clothed upon with the splendour of darkness! How "the army of unalterable law"—the glistening stars—rank on rank, did burn and burn above Belle and Bryan, as they sat spell-bound as with love and hushed with delight. There was nothing stirring save a gentle whispering of the summer airs among the "oatgrass and the sword-grass, and the bulrush in the pool."

Occasionally was heard the noiseless wheeling of the bat's wing skimming round the trees, or now and again the chirping of some field-cricket that possibly had lost its way back to its chine or chink in the kindly earth.

The language of love is at times, like that of flowers, inarticulate. Thus it was with these lovers—their eyes and lips for awhile did pledge each other deeper than all words.

'Do poor folk ever get into Chancery, dear?' she asked, looking with her soft, thoughtful eyes into his.

'No, Belle, darling; not if the Court knows it! Why should they?'

'Surely penniless orphans need protection as much as rich heiresses!'

'Certainly, sweet,' he said; 'more so, indeed, for they are defenceless. Yet whoever heard of the Court having a penniless orphan for its ward? The Court protects property, not the individual.'

'Then,' asks she, 'were I penniless, the Court would hardly concern itself about me?'

'No, not at all, darling; not even if some jail-bird cajoled you away for your sweet innocence and beauty's sake.'

She began to reflect again. She was silent. Her face began to betray her thoughts.

'What is it?' he asked.

'Bryan, dear, for your sake can I not forego my portion and become penniless, and then the law will have nothing more to do with us?'

'Dearest,' he said, 'the money may become useful to you, so perhaps it would be best for us to leave this happy spot soon after daybreak. We shall find a safer and more distant retreat, where we can learn all the manoeuvres of the enemy from my solicitor—young Osgathorpe of Sheffield until these dark threatening skies grow cloudless and happy again.'

So it happened that in the early morning they were driven off towards Chapel-en-le-Frith by old Neddy; and on the evening of that day Mr and Mrs O'Connor found themselves comfortably housed at 'The Tontine' in Liverpool, and on the following morning were well on the way to Limerick.

Mr Thomas Shout and Mr Dandelow Bantam, who had been sleeping over-night at Fox House, were up betimes on the morrow of Mr and Mrs Wolverton's departure from "old Neddy Guest's." They set off, intending to waylay Bryan as he went to the keeper's cottage, for they had got additional and more positive information that a young woman, exactly answering to the description of Miss Belle Bantam, had often been seen in the woods by old Neddy's, dressed in a loosely flowing garment of a russet colour, and wearing an old Gainsborough hat of faded and sun-dyed tints, which looked as if it had seen better days. Her appearance was represented to them as being "sweeter nor sweet pays or vilets in blume."

But Bryan and Belle had flown long before Tom and Dandy, armed with horsewhips, reached Longshawe Bottoms, though of course neither of these irate men were aware of it; so when they came to the bridle-path that leads up to old Neddy's, they conceal themselves behind the hedge of a little field or toft, fully persuaded that Bryan ere long would pass that way. They wait in ambush for an hour or two, but Bryan comes not, much to the disappointment of these angry bachelors.

There was something strangely incongruous in the natures of these men, yet for the nonce their spirits were fused as one. What had made them friends, that were once sworn un-friends? Was it not that Tom was writhing under the keen smart of having his long but vainly-coveted prize, Miss Belle Bantam, suddenly snatched from him? And was it not that Dandy, firmly believing that a ne'er-do-weel had off with his well-beloved sister, and firmly refusing to believe that they were duly "axed and parsoned," had made a sort of unholy compact with the former to horsewhip Bryan for his most scandalous conduct? Neither would have dared to embark upon such a perilous enterprise single-handed, but the twain of them felt quite equal to give the "rascal" a thrashing.

Tom was indefatigable in adding fuel to Dandy's wrath, and did not scruple to malign Bryan to the last degree; and so it was that these two, who hitherto had been divided by the sharp lines of hatred and distrust of each other, had become allies in their passionate desire to avenge themselves on their common enemy. But the enemy came not, as hour after hour they waited behind that thickset hedge for his appearance.

Their conversation drifted from one thing to another, until it verged upon a subject about which they were still "at daggers drawn." This was the mysterious disappearance of Captain Underwedge and Tom's father three years ago.

'He, if anybody does, kno's something about their disappearance. Yes, fair or foul, Kenneth kno's all about it,' says Tom.

'Rubbidge!' says Dandy. 'I kno' him better nor you, seein' as I lodged with him once up at Nether Edge. Kenneth's a gentleman born.'

'A sneaking coward!' added Tom. 'Why the deuce didn't he come back to the Forge after he got over that trumped-up accident of his? Ah! why indeed? Becos his conscience troubled him, that's why. And agen, what about Billy Benskin? Why, since we "sacked" him fro' t' works he's gone "cracked," and thinks hisself a prophet—taken to preachin' roarin' and rantin' i' t' chapel. Conscience agen! And what about old Mike, eh? Why, after we paid him off, he goes and turns consumptive and dies a lingerin' death. What! isn't that a judgment on him? Conscience agen! And what's more, Kenneth Millwood's mother died seemin'ly from a broken heart, becos her undutiful son had got wed to a penniless good-for-nowt; and poor old Millwood, the minister, had to give up his income, and go into a back street at Llandudno becos he couldn't abear to be near his unfilial son. And agen, who did Kenneth marry, eh?—a Miss Nobbody, as I said afore—a sister of this scamp we want to catch—a woman no better than she orter be, I'll warrant, which is sayin' a lot; and all I hope is that he's catched a Tartar—which I'm sure he has. Another judgment!'

Poor Dandy could hardly get a word in edgeways.

'It's my opinion,' continued Tom, 'that Kenneth Benskin and Mike should have been locked up on suspicion.'

'But,' interposed Dandy, 'wait a bit, man. Neither your father's nor the Captain's bodies have been found yet. It'll be time enoo to talk about lockin' folks up when t' bodies is found. It strikes me forcibly that you nivver heard tell o' t'abeas Corpus Act; but hush! 'sh! 'sh!' says Dandy; 'hark! I hear footsteps comin' down the lane. 'Sh, 'sh; be still!'

No one passes by, but suddenly through the gate of the toft a shaggy-haired, black, long-horned bull rushes full speed, and immediately a boy—a broad-faced, big-booted, billy-cocked, smock-frocked, bucolic-looking individual—bangs the gate to, and climbs on the top thereof to see how "Mester Bull" enjoys being isolated from his erewhile loving companions.

Now it so happened that Master Taurus had of late been guilty of causing indescribable alarm and confusion by making raids into certain forbidden territory, where good Farmer Jolliboys thought it so highly undesirable Taurus should never enter more, that he had sent his son with the bull to the bottom toft, to be quite out of sight of his quondam friends.

The bull, naturally enough, was mightily angered when he found himself shut up in this small enclosure or toft, and was in high disdain that a well-timed raid over some neighbouring fences should have been foiled by a young scarecrow sort of chaw-bacon. He pawed the turf, then lowered his horns, and rushed about the paddock wildly. No doubt it pained him to think that his loving protectorate over certain of his kith and kin had peradventure been given to another.

Jealousy having taken root in his heart, he began to tear round that small field like wildfire, so that young Jolliboys, lolling over the gate, remarked to himself—

'Dang it, he's stark mad—brussen up wi' rage, I reckin; but he'll not rootle through this 'ere fence in a hurry.'

The bull suddenly saw the two faces of Dandy and Tom peeping out of some long rank grass near an oak-tree in the corner of the meadow. They had been somewhat apprehensive of danger as soon as they had seen him enter the close; and their feelings of alarm were suddenly intensified when Master Bull, whisking his tail aloft, came thundering along towards them. Young Hodge, on his coign of vantage, the six-barred gate, saw the faces of these strangers and saw the bull tearing towards them, as also he saw the two quickly rush for their very lives behind the friendly oak. Dandy and Tom had never run so hard in their lives.

'He made 'em mizzle,' observed the boy to himself, with a quiet grin. 'Freightened o' t' bull seemin'ly,' he thought. When the bull reached the oak, he swerved round it, and made them dodge round the tree to avoid his horns. He fully meant to wreak his vengeance upon these two visitors, so round and round the oak he wheeled and bellowed; and the more he was baffled the more angry he became, until at last his eyes seemed to glare with rage.

For a minute or so he stood still, thinking they would break cover, and that he would exalt them over the hedge; but Dandy and Tom were too artful to risk the exposure of their posterior trouserings to any of Mr Bull's manners of argument.

Then again begun the roundabout business, and continued so long that both Tom and Dandy began to feel very hot by reason of their fright and wearisome quick manoeuvrings.

'Rare stirrin's!' shouts the boy; 'go it, fat un,' says he to poor fat Dandy, who is wellnigh exhausted.

'Come and drive him off!' shouts Tom to the boy.

'Naa, naa,' says the Derbyshire boy; 'he's not agoin' to toozle mea.'

Round and round they went, until both the bull and his imaginary foes grew dizzy; and the former began to lean more and more towards the tree, so that his tail often seemed to lap round the tree within reach of Dandy and Tom as they sidled round and round.

'I'll give you a sovereign, boy, if you'll call him away,' says Tom, puffing like a grampus.

'Will yer give me tew?' asks young Hodge, grinning.

'We will!' exclaims Dandy, almost faint with exhaustion.

'Well,' says the boy 'I can't call him away, but I can tell yer a road out o' this pickle, if yer'll chuck me the munny.'

Dandy threw his purse towards the boy; but to the credit of that boy be it said he did not go and help himself, but said with a contemptuous grin—

'Oi doant want yer brass! Jus lissen to me, d'ye hear, and do as Oi tells yer.'

'What's that?' they ask breathlessly.

'Sam owd on his tail, and then yo've got him, says the boy.

'Eh! what?' they ask.

'Sam owd on his tail,' the boy repeated; and at that very moment the bull gave them a chance of seizing his tail, so they both clutched hold of it, fast as grim death, and then—O ye powers! wasn't there a stampede round that toft! Away they went over hillock and hollock—helter-skelter—such a pace! Never yet had Dandy's fat little legs plied so quickly. Never yet had Tom Shout's liver had such a terrible shaking up.

'Waat till his bloomin' tail lathers,' grinned the boy.

At last the trio came to a standstill by the gate, thoroughly breathless and exhausted, but poor Dandy was just able to gasp out to the boy—

'Is he mad?'

'Mad!' says the boy, with a knowing grin. 'Waat till yer've yarked his tail off, and then you'll kno.'

This pithy rejoinder was not calculated to assuage the fears in, or inspire confidence into, either Tom's or Dandy's heroic breasts. It left so much to the imagination; and yet what was left unsaid seemed of such momentous and prophetic significance.

'What? wait till w-w-w-what?' stammers Tom, as if he was about to have a fit.

The boy nodded a malicious nod.

'O murder!' says Dandy; 'this'll never do!'

'A'! mesters!' exclaims the boy, more reassuringly, 'yo' needn't be afeared on him. Sticken yo' fast to old Runtle's tail, and then yo're safe as 'ouses; and when yo' gets close to t' bottom fence yonder—slip of t' tail, brust thro' t' hedge, and lammas up t' lane.'

Scarcely were these words of advice out of the boy's mouth when off "Old Runtle" starts again, more furiously than before, plunging down the croft at a terrific speed; and just as he came to the banks of the stream at the far corner of the meadow, his unwieldy bulk swerved round sharply, whilst at that moment Dandy stumbled over an old tree-stump, and over he fell, with Tom on the top of him. Luckily for them, they both rolled down the steep shelving bank of the stream, and fell with a tremendous splash into a rather deep pool or hole below.

'Dang it!' says young Hodge, getting off the gate; 't' gam's up; they've tumbled i' t' watter hoil.'

The bull stood as if stark, staring mad, as he saw them roll into the water, and as he watched them crawl out on the opposite bank, muddy, bruised, and drenched to the skin.

Young Jolliboys then sidled off home, and as he passed through the Brownstorth meadow, where the kine were peacefully browsing, he, after the manner of lonesome country cowboys, soliloquised—

'I'll lay tew thousan' to a 'a'-seed[8] as them tew chaps'll nivver lig long i' t' hedge bottom if they see old Runtle a-comin'.

Across the meadow came a sound as of distant heifers lowing, as it were, at some lamentable loss.

'Ay,' he soliloquised, 'yer may well begin lowin' an frettin'. Losh, if yer only knew what mischief's come to yer poor feyther's tail, yer hearts 'ud be brokken wi' sorrer.'

---

[8] hayseed

PART III

CHAPTER IX

EIGHTEEN MONTHS AFTER.

The arrows of hatred are ofttimes tipped, as it were, with steel, cold-chilled in bitter tears; whereas the shafts of love oft sing warm-feathered through the kind immensities.

Kenneth Millwood was again 'hard hit,' but not this time of love's sweet pain. He had lost an appointment which he had held since he left Otterclough Forge, under a firm of steel manufacturers and refiners, of the name of Petersen & Oughtibridge. This calamity had been brought about not a little by the dark hints and mysterious machinations on the part of Mr Thomas Shout and his friend Robert Underwedge, who had spared no pains to undermine Kenneth's position whenever chance offered.

They were members of the "inner circle" at the "Stannidge Pole," and so were Messieurs Petersen and Oughtibridge; and it was here that dark calumnious hints were often thrown out, which did not redound to Kenneth's credit. He always kept aloof from "Old Jerry's," or "Diggles'," and thereby gained for himself the unenviable reputation of being too proud to associate with his fellow-craftsmen in business.

But this must be said, neither Tom nor "Roberd" would have accomplished Kenneth's downfall had it not been for a very untoward event happening at a time when it was least expected. Kenneth, in a moment of unwise generosity, had put his name on the back of a bill to oblige a clever young acquaintance of his—his wife's cousin—who also was engaged in the Sheffield trade. The bill, which Kenneth had been made to believe was a genuine trade bill, was not met; and the bank who had discounted it came down upon Kenneth for the full amount of £570, for the clever acquaintance, together with the drawer of the bill, had run away when they found themselves unable to get it renewed. A writ was soon served upon Kenneth, which brought matters to a climax. He made a clean breast of his folly to his principals, and they, instead of helping him, told him that a man who could be so foolish as to endorse a bill to oblige a friend was not to be trusted. Explanations were futile. The partners were inexorable. What made matters worse was the fact that the defaulter was known to have undersold the whole "trade" by taking a Government order for files five per cent. below any other firm. Mr Oughtibridge had sworn at Kenneth an idle oath for his folly. Kenneth felt so sharply stung by his principal's rebuke that, when he went home, he had written, without saying a word to his dear wife Connie, and offered to resign. After three days his resignation was accepted, for the partners had, unluckily for Kenneth, conferred at "Diggles," where they had met Mr Thomas Shout and Mr Robert Underwedge, who shot their last bolt with dire effect.

Tom had said, 'Accommodation bill indeed! Umph! a man as'll put his name to such a dockyment, without security, orter be 'orse-whipped. Simply gettin' money by false pretences,— which allus means that, sooner or later, there's the deuce to pay. Why, gentlemen, do you know that young ambitious upstart has actually been tryin' to bamboozle that fool Dandelow Bantam into a partnership, to work out the precious patent he found out when my father and Captain Underwedge were sent to kingdom come. Who by, I wonder, eh? who by? I'd lay a thowsan' pound to a 'a'-seed as Kenneth Millwood was either an haccomplice or an hacissory in that terrible mystery?'

Kenneth's home was at Ranmoor, a delightful suburb of Sheffield, save when the dense smoke-clouds from the town, with the east wind for a helmsman, came sailing o'er Broomhill.

It was a bleak wintry day, and it so happened that the keen east wind, full charged with the reek and the dust from the revels of Old King Coal, came ravening up the valley, soughing among the gaunt bare limbs of the trees, that creaked and reeled in the rocking blast.

Hark, how it sings and whistles! strong as the groundwhirl of the hurrying winds of death that vex poor sinners, shivering by the lich-gates of the field of tombs, to an early repentance.

Kenneth and his sweet wife Connie draw nearer to the crackling branch coal fire in the grate. Little Bryan is playing on the hearth-rug, building him an "itta housie" with his wooden bricks; while the baby is asleep in a prettily dight[9] bassinet in the warmest corner of the parlour. There is an air of comfort as well as of refinement about the room. Connie has an artistic eye for everything, and had here been remarkably successful in her art. Simplicity and purity of style were studied by her. There were no hideous white antimacassars to glare at you as the whitened bones of the dead; no long white muslin curtains, that make you shudder and feel sick at heart as though you were being raveled in a shroud; no over-crowding of ornament—and, above all, there was nothing that painfully obtruded itself upon you as "havin' cos' munny." Homeliness and comfort reigned supreme— from the old oaken eight-day clock with its antique brazen face, to the old-fashioned arm-chair, carven of old by some chisel of love, not used to the craft of putty and veneer.

So Kenneth and Connie silently sat together by the cosy fire, while the cat was singing or "thrumming" close to the old brass fender.

____

[9] dressed/adorned

'What are you thinking of, love?' she asks, chaining her soft, white fingers together, and placing them gently on his shoulder, leaning and gazing lovingly into his eyes.

He turned his head, looking into their soft hazel depths, and kissed her, but he spoke not.

She drew her chair nearer to his, and entwined her right arm around his neck. She stroked his forehead. She kissed him.

Little Bryan looked up at that moment, and with a childish simplicity, asked—

'What for do oo tiss fader, mudder, dear? Is he pooloo?'

'Hush, darling, hush!' she said, patting his ample locks of gold. 'Poor father will be better soon.'

And she turned to him, and asked him so beseechingly, and yet so tenderly. Who could resist her?

'What is it, dear? Do tell me, Ken, darling.'

'Connie, my dear little woman,' he faltered.

'I cannot—I dare hardly tell you; but'—he paused as he looked again into those kind, sweet eyes— 'you *will* have to know—yes,' he sighed, 'you *will* have to know. Soon enough! Ay, too soon, my love, too soon.'

'Tell me,' she whispered; 'is it bad news from Bryan?'

'No, sweet; from Petersen & Oughtibridge. See,' said he, handing her the letter, 'this is what mostly troubles me.'

She read it over twice, gave it back to him, and kissing him again, said—

'Tell me, Ken, all about it? Do explain.'

Poor Kenneth felt constrained by her gentle sympathy, and little by little told her everything concluding—

'We shall have to leave this house at once, darling. The bank manager will give us no quarter. I have had an interview with him give to-day. He says he will sell up every stick about the place.'

Then followed a painful silence, during which Connie nestled closer to her husband, while her long wavy wealth of hair hung over his shoulders.

'Poor old darling!' she said at last, bursting into tears; 'but this, even this, is not so hard to bear as the dark noiseless shafts of calumny against your name, which have eaten into my very soul. Be brave, dearie. God lives to love. Forget not all His benefits.'

'What for do oo tie, mudder, dear?' asked little Bryan, leaving his bricks.

She stroked his pretty face and played with his lovelocks. But he clung to her dress, climbed upon her knee, soothingly lisping words of sweet, childish comfort—

'My itta, itta, poor itta pet lamb. Dere! dere!' he said, wiping her tears away; 'don't tie, mamsie, dear, don't tie.'

Kenneth kissed his little son, who wist not how dim were his father's eyes.

The evening wore on. The children were asleep in bed. Kenneth and Connie sat talking by the fire. The former felt some secret spring of strength well up in his heart as Connie won her way into its depths, and brushed away its sad forebodings. Yes, the shafts of love sing warm-feathered through the kind immensities.

'Ken, dear, if we leave this house next month, where do you think we shall have to go?'

'I cannot say, sweet; that depends upon what sort of work I get, and where,' he said sadly. 'Why, dearest, you have forgotten,' she exclaimed; 'there is that patent of yours, for which you said Mr Otto Schlesinger offered you four hundred pounds.'

'Yes, dear,' he said, painfully; 'but I will not sell that.'

'But why not, darling? It might save us from this terrible calamity of being sold up. Think of the children, dear, never mind me; but think of them, love, do. You know, dear, you can invent something else equally as good.'

'No, no, little woman; anything but this. This is as my birthright of the ages, given me of God, my priceless heritage. I never will sell it —never! not whilst I have hands to work for you, and a heart to love you. No, darling, no; not whilst your love can enkindle mine to win you bread—to slave for you—to cherish you—to die for you.'

'O Kenneth, Kenneth, darling Kenneth!' she said in tears, 'you are too good for me. But pray forgive me, Ken; I ought to have remembered what you told me a year or two ago. Dear,' she continued meditatively, 'have we no friends to help us?'

'None, darling, none; except it may be Dandelow Bantam, and I should be the last to take advantage of his good-heartedness and simplicity. Of course there is Bryan, but, as you know, he is in need, and already owes me about £200. He, I know, is a good soul, and would help if he could; but where is he?'

'Could not your fath—beg pardon, dear, I mean the Rev. Mr Millwood—help you a little? Surely he cannot be so ill provided for as it was represented at his chapel on his retirement, when they raised a handsome subscription for him to furnish a house at Llandudno, and pensioned him off.'

'Why, darling? Have you heard that he is well off?'

'Well, not exactly, dear. But the Barrowcloughs, who have a house at Llandudno, say that they have every reason to believe he is very well off, although he is very close and miserly in his ways.'

'My love,' said Kenneth, 'were he a millionaire and were I starving in the street, I would not beg or cadge a copper from his hoard. *He*,' said Kenneth, with lofty, scornful air, 'who married my poor mother when I was but five months old—ay, almost before he knew for certain that my father was dead. *He*, whose prayers were as froth, and whose hollow creaking faith was oiled with lust of gain, which he palmed off as a pure, unselfish, and heaven-hallowed love. *He*, who robbed me of mine inheritance—shall I cringe and sue before him? No, darling, no. God shall visit him; ay, God shall visit him!'

'Kenneth, love,' she gently whispered, pleadingly, on his arm, 'let us be kind—utterly kind. Think dearest, how can we afford to be otherwise, when to-morrow we may need so much kindness at our brothers' hands? May it not be that even *he* will yet repent, and give you back what should have been yours?'

Kenneth turned his head away and sighed a deep hopeless sigh, and shook his head, 'No, no, never!'

Later on, towards midnight, they stole softly together into their warm cosy bedroom. They went to Bryan's little cot. Lapt in peaceful slumber was he. Helplessly lay his erewhile restless hands on the fringe of the coverlet. Sweet was his sleep. His rose-soft cheek did cozen the pillow with a child's pure kiss. Adown the rose-leaf sweetness of his face a wanton lovelock strayed.

On the other side of the bed was the baby Gladys. Calm and still she lay, as if some slumberous spell had woven a wakeless weft on silken lid and dappled hand. Love walked upon that tiny face, from the wee kiss-suing lips that were sweet to the swan's-down flax of her hair. Her skin was as fair and soft as the petals of the wild-briar rose besprent with fairy beads of morning dew. Close clenched were the little fists. The lips, half apart and still, yet spoke as mouths of dumb sea-shells. Kenneth kissed her, and whispered to his wife—

'Heaven is here.'

She peeped at the sweet little face, and touched the velvety hands to feel if they were warm, and said—

'Surely it *is*, Ken. Isn't she an angel?'

'Soon afterwards Connie took a chair, and sat down near to the fire, and began to comb out the glossy tresses of her long wavy hair. Kenneth also drew a chair near to hers, and sat close by her, and rubbing his hands by the warm glowing fire, said after a sigh—

'This is a luxury, dear, *now*; we must say bye-bye to fires after this; we can't afford them.'

Connie ceased combing her luxuriant tresses. She began to gaze into that fire. They both gazed vacantly into it. Neither of them spoke for awhile, nor dare they venture to look into each other's pitiful eyes.

What could they see in that fire? Ah what could they *not* see? For them the mist of bygone years was haply brushed away, and once more as children they saw visions in the shimmering red caverns between the bars of the grate. Kenneth turned to his wife, still gazing with her soft misty eyes into the fire, and remembering the song that she once sang him five or six years ago, he half sang and half whispered into her ear, 'What are you dreaming of, auld Marie, auld Marie?'

She answered not, but buried her head, in her wealth of hair, on his shoulder. There was silence. Softly he stroked her hair, but spoke not. Somehow his voice was a little bit—. Well, you know, kind reader. He continued stroking, and stroking, and stroking.

'That is so nice, dear. It eases me so—my head, you know,' she said after awhile.

'Poor little woman! Does it ache?' he gently asked.

'Yes, Ken, dear, it always begins aching and throbbing when I am worried.'

'Be brave, sweet, and cheer up,' said he still softly stroking her forehead; 'remember what you told me downstairs—what was it? Forget not all—'

'His benefits,' she added; and then noiselessly she went to the bedside and knelt down. He crept there too; and the Allfather heard! For awhile there was peace in the hearts that were twain.

That night Kenneth had but little sleep, but Connie, after two or three hours of "restless-hearted rest," fell asleep. The room was lighted with a night-light, and by the flickering light from the fire. Kenneth, long after Connie had fallen asleep, kept awake, looking tenderly at her sweet face—yes, how passing sweet it was! How peaceful!

'Surely that is a deathless line of the bard's, "Sleep that knits up the raveled sleive of care," ' he thought; and yet the face was somewhat pale, and, as it were, a delicate pencilling or shadow of care served but to evoke in him a tender compassion for the one he loved so.

Unweariedly he kept vigil o'er his sleeping treasures, while many and tumultuous were the thoughts that flashed through his mind.

Dawn came, but not with rosy shafts of light, nor keen frost-boding beams.

Kenneth looked out of the window, and saw that it had been snowing for a long time, and that snow was still falling thick and fast—the white feathery flakes being driven by the keen wind.

Soon little Bryan awoke, and stood up tiptoe in his cot, astonished to see a white world.

His memory did not carry him so far back as the last snowstorm. He was puzzled.

'What—what—what,' said he, rubbing his eyes, 'what is it so dusty for, daddy?'

'It's the snow, dear, falling from the sky.'

The child appeared to reflect a second or two, and then asked—

'Doesn't Dod want it?'

'No, love; He sends it to keep the earth and the grass warm.'

Again the boy began to ruminate.

'What for does Dod send de earache, den?' asked he, doubtless thinking that the snow was like cotton-wool; and to his mind, of course, earache and cotton-wool were closely related.

Kenneth made no reply. Connie woke up. Little Bryan saw her eyes open, and said—

' 'Ook, mamsie, dear, 'ook. Dod's raining totton-woo' for de earache. And for de headache too, mudder, dear,' he added, as if to cheer her.

She kissed him for his thoughtfulness, and as she did so she felt a dizzy sensation come over her head, and it began to ache as if it would split.

When breakfast was over, Kenneth put on his top-coat, and got ready to be off.

'Surely, dear, you are not going to venture out in such a storm as this? Wherever are you going to?'

'I'm going to advertise for a situation in the Sheffield papers. I must go, love, to find work, you know.'

He kissed her and the children, and away he went into the blinding snowstorm.

He came back rather late in the evening, wet and cold. He had put advertisements into both the papers. He had also seen several of the heads of large iron and steel works, but had hardly received common courtesy from the most of them.

He had had a long interview with Mr Otto Schlesinger concerning the working of his patent, but the cautious Teuton had wanted too much of his own way, and had imposed conditions at which Kenneth's pride utterly rebelled.

Day after day passed by, and Kenneth's efforts to get employment proved futile. Not a solitary answer came in response to his advertisement save one, and that was from a firm which required "A smart, pushing gent as can influence orders for grease and oil among storekeepers at large ironworks and collieries. Commission accordin' to prices secured."

Poor Kenneth felt himself getting into low water. His resources were dwindling away, and the bank would not suspend execution more than three days longer. What was to be done? When he had broached the subject of working his patent to certain large iron and steel manufacturers, they had mostly ridiculed it, and one of them, a crusty old Hallamshire blade, had said,—

'A'! lad, we don't want none o' thy new-fangled schemes here. Thou'd better go and teach thy gran'muther.'

Kenneth little thought how deeply the slanders against his name had taken root. Nearly all the manufacturers he interviewed thought to themselves when they saw him, 'Why, this is the young upstart that's mixed up with "The Attercliffe Mystery." '

On the eve of the day on which execution was to be levied on his household effects, he came home flushed and excited; and poor Connie, as she let him in, and as they kissed, as was their wont, knew that he had something on his mind, yet she dare not ask him what. Hope and fear thrilled her through and through.

He kissed his children, and then sat down in the old armchair. Little Bryan clomb his knees, while baby Gladys crept close to his feet, but their father hardly heeded them.

'What for don't oo tittle us, daddy?' asked the boy.

'Father is weary and tired, dear,' said his mother.

Bryan gave a questioning, wondering look up into his father's face, and, kissing him, asked—

'Poor daddy! Are oo wollied? Does oor head ache, like mudder's?'

'No, my little man,' said his father. 'I'm not so worried now, and my headache is getting better'

'Any success to-day, dear?' ventured Connie, somewhat indifferently, as though she did not wish to pain him by wringing from him another sad negative—and yet how her heart longed to hear good news.

'Yes, darling,' he said; assuming a brighter face; 'I have found work and a house!'

'Work! A house!'

How her heart leapt within her, as she went to him, and kissing him, exclaimed thankfully—

'Thank God!'

There was silence. Kenneth looked pained, as if to say, 'Ah, she doesn't know all!'

'Tank Dod!' repeated the boy, and again he echoed it. 'Tank Dod—for what, mudder?'

'For work, love, for work,' said the mother to her son, and nestling closer to her husband, asked, 'Do tell me all about it, darling? Where have you taken a house?'

Most pitifully and most tenderly did he gaze into her face, and said, as cheerfully as he could—

'At Attercliffe.'

'Attercliffe! Attercliffe!'

A little wider she opened her eyes, which looked so timid, as timid as a bird's when a kestrel sweeps aloft. She seemed to shrink within herself at the bare thought of having to live in that unlovely and forever unlovable spot. It was a shock too great for her highly-strung nerves.

'Attercliffe!' she again exclaimed, folding her hands. 'Oh!' she sighed, 'O Kenneth, this is hard—too hard to bear!'

'Little woman,' he said cheerfully; ' 'twas you bade me be brave. And what else did you tell me—eh, my pet?' said he, smiling in spite of himself. 'Come, sweet, what was it? Tell me? God—lives to—'

'Lub,' chimed in little Bryan. 'I know dat tex' Mudder tell it me. I know anodder tex'.'

'What is it, darling?' asked his mother.

'Fordet—fordet—fordet,' he hesitated; 'fordet not all His —His—His— Fordet not all His— Mudder, I've fordotten the tex',' said he, appealing to her.

And the poor little child knew not why they kissed him so.

CHAPTER X

"Pitifully behold the sorrows of our hearts!" was the name of a picture being painted by Bryan Wolverton, who was then staying at a small village in the Deanery of Ballyragget. It was an eviction scene, and so enamoured was the artist with his subject, that as he put the finishing touches to his work, he felt conscious of success. The whole painting was full of tenderness, pathos, and poetry, and was over-brimming with life. His good wife Belle praised it unstintedly; and, indeed, the keen interest she took in his work, and her devotion to him, were the means of saving him from that gloomy pitfall of despair into which scores of young artists are so apt to fall.

Had Bryan and Belle but known that the picture nearing completion was as a prophecy then being, in a manner, fulfilled, and terribly visited upon Kenneth and Connie, how their hearts would have melted within them, and how their sympathy would have taken a practical shape; but as it was, neither of them had heard news from Sheffield for over three months, owing to the miscarriage of several letters—which, it afterwards was made clear, had not been re-directed to them, and this had led to a misunderstanding, so that Belle had said —'Well, if it is too much trouble for Connie and Kenneth to write to us, we had perhaps better wait until they awake from their apathy.'

Kenneth was allowed by the sheriff's officer who had taken possession of his household effects to take a few inferior articles of bedding, and what apparel was absolutely necessary. The officer had been instructed to act up to the very letter of the law and Kenneth's honest pride had forbidden his seeking an interview with the relentless bank manager, to ask him to act more leniently, and to allow them to take some of their wedding presents, and a few comparatively valueless articles of furniture. Thus it happened, when the sad hour for removal came, there was nothing to remove more than what a poor evicted labourer might possess.

Keen and bitter was the pang which Connie felt as she left behind those household gods and little belongings which she had treasured so. Especially keen was the smart of having to part with her piano —a cottage Erard, which Kenneth had bought her as his wedding present. As she touched the keys for the last time, and played softly "Dream Faces," her feelings were inexpressibly sad and tumultuous; but she brushed away the presumptuous tears that stole adown her cheek when she heard Kenneth's manly ringing voice—

'Connie, dear, everything is ready. The cab is here, and our little belongings are now well on the way. Come along, my brave little woman, come along,' said he, as if to cheer her, as he led her to the cab. 'You know we are going to live awhile, not amongst the drones, but amongst men that women who toil. It may be we may find that happiness is their lot, and will be ours too for the asking. Who knows?'

Away they rattled along the Ranmoor Road, down Broomhill and the Glossop Road, through the heart of Hallamshire, over the Don, along the Wicker, until they came in sight of the dreary, sunless, smoky hive of Attercliffe—that sulphurous-canopied, myriad-moted land, flanked and frowned upon by ramp on ramp of winged bastions of smoke, rolling slowly away, blotting out the wintry gleams from Phœbus' falchions, flashing through wild skies their ruddy westering way.

Great is the contrast between Belgravia and Wapping; far greater that between Ranmoor and Attercliffe.

Here, in this black stythying-place for the fiends of battle, are rows on rows of dirty brick houses, begrimed with soot and smoke—dingy, frowsy, utterly unlovable and appalling to the senses; and yet far away, and dimly discernible through the nebulous haze of smoke, and through the shimmering fusion of gaseous fumes that are belched from hundreds of fiery furnaces, are the faint sky-lines of lofty tree-capped hills, o'er which at times the sun glints forth with his all-vivifying beams to thrill with hope, it may be some sin-stricken soul below, travel-stained and aweary of the strife, heart-sick with the dust and clatter of Mammon's blood-stained chariot-wheels, home-sick for heaven!

Hither came Kenneth and his family to dwell.

A man who gets fifty shillings a week, and who has a wife and family, and has to be at his work at Attercliffe at six o'clock every morning, cannot afford to live at Ranmoor. He cannot pick and choose.

Kenneth had found work as a foreman steel melter at the small manufactory of one named Mr Locksley Lynnacre, who up to now had been what is generally known in Sheffield as a "little mester"; but being a man of thrift, and a sober, long-headed Yorkshireman, he had saved enough money to build him a twelve-holed furnace for melting cast steel. Although he had been warned not to employ Kenneth, he had thought well to be charitable, and exercise his own discretion. Mr Lynnacre had offered Kenneth fifty shillings a week to begin with, and Kenneth, feeling anxious to be in a position where he would have every opportunity of adding more to his knowledge of the steel trade, had accepted it.

Mr Lynnacre was favourably impressed with Kenneth's ability as to the melting of the different "tempers" of steel, so necessary for his growing business; and he soon found out that his opinions were well founded, for Kenneth soon proved himself to be a thoroughly practical and efficient man of business, so much so, indeed, that Mr Lynnacre, being more and more inclined towards him, raised his salary to three pounds per week at the end of three months.

Somewhat unfortunately for Kenneth, Mr Lynnacre's manufactory was not on an extensive scale, and therefore was not suited for the working out of Kenneth's patent. Otherwise Mr Lynnacre would have been only too happy to allow him to continue his former experiments.

Kenneth's cottage was in Bessemer Street, and after he had been there three months it began to look cosy and comfortable inside, albeit the outside was of course unavoidably dingy.

Connie, in spite of failing health, had done her very best to make her husband happy and comfortable in his new surroundings; and indeed they had found secret joys which before they had never experienced.

Hard work—for they both worked hard—not only brought the priceless dowers of good appetite and sound sleep, but the altogether sweet consciousness that they were living in communion with Him, who, if aught be true, long ago had changed the curse of labour into the most desirable of blessings, for which all true workers should thank God continually. Moreover, instead of finding themselves dwelling amongst a colony of rough, uncouth iron-workers and artisans, they had found themselves denizens amongst men and women who were gentle, kind, and true at heart, though often with a ruggedness of manner and exterior that concealed the sovereign worth of their ready sympathy.

Poor Connie had had a good deal of note-paper sympathy from her quondam friends up in the West End. She now experienced some of that practical ready sympathy from some of her poorer neighbours in Bessemer Street. The poor oft give of their very best—body and soul—ungrudgingly; whereas the well-to-do oft give what costs them nothing, or it may be, at best, some effervescent tear-drops of sympathy done up in best "cream-laid."

Mrs Martha Stallybrass, an iron-roller's wife, and Mrs Ruth Pimpernel, an artisan's wife, were neighbours of Mrs Millwood. They had "sorter taken to her" from the very first day of her arrival, and these two estimable parties had ever since vied with each other in a friendly emulation as to which could rub and scrub her doorstep or her "har'-stone"[10] the best and tidiest. Also they were next kin to being jealous of each other's attentions to the baby Gladys, while they both fell to tears the first night they heard little Bryan, low-bending at his mother's knee, sweetly lisp his evening prayer—

'P'way, Dod, b'ess fader and mudder, and itta Dadys, and Mrs 'Tallyb'ass and Mr 'Tallyb'ass, wif de pooloo leg, and Mrs Pimperwewes, and all de itta Pimperwewes, and div dem a dood p'wace in dy tin'dom of lub.'

One Sunday afternoon Mrs Stallybrass, who was a very stout woman of about fifty-five summers, and Mrs Ruth Pimpernel, who was an exceeding lean personage, with a shrill, piercing voice, with little eyes, and with sharp angular features, and whose age had been "risin' forty" for an uncertain number of years, sat chatting and crooning alone on the har'-stone of the former's house, while Mr Luke Stallybrass was having a snooze on the bed in the little room adjoining—he, poor man, having lately had his foot crushed at the "Cyclops,"[11] was on sick pay.

'Well, Martha,' said Ruth, 'she railly looks wuss an' wuss an' wuss, an' I think she's in a decline.'

'Ah, pore thing!' said Martha, with an ominous shake of the head, and a deep-drawn sigh; 'there's summat wrong, for sartin. It's my belief as she's too good for this world. Why, Ruth, she's angillic—pos'tiv'ly angillic!'

---

[10] hearthstone

[11] Cyclops works

'Ay,' said Ruth, capping Martha's sigh with one far deeper; 'she's seen better daze, pore dear, an' it's my belief she's some secret sorrer a-gnawin' at her heart.'

'An' yet,' said Martha, 'when Mr Millwood comes home, bless me, if she don't look bright as a daffy-downdilly or as 'appy as a throssle[12] on a strawb'ry bed.'

'O' coorse she does,' said Ruth; 'but that's all "put on" — mak' b'lieve, yer kno'; why, she's that angillic, she don't want to sodder[13] him in his coffin we scaldin' tears an' chokin' sighs, as some folks would.'

'But he must kno' as she suffers, seein' as he axed Dr Tickle to see her on Wednesday.'

'Ay, surely,' said Ruth; 'but that was for the fit of dizziness which came over her. He saw it himself, and was freightened. But we kno' how the pore thing suffers. Why, when I went in yester-mornin she could neither stand nor see, she waz that dazed wi t' headache.'

'Yes, it's my opinion there's summat wrong here,' said Martha, touching her forehead.

'Mebbe there is, seein' as she has had so much trouble; and railly, Martha, when she met me crossin' t' Wicker[14] she didn't reckonize me.'

'Well!' said Mrs Stallybrass, 'summat'll have to be done to mend her afore long, for she's fairly fadin' away, the pore, pretty thing, an' she's like to die.'

'An' so young too!' sighed Mrs Pimpernel. 'An' helpless!'

'An' wake!'

'An' yit so ladylike!'

'A' deary me! what's to be done, Martha?'

'Why, I votes we helps her all we can, seein' as none of her own acquentance does.'

'Ay, lass, that we will,' added Ruth.

----

[12] thrush

[13] bury

[14] The Wicker – a main street near the Don river crossing

'Thumpin', rantin', groanin', an' shoutin' i' t' reekin' hot chapil may be raligion,' said Mrs Stallybrass, 'but to my thinkin', Ruth, helpin' the misforthunate an' them that's afflicted is the only raligion as'll wesh; but, hark there's somady at t' dooar.'

'Ay, oppen it, lass.'

Mrs Stallybrass went and opened it.

'Bless his little 'eart! Why, it's little Brine! Come in, there's a darlin'. Bless his little soul!' said she, kissing him. 'Come and sit thee down i' t' little child's rocking-chair afore t' fire.'

'Tank oo, Mrs 'Tallyb'ass. It is so dood of oo to let me have dis comfy itta chair,' said little Bryan. And he sat down between them, and crossed his legs before the fire, his long fair locks hanging loosely over his little plum-coloured velvet jacket, which was set off by a white lace collar and frills to the sleeves. This garment, and his knickers too, were relics of more prosperous days. Diving his hands deep down into his pockets, he asked—

'Do oo know Doctor Tittle?'

'Doctor Tickle? Yes, little dear; he's our doctor,' said Mrs Stallybrass.

'He is ours too,' said Bryan; 'and he has tum to see dear mudder.'

'Deary me!' exclaimed Mrs Stallybrass; 'an' is yer ma ill?'

'Yes, my mudder is velly pooloo—velly pooloo,' he said, looking sweetly compassionate.

'What's the matter with her?' asked Mrs Pimpernel.

'I do not know,' said little Bryan, 'but Dod knows; fader says so. She has been velly sick, and tieing, and she tan't stand, and I am so solly for her —so solly; but I tan't make her better. But p'waps Dod tan't hear me when I p'way to Him to make her better. Will oo ask Him? P'waps He knows oo better dan me. Oo are older dan I. I am only four years old. Tan oo p'way, Mrs Pimperwewe?'

'Oh yes, dear,' said Mrs Pimpernel, very doubtfully; 'but God will lissen to your prayers sooner than to ours. We are only pore mis'rable sinners.'

The child seemed puzzled. He could not understand.

'What do oo say?' he asked.

'Pore mis'rable sinners,' said Ruth.

'Nonsense! Rubbidge!' exclaimed a husky voice behind them, which made them start. It was Mr Luke Stallybrass, who had just awoke from his nap, and who came into the room, supported by crutches, and with his big bandaged foot held by a sling round his neck. He was a tall, powerfully-built Yorkshireman, with grisly hair. There was a worn and haggard expression about his intellectual face, an expression which did not seem natural to him. His voice was very deep, and it quite startled little Bryan.

'Aw'm a mis'rable sinner if you like, an' allus shall be—but you? How have you offended t' Almighty? Two honest women—kind-hearted and trew: pray what have you done to earn sich a bad name? Has t' minister been scarrin' yer wi' his brimstone fiery bogeys agen? Aw wish he'd do more wark and less rant.'

'Mr Stallybrass, you don't understand. We are all born in sin,' said Mrs Pimpernel rather sharply.

'Eh? what? who sez so? Mean to tell me as this ere little lad's born in sin? Does he look as if he'd been hammered and tilted, cogged and rolled in the devil's mill? What no? Sh'd think not, indeed! Some o' you religious folks thinks that t' Almighty's got nowt to do but ter mak wasters; for shame of yourselves! for shame!'

When Mr Luke Stallybrass got fairly wound up to "go it" on matters theological, he did "go it," and there was generally no stopping him; but little Bryan stopped him, for he went gently up to him, and looking with his soft blue eyes full into Mr Stallybrass's, he said—

'P'ease, sir, tan oo p'way, sir?'

'Praay? Noa, lad, but aw can sing.'

'P'ease, sir, do sing me a nice itta hymn den.'

'Well,' said Luke, scratching his grisly head, 'aw'll do owt to 'blige thee, lad. Martha, luv, where's t' hymn-buke?'

Martha looked *so* astonished. It was such a long time since *she* had been "luved," and as for the hymn-book, it had been put by on the shelf for years. However, she got it down, and wiped it with a duster, as it was so very dusty.

'What for is oor hymn-book so dusty, Mr 'Tallyb'ass?' asked Bryan, with a sweet innocence of expression.

'Becos it's been on t' shelf so long,' said Luke.

'But why?' asked the child, wonderingly.

'A'! lad, thou axes me a funny question; but what shall I sing for thee, eh?'

'Anything about Dod, sir,' he answered. Luke turned over the pages of the book, in which the hymns were set to music. It was thumb-marked and very dirty.

'Here's one,' said Luke, tuning up his voice, and then he began lustily to sing—

'Sound the loud timbrel o'er Egypt's dark sea,
Jehovah hath triumphed, His people are free.'

He had a voice of marvellous depth and power—a good old Yorkshire voice, such as one hears about the wolds, and he had a complete mastery over it. He sang as if he had been trained to singing—as he had, long ago; for he was once a chorister in Sheffield's grand old parish church.

When he had finished his wife remarked, 'Well done, lad! you mak t' pots an' t' pans to dither an dirl, anyway.'

Bryan said, 'Tank oo, Mr 'Tallyb'ass; I'm so 'bliged to oo. Will oo p'ease sing anodder?

'Perhaps there is nothing so infectious as music— a thousand times more so than the measles, for before he had time to find another hymn two of his neighbours, hearing the glad sound, dropped in. One was armed with a fiddle, and the other with a "chello." There is music in a Yorkshireman, whatever his trade! Before many minutes had passed, there was enough music in that clean sand-strewn kitchen to fill a good-sized barn. After a while they chose a hymn with a chorus, a well-known one of Montgomery's, "Hark! the song of jubilee." All joined in the singing, even the shrilly-voiced Ruth to the tremulous contralto of Martha, and little Bryan, who caught the infection, ventured a "Alleluia" on his own account.

That night it was whispered abroad down Bessemer Street, and even to the gates of "Mount Tabor," the chapel, that Luke Stallybrass was "bein' convarted."

They sang on and on, hymn after hymn, until Martha asked her husband to sing a hymn which he had loved to sing when a choir-boy.

He began, with his powerful voice, clear and strong, "How shall a contrite sinner pray"; but ere he had got half-way through his voice faltered. He broke down. His limbs trembled. Luke had seen a terrible vision. His eyeballs glared, and then waxed hazy. Was he going to faint?

'Luke Luke!' exclaimed Mrs Stallybrass, 'what's the matter?'

'Nowt, lass, nowt,' said he, rubbing his eyes; 'but, dang it! who ha' thowt that singin' an owd hymn tune 'ud have given me the staggers? Ah!' he half gasped and sighed, 'they'll not catch me singin' hymns agen in a hurry. There!' said he, hurling the book into the fire, and thrusting it deep into the blazing flames with his crutch, to make it burn all the faster; 'there! that buke'll mak' a fule o' me no more.' Mrs Stallybrass came to the rescue, and with difficulty succeeded in saving the old volume of hymns from being burnt to ashes.

All looked aghast and were speechless.

Little Bryan looked wonderingly, as if he couldn't understand. Luke sank back in his chair, and buried his face in his hands.

The visitors whispered 'Good-night.' Mrs Pimpernel sidled off. Mr Stallybrass had been queer for some years. They thought he was going to have one of his "queer bouts," so they left him.

After a minute or two's silence, little Bryan went softly up to Luke, and taking hold of his hand asked, 'Are oo ill, Mr 'Tallyb'ass?' No answer. He repeated the question. Still no answer. Then with his little soft hand he stroked the strong man's forehead, brushing back his grisly locks. Haply he had seen his father do this to his mother, so he went on stroking. Mrs Stallybrass left them alone for awhile. She knew that she could not control Luke's tantrums, but she knew that little Bryan had, for the last few weeks, been winning a strange influence over him, that was quite a marvel and a mystery to her absolutely inexplicable. There was silence, save the tick-tick-ticking of the clock and the merry chirping of the crickets.

'Mr 'Tallyb'ass.'

'What, luv?' said he, looking around to see if they were alone.

'Do oo tink dat de men who fell into de big furnace at Ottertuff Ford will doe to heaven?'

' 'Sh, darlin', 'sh! that was only a tale. 'Sh! don't talk about it agen.'

'But, Mr 'Tallyb'ass, what for did dey fall into dat fierwy furnace?'

' 'Sh, 'sh! 'sh! we musn't tell tales on a Sunday. It's wicked, very wicked,' whispered Luke in alarm.

'Tell me to-mollow, den, and I will tell oo about Sadac, Meset, and Bendido. It's a t'ue tale.'

'Very well, luv; very well. Come in to-morrer an' see.'

'Tank oo, sir I will doe home now to see mudder and fader. Dood-night, Mr 'Tallyb'ass; when I doe to bed to-night I will ask Dod to div oo a dood pwace in his tin'dom of lub. Dood-night.'

'Good-night, and God bless thee, lad,' said Luke, kissing the child's face that was so innocently held up to him. Ere little Bryan fell asleep that night, he must needs look out of his bedroom window, just to see if the furnaces at Otterclough Forge were in blast.

Yes, there they were, blazing away. His mind was much excited by the tale Mr Stallybrass had told him so thoughtlessly. He could not sleep for thinking about it.

'But it's only a tale; it didn't leally happen,' he said to console himself. 'But why is it velly wicked to tell tales on a Sunday? My mudder tells me tales on Sunday, and s'e is not wicked.'

After little Bryan had gone home Luke Stallybrass said to himself—

'Bless my soul! what a memory that lad's gotten. I wish aw hadn't told him any tales at all. What a fool I was to give a child a sorter clue to my terrible secret, but some'oworruther I nivver thowt he'd think owt more about it!'

CHAPTER XI

Algernon Tickle, M.D., of Bart's, London, had first started in practice in the Glossop Road. He was a little man, exceedingly plain-looking and club-footed. His sharply turned-up nose was painfully prominent, but his face was relieved by a pair of intellectual-looking and jewel-bright eyes.

He was very clever, but no one would believe it; at least, this is certain, he was hardly ever "called in." No, the gentlefolk of the West End did not choose to patronise Tickle; so he waited and waited for twelve months, and only had eight or nine patients, who seemed to be of opinion that a young doctor's services should be given gratuitously for the first year or two. But the upper ten, the elite, what did they do? Why, they left him severely alone.

'What!' they said in their hearts, 'call in a plain little insignificant man, bearing the name of Tickle! Preposterous! Nonsense!' Mothers and marriageable daughters rebelled—the idea was too utterly ludicrous!

So it happened that Dr Tickle, finding the well-to-do folk of the West End sought not his advice nor took counsel with him at all, he, nothing daunted, determined to see if the good folk of Attercliffe would come to his rescue. Thus it was he restarted in practice there. He cheerfully argued with himself, after the manner of Mahomet of old. 'Well, if the people won't come to Tickle, Tickle'll go to the people. Why should Tickle wait?'

Moreover, Dr Tickle was not absolutely dependent on his practice, he having a small income under his grandfather's will; and so he further argued—

'Well, if the sons of Atlas, Cyclops, cannot pay my bills, and will have none of me, I shall neither be destitute nor miserable. True I may never make my "pile," but the

knowledge from an experience of my fellow-man's needs, and
gratitude from kindly hearts—these may yet be mine, and no
small guerdon these!'

He was a chatty, cheerful little man, and so kind-hearted.
He soon began to win his way into the hearts and affections of
the "great unwashed" of Attercliffe.

'He was a proper doctor,' they said one to another; 'not a
Dr Gallypot, with a false handle to his name.'

Kenneth Millwood was pleased with the doctor on his first
visit to his wife. He found him a well-read man, who could
talk well—a man whom he felt shared his sympathies.
Moreover, he was brimful of love for his profession, and had
such a quiet, fascinating influence or charm that he made
converts to, if not enthusiasts in, his belief that surgery and
medicine were the loftiest of sciences in the world, and that, as
he rightly argued, the medical profession was utterly peerless.

Kenneth and the doctor were seated in the latter's small
consulting-room. He had come once more to consult the
doctor about Connie, whose headaches were getting more
frequent and more intense, whilst her eyesight and hearing
were seriously affected.

'Ah! that explains a good deal,' said the doctor; 'in fact, I
should say that it solves the difficulty, and is the origin of the
trouble. Pray how long is it since she had this fall?'

'About eighteen months ago, but really we thought it was
not serious at the time. The horse shied at a destestable
traction-engine just beyond Owler Bar, and would have bolted
down the hill, but I managed to turn him through an open
gateway into a sort of rough moorland field, where the gig was
speedily upset as the ground was very uneven. We were both
pitched out, and I was apparently uninjured; but she fell rather
heavily upon her head and was stunned by the fall. For a while
she was unconscious, but soon recovered, and we walked back
to the inn together, where I gave her some brandy. She
complained of considerable pain in the head, and on my

examining it, I found a slight scalp wound, and a swelling about as large as a half-crown.

'She appeared fairly well and cheerful for the remainder of that day, with the exception of having a sharp pain where the swelling was, but the pain gradually passed away.

'The next day I noticed that the swelling had disappeared, but the skin was slightly abraded; and there was a small well-defined indentation or dint in the centre of the wound, as if a sharp flint, or some other equally hard substance, had pierced the bone somewhat; but in a few days' time the whole thing healed up, and there was nothing left but a little scar, with a slight depression in the middle of it.'

'Yes,' said the doctor; 'doubtless the mark is there now, and it is highly probable that that spot is the seat of all the mischief. There is undoubtedly something pressing upon the brain, and this may be from a growth superinduced by the effects of that fall.'

Kenneth seemed pained, and looked nervous, and asked— 'What sort of a growth?'

'Oh, don't be alarmed,' said the doctor, knowing that Kenneth's sympathies were so easily excited, 'don't be alarmed; such cases are not uncommon—the growth may be an ordinary tumour, resulting from that fall; and if so, it is possible to have it removed, especially as we have now reason to know the seat or location of the disease.'

Poor Kenneth turned somewhat paler, and his face was the picture of sorrow as he gazed piteously into the doctor's sparkling little eyes.

'Surgery, you know, Mr Millwood, has advanced by leaps and bounds during the last few years; and we now think no more of operating on the brain than amputating a finger, only, of course, the element of danger destroys what parallel may exist the two cases.'

'Have you removed many tumours from the brain?' asked Kenneth, as his heart sank deeper and deeper within him.

'Only five,' said the doctor.

'Successfully?' asked Kenneth, vainly trying to assume a nonchalant professional air.

'Yes, very. They were splendid cases. True, the first three cases were fatal, nevertheless the operations were attended with remarkably successful results.'

'I do not quite understand,' said Mr Millwood.

'No, perhaps not. I should have explained that the first three cases were practically hopeless ones, as the patients were brought into the hospital as a last resort. The disease had advanced too far to allow of a cure being possible. The last two cases were not so interesting from a pathological point of view, but happily they were not attended with fatal results. One of them was a hammer-man at the "Atlas," and the other was a file-forger at Otterclough Forge.'

'Pray what was his name—the file-forger's, I mean?' asked Kenneth.

'Dan Riley.'

'Dan Riley! How strange! I knew him when he was a workman apprentice,' said Kenneth.

'Well, he's a good example of a perfect cure; but I didn't let the thing go too far. It's of no use attempting or hoping for cures when cases are left until the patient is absolutely exhausted; perhaps in a sort of chronic comatose state, enlivened by occasional convulsions and other complications; but, Mr Millwood, I see that you are nervous. Now, no good can come of being alarmed over this case of your wife's. Let us look at matters in a happy light. Now, might it not be advisable to call in a second opinion?'

'Yes, as the case seems to be so serious,' said Kenneth, 'perhaps it would be better to have a consultation. No doubt you know the most likely man. I only know Redmires.'

'Redmires—the very man!' exclaimed the doctor. 'Not as an operator, mind— O no! far too nervous; but as a thoroughly painstaking man, accurate in his diagnosis, he hasn't his equal in Sheffield. Shall I drop him a line to-night to ask him to meet me at yours to-morrow at noon?

'I should be glad if you would,' said Kenneth; 'the suspense is killing me.'

And so it was arranged that Dr Redmires, if disengaged, should meet Dr Tickle at Mr Millwood's on the following day.

Then Kenneth went home, and told his wife quietly, so as not to alarm her, that Redmires was coming to see her on the morrow.

'Redmires?' she said, 'Redmires?' She shook her head. She didn't remember. Kenneth looked at her compassionately.

'Poor darling!' he thought; 'she must be bad indeed not to remember the doctor who brought both Bryan and Gladys into the world.'

He noticed that the former was trying to attract his mother's attention by tickling one of her feet, from which the slipper had slid off, unheeded by her. She was formerly very sensitive at these extremities, but she now appeared to be quite insensible to touch. Next morning Kenneth told the doctor this. 'Ah!' said Tickle, 'we call that anaesthesia, merely a sensory disturbance indicative of— But, bless me! here comes Redmires!'

The two doctors chatted cheerfully together for a minute or two, and then went upstairs, leaving Kenneth with little Bryan, whilst the nursemaid took baby out in her perambulator for a little fresh air, if haply any there was in the dingy smoke-begrimed hamlet of Brightside.

Kenneth and Bryan were thus left alone whilst the doctors were in the room above. How the former's whole being was then literally torn asunder, and utterly convulsed, by the warfare which hope and fear waged within him! how in his inmost soul he prayed that all might yet be well!

'Fader,' said little Bryan softly. 'I tan see Ottertuff Forde and de big b'ast furnaces blazing away.'

'Can you?' said his father, but he heard not what his son said.

'Yes, fader,' the boy continued; 'two men fell into one of dose bid furnaces; Mr 'Tallyb'ass says so.'

'Does he really?' said Kenneth, but his heart was upstairs, and again he heeded not what his son did say.

'Would dey fizzle, fader?' the boy persisted.

'I do not know, dear,' said his father abstractedly.

'Perhaps dey wouldn't fizzle,' said the lad. 'S'ad'at, Meset, and Bendido didn't fizzle, did dey?'

'No, darling, no; they were so *gooa*, you know; but don't talk, dear,' said Kenneth, as he listened to the footsteps of those in the room above.

But the child was bent on talking about something, and asked—

'What for has dat odder bid doctor tum— de doctor wid de bid red face?'

'To see poor mother, love. She is so very ill,' said Kenneth, kissing the little questioning face.

'Fader,' said the lad after a pause.

'Yes, love.'

'Mudder has diven me somet'ing to teep in my top d'awer.'

'Has she? What is it, dear?'

'Her Bible book, and some of her pretty hair in a locket.'

'Anything else?' asked the father, who was now deeply touched by what his son said.

'No, fader; not'ing else; 'cause s'ee said s'ee had not'ing else to div, and s'ee tied when s'ee dave dem to me, and s'ee tissed me so sweet, and s'ee told me not to tie when dey took her away. Fader,' said he, looking up with his soft innocent eyes into his father's, 'where is s'ee doing to? Do oo know, fader, dear?

'O child!' said Kenneth, fondly kissing his boy, and almost concealing his face among the lad's silken hair. 'I do not know. God knows, God knows.'

The child seemed lost in thought for awhile, and then—
'What for do oo tie, daddy?' he asked.

Kenneth turned his face towards the window. He could not speak. His eyes seemed rivetted on some-thing in the valley below. Was it old Otterclough Forge, or the dun sailing clouds of smoke? No, it was nothing, absolutely nothing.

Little Bryan came softly up to his father and pulled his arm.

'Fader, dear, it's dinner-time. Are oo hungry?'

'No, not at all; are *you*, love?' he asked, as he blew his nose and wiped dry his brimming eyes.

'Yes, daddy; I feel twite empty.'

'Poor little fellow!' exclaimed his father, who had entirely forgotten to arrange for the boy's dinner. 'What shall I give you? A biscuit? Yes. Here are some; help yourself, darling,' said his father, handing him a tin box full of biscuits.

Bryan sat on the hearthrug. He began to be very quiet. Bryan was happy.

'Hark! they are coming downstairs,' said Kenneth, and as he opened the room door to let them in, he felt a nameless sinking of the heart. He feared the worst. Men are not always brave.

'Well,' said Doctor Tickle, with a cheerful, ringing voice, 'we have made a thorough examination, and if you don't mind going upstairs to Mrs Millwood, we will have a few minutes' confab. What? Take the boy? Oh, no; let him stay here. He's all right, the rascal. Let him crunch away!'

'Let me stay here, daddy. I'm twite comfy,' said the boy as he hugged him somewhat closer to that biscuit-box. 'Twite comfy,' he said, as the door closed.

'Well,' said Doctor Tickle to Doctor Redmires 'what's to be done?'

'Sir,' said Redmires gravely, 'there's nothing for it but the trephine.'

'Precisely so,' said Tickle; 'that's my only opinion about the case—there can be no other. These convulsions and changes in the eye, and other sensory disturbances, prove beyond doubt the nature of the disease.

'What I fear most,' said Redmires, 'is that serious complications might ensue. She is not strong. Trouble has worn her away so. By-the-bye, do you propose performing the operation yourself, as you know I am not quite *au fait*, and am not so young as—'

'Nonsense! rubbish! but really I was going to suggest that an old Bart's chum of mine should be chief, a young fellow called Herman Darrell. Do you know him?'

'No, I do not; but I must say that I had rather not operate. The strain would be too great for my nerves, and you know nervous exhaustion is my bane.'

They chatted for a few minutes longer, and then agreed that it would be better to tell Mr Millwood straight out the result of their deliberations.

'My little man,' said Doctor Redmires to little Bryan, 'are you making your dinner off these biscuits, eh?'

'Yes, sir; I am twite full now, right up to de top of de troat.'

'Bravo, Bryan,' said Doctor Tickle; 'just go and tell your father we want him; go softly, mind, or you'll perhaps disturb your mother.' Bryan crept gently upstairs, and as he went he said, 'Tank Dod for my dood dinner, Amen.' He opened the bedroom door. He peeped inside.

'Fader,' he said; but no answer came. He toddled round to the other side of the bed.

His father was there on his knees, kissing his mother's hand, that was hanging loosely by the side of the bed.

She was asleep. The examination had wearied her. She looked so fair, and so sweet, and yet so very pale—as if cold death were planting his ensigns one by one on one-time damask cheek and rosebud lip, that erewhile quivered and were thrilled with very joy to be kissed of him, her husband.

' 'Sh, 'sh, 'sh,' he said to Bryan; 'mother sleeps.'

'Fader, dear,' whispered the lad, 'de doctors want to see oo.'

Kenneth went downstairs, and was in a terrible state of suspense when he came into the tiny parlour where the doctors were, and was almost breathless from anxiety as he asked as composedly as he could—

'Well, gentlemen, have you decided what is the best to be done?'

'We have, Mr Millwood,' said Doctor Tickle. 'We are of one mind that nothing but an operation can save your wife's life; and that operation is known as trepanning or trephining, and is of a serious nature, as you know.'

'Nor should it be long delayed,' added Doctor Redmires.

'In the first place,' said Tickle, 'we recommend that two duly-qualified hospital nurses be sent for immediately.'

Doctor Redmires nodded a grave 'Yes.'

'And we further think that, with your approval, the operation should take place this week.'

'This week!' exclaimed Kenneth, with a painful look of surprise.

'Yes, this week,' said Redmires; 'we think it would be best not to delay the operation, as to do so would only be to lessen the chances of a successful issue. My friend Doctor Tickle knows a specialist in London, who is well up in these cases, and I should advise you to secure his services. He is younger than I am, and I must confess that I have some diffidence in performing such an operation, although I will gladly render all the assistance I can.

'Yes,' said Tickle, 'my friend Herman Darrell of Harley Street is the best man I know of in a case of this sort, and I know he would do anything in his power to oblige me.'

'But,' said Kenneth hesitatingly, 'all this means such a heavy expense, that I fear I shall not be able to bear it. Not that I would not give everything I possessed—and even draw largely upon the future—to effect a cure; but, God knows, I am now poor, and am hardly possessed of a shilling that I can call my own; and even my little ones are being neglected through not having their mother's care, and I—'

The poor fellow seemed to break down from excessive emotion, and with his elbows on the table, and with his hands supporting his head, hardly seemed able to go on.

'Cheer up, old man,' said Tickle, laying his hand gently on Kenneth's shoulder; 'we know you have been hard hit, and we are downright sorry for you; but you mustn't suppose that we are going to bleed you to death. I'm sure if we thought you were only possessed of a solitary sixpence wherewith to pay our fees, we should still do our level best for you. My dear fellow, trust us and we'll trust you; and if you are "hard up" for a tanner or two, I know a friend who'll help you.'

'Ay, brother Millwood, you must not forget that even in Sheffield we can act on the square to each other,' said Redmires, holding out his hand.

Kenneth grasped it. They had a good, hearty, old-fashioned grip.

'Do you know,' said Redmires, 'that Mr Dandelow Bantam has joined our Lodge, and I'd bet a million pounds to a hayseed, if Dandy knew you were hard up, he'd neither eat, drink, nor sleep, before he'd made you aware you had a friend indeed. Why, Dandy's one in a thousand.'

'But whatever made him join the masonic brotherhood?' asked Kenneth. 'He once poohed-poohed it utterly.'

'Yes,' said Tickle; 'but a man who never changes his opinions is oft the veriest fool; and although Dandy is reckoned to be somewhat slow, he is nevertheless as true as his double shear steel, and he has more sense in his little finger than his partners have in all their heads put together.'

'By-the-bye,' said Tickle cheerfully, 'I met Mr Lynnacre last night, and he said how delighted his wife would be to look after your little ones for awhile. She is a most estimable and charming woman.'

'It is exceedingly good of her,' said Kenneth; 'I feel quite undeserving—indeed, quite overcome—by such considerate kindness.'

After the two doctors and Kenneth had fixed the day for the operation, the former took kindly leave of him, and in doing so, they wellnigh made him forget his troubles, and almost made him cheerful in spite of himself. But when he found himself alone, a feeling of unutterable grief crept slowly over him. He knew the terrible nature of the operation to be performed, and in spite of hope's cheery dulcet carollings, he in a measure realised by anticipation the keenness of the pang of having to part from Connie, whom he had loved so long and so well.

He felt his feelings were getting the mastery over him, so he arose from his chair and went upstairs. He opened the bedroom door very gently. He went into the room on tiptoe. She was asleep. He gazed at her lovingly. He saw that her lips twitched slightly. He feared to kiss her face or hand lest he should wake her; but he kissed a long stray tress of her hair instead, and then quite noiselessly he went downstairs again, and spoke to his only servant, who cheerfully, and uncomplainingly, and successfully coped with the duties of nurse-maid, scullery-maid, house-maid, cook, and general servant.

'Cathie,' said he, 'I shall be home again in an hour or two. I am going to fetch two nurses. Your mistress is ill, seriously ill, so will you kindly keep the little ones quiet? and, Cathie, would you mind making up the small bed for me—the "shake-down" I mean—in the corner of the kitchen?'

'The kitchen, sir!' she exclaimed in surprise.

He put his hand upon her shoulder, and said somewhat pitifully—

'Yes, Cathie, I shall sleep best in the kitchen; indeed, there will be no other place for me.'

Away he went, and left poor Cathie in a high state of bewilderment—utterly amazed.

'Deary me!' she exclaimed. 'Him shleep? Blest if there's a wink o' shleep in him. But faix,' she soliloquised, 'he's a jewil, he is. No bullyraggin' a pore slavey's wits out av her. Troth, I'd liefer be his dhoor-mat nor Miss Barbara Shout's parley-maid any day. *He* don't cuss wid his mouf shut, as some folks do. Faix, it's some so-called ladies'll gnatter and gnash the immorthal sperit out av yer, if yer'll only let 'em!'

After Kenneth Millwood had arranged for the nurses to attend his wife, he set off to walk back to Bessemer Street, and as he came nearer to the manufactory of Messieurs Otto Schlesinger & Co. he thought that there was yet one way whereby he might get over his difficulties from a monetary point of view; and that was by accepting the offer of Mr Schlesinger to buy his patent rights for dealing with crude and molten iron.

To preserve his independence at all cost had been Kenneth's ambition for many years; but now it seemed to him as if his spirit of independence was to be broken down for ever. 'What!' he thought, 'am I going to surrender my guns at the first brush of the fight; by borrowing and pledging my present and my future credit?—by becoming more and more indebted to my fellow-men?—and perhaps then to sink deeper and deeper into the quagmires of debt and despair ;—and then, it may be, to be shunned and shunted by the scoffing world; to be held up to scorn as one that cheats his creditors; while perchance the shiftless finger of some soulless religionist may point at me, as if to say, "There goes a poor wastrel, drifting hellward!" '

Such were the thoughts that flashed and re-flashed across Kenneth's mental vision, until they thrilled his whole being with alarm and with pain. 'But ah!' he thought, 'shall she, my dearly beloved one, lack aught that may cure her? No, no! I would beg and cringe, nay almost grovel, at the feet of the pitiless gods of this world, rather than that she should die from lack of the best means to restore her to health.'

'What!' he soliloquised; 'shall I put off till it is too late? Shall my pride wax humble when dumb lips speak, and those sweet tell-tale eyes are for ever sealed in the sleep that awakes no more? Pride and ambition, get ye behind me! *Rethro me, Sathana!* What! was it not these that steeled my heart when I could have sold my patent rights, and when my beloved one asked me to do so? Might she not have been strong and happy to-day had I but sold these rights, and enabled her to live away from the smoke, the dust, the forever-enduring clang and throb of this mighty stythying-place for the fiends of war? Alas! is it not now the dawn of summer—the time she loved so? Might she not now have been happy and strong, spell-bound with sweet flowers and "fair limbs of the tree," while her sunburnt face was kissed of playful winds, or the quickening beams of the sun? O that we were handfast and heartfast again by the shining sea—far away, by the cliffs of Flambro' or Speeton, whither she loved to spend the summer days! Would that we were once more on the soft silk sands by the green sea's fringe—

> *'When the sea has the wind for a harper,*
> *And the wind has the sea for a lyre.'*

O that the day might come again wherein, as young lovers, we clomb the dewy slopes to see the sun uprise, and as children of God, hand in hand, lovingly watched his orient beams enkindle the waves in one wide Appian way of gold! O to think—

'Hello! is that you, Mr Millwood?' said a voice behind him.

Kenneth turned round sharply. It was Mr Otto Schlesinger. They shook hands.

'I was just coming in to see you,' said Kenneth.

'All right; I have half an hour to spare,' said Mr Schlesinger, pulling out his watch.

'Five minutes will do,' said Kenneth.

They went into the private office and sat down.

'Changed your mind yet? Going to sell, eh?' asked Mr Schlesinger.

'Yes, sir, that is my business,' said Kenneth; and he thereupon proceeded to tell Mr Schlesinger the sad circumstances which had made it necessary for him to sell his patent rights. He explained everything frankly and fully.

'Oh!' exclaimed Mr Schlesinger, who spoke in broken English to the following effect, '*you're* a nice man of business indeed! You'll prosper, *you will*. Why, sir, this is my first experience in this country of an Englishman saying outright that he really wishes to sell something valuable. It has always been my experience, sir—in this town at any rate—that a man who really wishes to sell feigns the contrary; and when a man wishes to buy, he says, "It is nought, it is nought." In other words, sir, the buyer pooh-poohs solid cast steel and extols the "roaky,"[15] to further his ends, whereas the seller makes everything look ridiculously valueless by the side of the thing which of course he would not sell for love nor money. Not he, except it may be at double its worth to a bosom friend! In fact, sir, all men are liars, and seem to be so fond of "going out of self," as they call it, that they would compass heaven and earth to get twenty-one shillings for every sovereign they possess, or, it may be, secretly to undersell a neighbour in the hope of ruining him, or to curry favour with his customers. This is the way of the world, sir; and pray why should not I make a lever of your necessities? Eh, Mr Millwood, tell me that? Look here, young man; your patent is not worth *that*,' said he, snapping his fingers. But,' said Kenneth, 'you offered me *four* hundred.'

---

[15] now obselete adjective used to describe an inferior steel

'Ay, *then* I did; but *now* I'm on your track. I've found out *most* of your secret. I know the right "physic" to use now, and —'

'Then is your offer withdrawn?' asked Kenneth, interrupting.

'Certainly,' said Mr Schlesinger; 'but what would you be willing to accept, supposing that I were still a buyer?'

'Whatever you like to offer in reason, sir,' said Kenneth.

'Then I'm buyer and seller too?'

'Yes.'

Mr Otto Schlesinger then went to his desk and wrote out a cheque and put it inside an envelope, and fastened it up.

'There!' said he; 'take that home and look at it, and if you are not satisfied, return it, and remember this: you're the only Sheffielder that I ever gave an open cheque of that amount without first having an agreement in writing with him. I can trust *your* word, sir, although, mind this, my business would never prosper if I copied *your* example of salesmanship. I'm a man of the world, sir, and like to buy things as cheap as I buy your patent.'

When Kenneth reached home he opened the envelope, and there, to his extreme surprise, he found that Schlesinger's cheque was for £500, or £100 more than he had offered him formerly.

CHAPTER XII

It were perhaps undesirable in these pages to enter into the details of the serious operation which Mrs Millwood had to undergo. Let it suffice that, besides being of a very dangerous nature to the unconscious patient, it was an operation very fatiguing to the doctors, and it took them three hours to perform. After the foreign growth had been removed from where they thought to find it, and after every requisite of sound treatment had been used, the doctors left the patient in the charge of the nurses, until she recovered from the effects of the ether, etc., which they had had to use. Kenneth's highly-strung nerves had been tried to the utmost during the operation. His feelings of anxiety, pain, and suspense were indescribable, but when the doctors came downstairs and told him that his wife was going on as well as might be expected, and that she had known nothing whatever of the operation, he felt more relieved. Half and hour later on he entered the sick-room, and as he did so he experienced considerable misgivings and pain, and seemed almost afraid to look at the features of his well-beloved. He whispered something to the nurses and drew nearer the bedside. He saw the sweet wan face peeping through the bandages. He drew nearer. 'How pale!' he whispered, as he kissed her so gently. He saw that some of her lovely hair had been removed, and the thought of it of course pained him. He smelled the strong pervading odour of iodoform and other antiseptics. It was oppressive to him. The room was so still, too, and so clean and tidy, as if nothing had happened. The nurses, in their clean white caps and aprons, seemed as angels whose serenity nothing could mar.

'She will be coming round soon,' said Nurse Gwendolen, the elder of the two.

'Yes, Mr Millwood, you may just come in for a little while when she wakes,' said Nurse Evelyn.

He turned from the bedside, and as he did so his eyes caught sight of five splendid long locks of hair on the dressing-table.

'Dr Tickle removed them so carefully,' said Nurse Gwendolen; 'he said he knew you would value them so.'

Kenneth took the hair in his hand and went out of the room. He pressed the soft silken tresses to his lips as he went downstairs. Yes, they were very precious. He went and locked them up in the drawer of an old oaken bureau.

About two hours after the doctors had gone, Mrs Stallybrass and Mrs Pimpernel made a call, to enquire if everything was going on right, and to wish the patient "God speed."

Kenneth received them most courteously, shaking hands with them both, and telling them all he knew about the case; and so obviously sincere were the thanks that he gave them for their kindly attentions to his wife and children, that they forgave him unaware for the feelings of annoy at being slighted, as they thought, when it was told them that two trained hospital nurses were coming in their stead.

The neighbours in Bessemer Street were very considerate. Not only did the women folk forbid their children to play near "Mrs Millwood's," but the cutlers, filesmiths, and file-cutters in some small workshops opposite the house, ceased work earlier than usual that Saturday lest their hammerings and tinkerings should "mak her lig wakken as orter lig quiet." Yes, even the toilers and moilers of Babylon may be kind, whereas it may hap that some of our modern red-rag fanatics of religion forget to be so, for ofttimes does it not come about that even our little ones are rudely awakened by some trumpet-blast, or a thundering drum, long after they have been hushed to sleep by a weary mother's loving care?

It happened that at the time Mrs Stallybrass and Mrs Pimpernel were talking to Kenneth, another lady visitor was on her way to Bessemer Street. She was being driven thither in a carriage drawn by a pair of horses, and by her side sat a man well known in Sheffield. As they passed by the Norfolk Market Hall, they were recognised by Mr Thomas Shout and Mr Robert Underwedge, returning from business.

'Well I never! exclaimed Tom; 'if that isn't Belle Bantam and Dandy I'm jiggered!'

'What a pace they're travellin' at!' said Robert; 'but where the deuce are they off to?'

They watched the carriage disappear in the direction of Attercliffe.

'I kno' their game,' said Tom; 'they're goin' to that scoundrel's—Kenneth Millwood's.'

'Why so?' asked Robert. 'Because I heard that cackling 'pothecary Tickle talkin' to Dandy about Missis Millwood, who's took ill, seemin'ly.'

'What!' sneered Robert; 'he's smittled agen, is he? Sympathy, I reckin! Pheugh! Dandy allus was a bit cracked.'

'Ay, lad,' said Tom; 'his 'eart's softer nor souse an' his 'ead is like a crop-eared barm-dumplin'.'

'More's the pity,' said Robert; 'but, by jingo, Tom! wasn't Belle lookin' in rare fettle, eh?'

'Ay, Roberd; I should just like to screw that wild Irishman's neck round. Bryan Wolverton's a robber. Belle was "comin' to" bit by bit, an' then he comes deer-stalkin' an' moonlightenin' with his Irish blather, dang him! But I reck'n they're spliced now. I kno' the Court o' Chancery has condoned the scoundrel's offence—but here comes t' Broom'ill 'bus, Roberd: jump up. Let's go to t' prominade at t' Gardens.'

Kenneth was not a little surprised to see Mr Dandelow Bantam, accompanied by his lovely sister Belle, step out of the carriage. The event caused quite a consternation in Bessemer Street. The news soon spread that it was the late Mr Stanislaus

Bantam's carriage and coachman, and that the visitors were his children.'

Dandy seemed to be much affected when he saw Kenneth's thin, pale, careworn, cavernous cheeks. They shook hands, yet neither of them spoke, but Belle, after a few moments, whispered softly—

'And how is Connie, Kenneth? Is she going on well?'

'I hope so, Belle; but she really has not come round yet. The doctors have not been long gone, and the nurses are now looking after her.'

'O why didn't you send for me, Ken? I would have come so gladly,' she said.

'But we wrote to you three or four times, and you never replied,' said Kenneth.

'How strange! I'm sure we never received your letters; and O how very unkind of us to think that you had forgotten us! There must have been some miscarriage of letters, I fear.'

'Does Bryan know anything about Connie's illness?' asked Kenneth. 'Not a word,' she replied. 'How grieved he will be when he knows! He is now in London, and has written to me this morning to say that he has sold his Academy picture for £700.

'What picture?' asked Kenneth.

'The Eviction,' said Belle. 'But haven't you heard of it in the papers?'

'No, I have not. In fact, I rarely see the newspapers; we have had to cut down our expenses so much, that we only bought the *Sheffield Daily Standard* on Saturdays. But really, Belle, I am so glad to hear of old Bryan's success. He will be in clover now.'

'Yes,' said Belle; 'but we owe you two hundred pounds or more; and if you will let me, I will now repay you with interest, and what is more, with my very, very best thanks.'

'I thank you,' said Kenneth; 'but really, Belle, I am not now so poor as I was. I have sold my patent to Mr Otto Schlesinger for £500.'

'The dickens you have!' exclaimed Dandy.

' 'Sh, 'sh, 'sh not so loud,' whispered Kenneth.

'But do you kno', said Dandy, 'that I have given notice to withdraw from the partnership at Otterclough Forge, thinkin' that you and me might work that patent somehoworuther, and become partners some day? I'm sick o' the Shouts.'

'But are you not engaged to one of them?' asked Kenneth. 'No, thank my stars! not *now*. I'm sick o' Barbara.'

'But why?' asked Kenneth, almost raising a smile.

'Becos, when I stayed at their 'ouse for a week, I couldn't stan' her naggin' an' her gnatterin' ways. Thowt I to meself, "If she carries on in this fashion afore we're wed, what'll she do after?" But it's off! thank God, it's off—an' no bones broken! Yes, I'm going to leave Otterclough Forge. I'm sick o' the Shouts,' said he. 'But whatever made you sell out, Kenneth, eh?—the patent, I mean?'

'For Connie's sake,' he said. 'I would not have her starve or lack the means to get over this most serious operation. You may be sure I had no alternative plan, or I would not have sold my patent.

'A' dear!' exclaimed Dandy; 'I wish some folks wouldn't be so mighty hindependent. Why, man alive! if you'd only held up your little finger to me, I'd ha' lent you a thousan'. I'd rather go bail for you than t' Archbishop o' York any day' he exclaimed, with considerable emphasis.

' 'Sh, 'sh, 'sh' said Belle softly 'not so loud, my good boy. Remember we are in a miniature cottage and there is a patient it upstairs.'

'A milliond pardons, Ken,' said Dandy; 'but it maks me wild to think you should have never axed me for a fardin' when I'd hundreds russin' t' bank.'

'Dandy,' said Kenneth, holding out his hand, 'you're a good old soul; I take the will for the deed, and I'll not forget your kindness— no, never, brother Bantam, never!'

'What! eh? has it come to this?' asked Dandy, smiling.

'Yes, long ago,' said Kenneth. 'I was made a Mason when I was twenty-one.'

'An' no waster either,' said Dandy. 'You're a reit un, I'll be bound, as we say in Shevvild, eh, Belle?'

'Speak for yourself, Dandy,' she replied. 'You, I am sure, need no prompting in the dialect of your mother-tongue.'

Dandelow Bantam, as will have been observed, was not ashamed of using his mother-tongue. Had he so chosen, he could have spoken more after a cosmopolitan manner, but he loved the language of his fathers and of his fellow-craftsmen at the Forge.

'And where are the children?' asked Belle, after a pause.

'They are staying with Mrs Lynnacre up at Bell Hagg. She kindly offered to take them during this trouble.'

'How good of her! Do you know, Ken, we christened our boy after you?'

'Your boy!' exclaimed Kenneth; 'we never heard.'

'But it was in the Sheffield papers,' she interrupted.

'How strange,' said he, 'that neither Connie nor myself heard anything of it—but hush! hark! someone is coming downstairs.'

It was Nurse Gwendolen, who came into the room and said to Kenneth—

'Mrs Millwood is now awake, and has just asked for you, sir, so perhaps you had better see her for a minute or two.'

'I will come now,' he said, as, turning to Belle and Dandy, he asked, 'Will you wait till I come down?'

'Oh dear no, Ken we must be off. Besides we are only in the way—hinderers, not helpers.'

They left the house after saying good-bye, and then Kenneth went upstairs, and as he did so Nurse Gwendolen whispered to him—

'Mr Millwood, please do not show the slightest emotion, except to seem glad, when you enter the room, and do not contradict Mrs Millwood, as she appears to be labouring under a slight delusion.'

As he went into the sick-room, immediately his wife's eyes turned gladly towards him, and brightened up. He went up to the bedside, and kissed her. 'Aren't you glad, darling, that it's a boy?' she whispered softly.

The nurse nudged his elbow slightly.

'Yes, darling, I am delighted,' said Kenneth, assuming a pleased expression, and kissing her again.

'I knew you would be. You wanted a boy, didn't you, love?' she said. 'But I cannot speak much. I am weary, love, so weary; yet I hear such sweet music such sweet—sweet music —as if I was listening to the sound of sea-shells, hollow sea-shells—sea-shells; but, Ken, love, let me sleep awhile, just a little while, and then—'

She closed her eyes. He stood looking at her for a minute or so, and then left the room. Nurse Gwendolen followed him, and said to him on the little landing—

'You did quite right to agree with her, Mr Millwood. We must not undeceive her. This is a happy hallucination, which we may turn to good account. What shall we christen him?' she asked, while a sweetly innocent smile stole across her face, that was very fair.

'Basil,' he said, 'I know she loves the name of Basil. But what if she should ask for him?'

'Oh, we will arrange all that,' she said; 'perhaps Dr Tickle's knowledge, of this neighbourhood may help us in this matter.'

Kenneth's hopes rose considerably after his short interview with Connie. His conscience did not accuse him in the slightest of having been a party to any deception. When Dr

Tickle came in again later on they had a good laugh over the baby.

'Believe me,' Mr Millwood said to Tickle, 'this is the luckiest form of hallucination that could have happened. Why, it will keep her *quiet* for a month, at least, and that's half the battle. 'Yes, but what about the baby?' asked Kenneth.

'Oh!' said the doctor, 'that's easily arranged. I know of one just to hand, three weeks old, a bonny boy, as fine a chanceling as ever breathed.'

'But do you think it right, Doctor, to keep up the deception?'

'Assuredly I do,' said Tickle; 'just as right as it would be to go bail for your great-grandmother on the Sabbath. Why, sir, I have a lady patient of considerable talent and means, and about sixty-five years old, who has had the nurse within call for over five years; and the joke is, she is sure it's a boy absolutely certain! and she is going to call him Æneas, so between us we have slyly re-christened the old nurse-in-waiting *Æneas nutrix.*'

'But surely it would be better to disillusionise the lady, if I may use such a word,' said Kenneth.

'Oh dear no; not at all,' exclaimed Tickle. 'Her hallucination is as happy as it is harmless; and she is so careful in her diet *now*, whereas formerly'—he shook his head— 'well, there was room for considerable improvement. Moreover, she has a very weak heart, and to undeceive her might upset her nervous system, which might be fatal.'

So it was arranged to keep up the illusion; but alas for human ingenuity! little did they think what an enormous superstructure of innocent lies they would soon have to "shore" up.

Dr Tickle had no difficulty, as heretofore explained, about the baby boy. He came, and his mother too a sweet-faced girlish-looking mother, called Yewniss (Eunice).

A bassinet was soon forthcoming, and certain soft lawn robes were ferreted from their hiding-places, and before the lapse of many hours the little lad, who had come into this world "asklent,"[16] had two nurses to, supervise him, two mothers to love him, a physician's care, and perhaps an Allfather's tender pity. Who can say? for where love is the measure of faith, wide are the wings of hope.

Day by day Mrs Millwood got both mentally and physically stronger, and day by day her innumerable questions became more difficult to answer. Of course they nearly all related to the baby and herself. 'It was so strange,' she thought, 'that I never had the remotest conception of the thing; but all! my poor, poor head! I am afraid it has been at sea, sadly at sea.' One day she asked Nurse Eunice 'Whom do you think baby resembles most?'

'Well,' said Eunice, 'I don't think he favours either of you. Excuse me saying it, mum, but he's a lot handsomer altogether, bless him.'

Nurse Gwendolen smiled as she sat at the foot of the bed doing some needlework.

Mrs Millwood's mind again began to be exercised, and she said—

'Do you know, Sister Gwendolen, that it seems quite an age since I went to bed.'

'I am not at all surprised at your thoughts,' she replied. 'Your memory has been quite at fault; indeed, your mind has been a-wool-gathering for a long time.'

This was the way whereby Nurse Gwendolen satisfied Mrs Millwood's ever-growing inquisitiveness.

'Of course, of course,' she said; 'I ought to have known that my head was queer. Doubtless that is why, they cut off my hair, and put these bandages round it.

'Precisely so,' said the sister; 'but you are getting all right again now, and maybe in a week or two you will be strong

---

[16] aslant – "come to the warld asklent" quote from Robert Burns.

enough to get up; and then Mr Millwood is going to take you over to Filey Bay or to Burlington for a change. Won't that be delightful?'

'Oh yes,' said Connie, as her eyes flashed with keen delight; 'he is *so* kind, so kind. Ah yes! I remember how good he was when he brought me to live here. He was ever so thoughtful, nurse, and so kind to the little ones— and I? —I? Yes, I was very weak, and had a bad headache, and could only cry when he was gone to the works. Yes, my illness was beginning then. I remember turning dizzy as I was putting up those curtains on the steps. I fell, but I did not tell my husband, No, I didn't want to worry him. Poor Kenneth!'

She ceased talking, and began to reflect awhile, and seemed lost in deep thought, staring at nothing; but the noise of the rapturous kisses which Eunice was bestowing upon baby awoke her from her reverie. She began to eye the nurse eagerly, keenly watching her every movement; and as she saw her bending over the sweet warm curves of his soft rose-leaf limbs, literally eating him up with kisses, a momentary feeling of jealousy stole over her as she thought—'How she loves him! How he loves *her*! but I—?'

She became somewhat impatient at the nurse's volleys of kisses and endless caresses, and so she spoke somewhat sharply to the nurse—

'Eunice, bring me my little aroon, or it's slain with your kisses he'll be.'

This was the first time she had used any Irish idiom or word since the operation. Nurse Gwendolen noticed it, and looked up in surprise; but she continued her needlework, saying to herself, 'Yes, she'll soon be herself again.'

Eunice brought the baby, and laid him in the warm bed by Mrs Millwood's side, and as she did so, the latter saw that Eunice was crying.

'Dear me, what is the matter, child? Surely you don't mind my having my own child for minute or two? Must I not love my own precious?

'Yes, mum, yes,' she sobbed; 'I'd as lief you had him as me, mum. I kno' you'll allus love him, the little sweetheart.'

'But tell me, Eunice, why do you cry? 'asked Mrs Millwood.

The poor girl looked very sad, and through her tears her eyes looked red and swollen.

'Becos,' she sobbed, 'my mother and father, and my brothers and sisters are all so unkind to me. They'll never let me darken their threshhoud agen, they say— never agen!'

'But surely they will forgive you, Eunice. Go and ask them. Tell them I say so. They know the child is *deaa*, don't they?'

'No, mum, no,' she said; 'I haven't told 'em that.'

'What a foolish child you are!' exclaimed Mrs Millwood. 'Now just you go and tell your mother I want to speak to her at once, and I will try and smooth your path for you.'

Two hours afterwards darkness came on, and Mrs Millwood fell asleep, and baby was put back into his bassinet after Eunice had attended to the little fellow's ravenous appetite. She was still crying. Her eyes were more swollen than ever. Her mother had been harsh with her. Nurse Gwendolen noticed how distressed she was, and therefore spoke very kindly to her.

'Have they been cross with you, dear?' she asked in a sweet, low voice.

'Yes, nurse,' she half sobbed and half whispered back; 'my mother says that God will punish me everlastin'ly, and that my child will go to go to—'

She could not finish the sentence. She buried her face in her apron, and wept bitterly. Sister Gwendolen was very much touched, and went nearer to Eunice to comfort her.

'Fear not what they tell you, child,' she said; 'God lives to love you still, and your little boy too. He is kind, very kind. Do not tremble and fear. Ask Him to forgive, and He will say to your heart, 'Go in peace; go, and sin no more.'

Later on in the evening, while Nurse Gwendolen was at supper, Eunice stole softly to the baby's bassinet. She saw his sweet wee face by the ruddy light of the bedroom fire. Lovingly she gazed at the little clenched fists and the sweet close-pressed lips. She bent over him and kissed him in his sleep, and as she did so hot, burning tears fell down her cheeks. She would never kiss him more!

Mrs Millwood was calmly sleeping, as poor Eunice turned towards her, whispering from her heart—

'God bless you, mum! God bless you! May you be to him a mother indeed.'

She went out of the room, and stole very softly downstairs. Noiselessly she opened the back door. Away she hurried across the courtyard, and disappeared down the jennel or entrance on the other side. Blind with compassion, choking with grief trembling and affrighted at some terrible, vengeance-loving god, away she hurries into the night; and as a bird, hard-stricken of death, towers aloft towards the gates of heaven ere it falls to earth, so did her spirit soar aloft for awhile as it cried out in unutterable anguish, 'God, be merciful to my child.'

CHAPTER XIII

'Who has told her this?' asked Doctor Tickle, sharply and angrily.

'Eunice's mother; there has been quite a scene,' replied Nurse Gwendolen.

'Couldn't you have stopped her?' said he, with a sharp accent of annoy.

'No, doctor; she persisted in telling the truth. She blurted it out with pious ejaculations. She told Mrs Millwood that the child was the devil's own,' and said that Mr Millwood was little short of a murderer.

'The impious old hypocrite!' exclaimed Dr Tickle; 'why didn't you gag her?'

'Sir!' said the nurse, assuming a sort of severe, yet kind expression.

'I beg your pardon,' said he, seeing that he had gone too far; 'but I really am downright vexed. However, the mischief's done, and we must try and mend it.'

The foregoing conversation took place downstairs on the morrow after the night in which Eunice's mother had had an interview with Mrs Millwood, at the latter's request.

As soon as the doctor went into the sick-room he could see that something had gone wrong with his patient. Her face looked flushed and excited, and her eyes had a wild and wandering expression. He felt her pulse. It was quick and feverish. He then took her temperature. The thermometer registered 105. He put it back into its case and sighed, and then turning to his patient, asked—

'Are you thirsty?' She made no reply.

'Does your head ache?' She stared at him, but did not speak. He then addressed Nurse Gwendolen. 'Has she been out of bed?'

'Yes, once; last night. She was so angry with Eunice's mother, that, when the latter hinted at Mr Millwood being an accomplice of murderers, she shrieked and sprang out of bed, and in doing so, she fell with her head on the floor.'

He looked very grave, and went out of the room. At the foot of the stairs he met Mr Millwood, who had just returned from the works, and who was anxiously waiting to hear the result of the doctor's visit.

'Come along with me, Mr Millwood; we had better fetch Redmires,' said the doctor to him as cheerfully as he could, although Kenneth could see he was "upset." 'There's something wrong upstairs.'

'What is it?' asked Kenneth, whose hands turned clammy, while his heart seemed to leap to his throat.

'A little brain trouble, I fear that's all,' said the doctor; 'that's all,' he repeated, with a shrug of his shoulders, and an ominous sound in his voice, which seemed to say, 'ay, and more than enough—more than enough.'

Fortunately they found Dr Redmires at home. He drove back with them in Dr Tickle's dogcart, and on their way they called at Gaskell's in the market-place to get some ice. They soon got back to Bessemer Street, and the doctors went upstairs. Poor Kenneth thought that they never would come down again. An hour seemed as long as four to him, waiting as he was in such terrible suspense.

The two doctors were using every available means to reduce Mrs Millwood's temperature, by applying ice-bags, etc. When they came upstairs they found that it had gone up to 106. After an hour's time they succeeded in getting it half a degree lower. At last they left the bedroom, and as they were on the little landing outside Dr Redmires shook his head gravely and whispered—

'She'll hardly last through the night. We had better tell him all.'

Dr Tickle nodded. 'Yes,'; and as he did so there was a little dimness in the eyes that usually flashed so very brightly. However, when he got into the room below, his eyes shone clear, bright, and kindly as ever, as he said to Kenneth, 'You had better go upstairs, and see your wife, Mr Millwood; she is dangerously ill, but of course there is hope.'

'But not much— not much,' added Redmires gravely, 'your wife has got acute meningitis. That fall on the floor has done irreparable mischief, I fear. Perhaps she may recognise you. She does not seem to know either of us at present.' As soon as Kenneth went into the sick-room, Connie's eyes were fixed upon him, and they followed him as he came to the bed-side. He kissed her feverish brow, and stroked it gently. She seemed to wish to speak, but was unable to do so. She kissed her hand and pointed to the child in the bassinet. Nurse Gwendolen brought the baby to her. She kissed the child, and then looked pitifully at Kenneth, as much as to say, 'Have pity on him, the precious!'

Then her eyes wandered round the room as if she wished to see little Bryan and Gladys, who were away; and then, after looking up at her husband with soft piteous eyes, she closed them, while her lips seemed to try to say something in prayer. Kenneth noticed that her breathing was quick and laboured. He again stroked her forehead. It was very dry and hot. He kissed her face, and gently took her hand in his, and Nurse Gwendolen left the room. He knelt down by the bed-side, still holding her hand. He had borne up very bravely until then, but his feelings suddenly got the mastery over him. For half an hour or so there was silence in that room—unbroken silence —love's tears fall still, so very still.

Nurse Gwendolen came to the door and knocked. She opened it and walked into the room. She had a card in her hand from somebody. She said, 'The gentleman is waiting downstairs.'

Kenneth looked at the card. It was Bryan Wolverton's. He left the bedroom and went below.

Bryan could hardly believe his eyes when he saw Kenneth. 'What!' he thought, 'could this be dear old Ken—the strong, lithe fellow he had last seen near Grindleford Bridge?'

Then he was tanned by the wind and the sun—a handsome, cheerful, light-hearted fellow; but now he was pale, thin, and quite "chapfallen" ; indeed, he seemed as if he was half starved.

Bryan, on the contrary, was the very picture of health; whilst his sunburnt visage, his well-trimmed wavy beard, his loose shooting-jacket and knicker-bockers, his heather-coloured stockings that set off the shape of his legs, his loose-flowing necktie, and his old sun-faded and broad-brimmed hat, all seemed to remind one of crag and fen, and moor and wold. The smell of the woods and fields seemed to be upon his very raiment.

The contrast between the two men was most marked. After the usual kindly salutations, Bryan asked,—

'May I see her, Ken?'

'Yes, Bryan, if you wish to do so; but she may not recognise you. She is worse, much worse, In fact, she is dying; the doctors know it, but hardly like to say so.'

Bryan seemed thunderstruck. He had not heard of the sudden change in his sister's condition. He had hoped to find her approaching convalescence, and to cheer her up with a few sprightly anecdotes which he had learnt near Ballyragget.

'Ken, old man,' said he, looking very much touched, while the colour faded from his lips, 'I was not prepared for this. I was not told that she was so bad. Poor Connie!' he exclaimed; 'how we loved each other! Ken, I really feel afraid to go upstairs. I am not used to look upon painful scenes; but I must see her, Ken. Yes, you lead the way; honest soul, you lead the way.'

Bryan, who had just been painfully surprised to see poor Kenneth looking so worn and haggard, was inwardly overwhelmed with grief and compassion when he saw his sister's face, and her thin white hands and wrists.

He stood speechless by the bedside for a while 'What! is this the face that once was lit warm with love and smiles?' he thought. 'Is this the darling whom I counted fairer and sweeter than any?'

He gazed as one stupefied on the eyes that were closed, on the lips that were once ruddier than the cherry, on the long dark lashes that enfringed those pity-speaking eyes, that oft would plead for him in the days when he, a mischievous lad, had chanced to get his worthy pedagogue's "dandher up." 'Were those the hands,' he thought, 'that came to succour me when Shamus Murphy was "welting" the daylight out of me?'

He drew nearer to her. He heard her quick, heavy, laboured breathing. He whispered 'Connie.' But she opened not her eyes.

'Connie, Connie, love!' he pleaded in a louder voice, but she seemed not to hear. Then he bethought him of certain terms of endearment which they had used in their school-days. He took hold of her hand. 'O how hot it was!' he thought. He whispered close to her ear—

'Connie, adheelish! Connie, alanna! It's Bryan come back to you, aroon, just to give you one sleusther of love. Look up at me, jewil; spayke to me now, acushla machree.'

She opened her eyes, and rivetted them on to Bryan, with a strange, wondering expression.

She seemed to recognise him. Her lips parted and quivered, but were dumb. Again they quivered, as she tried to speak, but she could not, while tears ran down her cheeks that were so wan.

The strong-built man was very much touched at this. The sight of those dumb pleading lips quite unmanned him—or perhaps we should say, they smote too heavily upon the chords of his human heart. His dim rainy eyes looked tenderly into his sister's. He leaned over the bed, and kissed her dry pale lips, and said in a deep, smothered voice—

'God bless you, darling. God bless you, my sweet.' Then he thoughtfully left the room, because he thought it were akin to abandoning all hope to give way to sorrow before a patient in a sick-room, and furthermore he thought, 'Perhaps poor Ken wants to be alone.'

So Bryan went and sat down in the arm-chair in the little parlour below, and buried his face in his hands and many and tumultuous were the thoughts that crowded and surged upon his over-wrought brain.

Not infrequently on such occasions as this fond memory carries us back to the little far-away touches of nature that gladdened our hearts in the sweet springtide of life. So it was with Bryan. Instinctively his mind roved back to the happy innocent days of their earlier years, and, as the tangled skein of memory unwove, he seemed to be playing with his sister once more by babbling brook or dewy mead. How they loved each other again! How she cried, he remembered, when he read to her about Rebecca in Torquilstone Castle! How valiantly he chaperoned her to school, as, hand in hand, they thridded through the dusky woods of Ballysheen Yes, he thought, the hour of wedded bliss is very sweet, but who shall say that this is not sweeter, purer, lovelier far— "the hour of sisterly sweet hand in hand"?

Bryan was aroused from the tender spell of his poetic dream of happy bygone days by the sudden appearance of Doctor Tickle, who came into the room abruptly, without knocking at the door. He put his hat and stick on the table, muttered a hurried 'Good evening,' although he had never seen Bryan before, and then, although he was lame, he hobbled upstairs in a trice. Doctors, although they may at times be over-punctilious about matters of professional etiquette, do not as a rule stand on ceremony when they come into a patient's house.

He did not remain long upstairs. When he came down he said to Bryan—

'You are Mrs Millwood's brother, I hear?'

'Yes, sir, I am. How is she now?'

'Sir,' said Doctor Tickle gravely, as he put his hand on to Bryan's broad shoulder. 'She cannot go on at this temperature much longer. The strain is too great. I must tell you there is no hope; but I shall be here again in an hour or two,' said he, and then he left the house.

Although a sunset in Attercliffe is a phenomenon hardly ever to be witnessed, as the mighty town of Sheffield lies between that unlovely neighbourhood and the west, yet Attercliffe can boast of a sunrise of its own, for—

> *"As Phoebus 'gins arise,*
> *His steeds to water at those springs,*
> *On chaliced flowers that lies,"*

he remembers poor Attercliffe, and through wind-riven chinks in the billowy, smoky haze the sheen of his falchions flashes from the glorious east, lightening up the hovels of the poor, and for awhile putting Old King Coal and his merry fiddlers to utter rout and shame.

And it happed on this quiet Sunday morning in the month of June. It was about four o'clock. The sun was shining on the happy abodes of life and the sad abodes of death. The whirring, of wheels was still. The tilt-hammer, and rolling-mill were not heard. No anvils rang a joyous pæn to skies. The stythies were quiet. The swart-limbed sons of Vulcan were lapt in peaceful dreams. The monotonous sound of the dog-hammer of the file-cutter was not. The streets were silent as death but for the grating chirp of the sparrow.

Kenneth looked out of his bedroom window towards, Otterclough forge. The furnaces were in blast, and from some dozen tall chimneys long trails of smoke went sailing in the summer air; but he did not notice these things; his heart was molten with a grief unspeakable. His beloved wife was fast asleep! Fast asleep! How still was the house! The pulling down of the blinds seemed to make quite a loud grating noise. He went down to his tiny back parlour where he found that the thoughtful Mrs Martha Stallybrass had prepared food for him, having provided some toast and a bloater and a pot of tea. She had the good sense not to break the solemnity of his sorrow by idle words, and left him alone. How plainly the clock ticked! He sat down to the first meal he had had before him for twenty-four hours. After the manner of the simple faith which they had loved to follow, he asked the Allfather to bless the simple food. With him every meal was a sacrament blessed of Heaven. He ate his early breakfast quietly. He even relished it. The terrible suspense was over. He felt a longing to see his children. They would comfort him, he thought, and yet how would they fare without her—she who had loved hem so—the little ones on life's untrodden brink—the motherless? The salt tears trickled down his cheeks, even on to the toast in his hand, and yet he went on eating; nay he almost enjoyed that frugal meal. Happily for him, neither the edge of his sorrow nor the edge of his appetite had been dulled by seeking nepenthe in something stronger than water. He knew full well that this was one of the commonest yet the very worst of panaceas to which sorrow stricken men do fly.

After his early meal was over he thanked God in his heart, more than if he had feasted with kings. He got up from the table and went into the kitchen, feeling more resigned than he had felt for many days and weeks.

'Mrs Stallybrass, where is the baby?' He asked.

'The baby, sir?' Why, sir, Mrs Pimpernel has it, sir; and she's goin' to teck it to the workus, as its grandmother'll have nothink to do with it. She called it "a limb of the d—" '

'Oh!' said Kenneth in astonishment; 'the workhouse?'

'Yes, sir; the workus,' she nodded.

'And who has suggested that?' he asked.

'Mrs Pimpernel and the doctor, sir,' she replied.

Kenneth seemed to reflect a minute or so, and then said—

'Mrs Stallybrass, I want you to do me a great favour. Will you?'

'Ay, that I will; a milliond sir,' she said.

'I thank you heartily,' he said; 'will you look well after the child for me, until we get settled down again? *I* will be the lad's father.'

'Heaven bless yer, sir!' she exclaimed.

'And him too,' he quietly added, as he put a five-pound note into her hand and left the room.

'Well I never! there I never!' she exclaimed, whatever that may mean. 'Him as orter be gnashin' an' wailin' o'er the dead is worritin' hisself about the livin'—a chancelin' too! I never!'

PART IV

CHAPTER XIV

A SHORT TIME AFTERWARDS.

Dandelow Bantam, Esq., had started housekeeping. An old aunt of his had died, and left him a good round sum of money, and a little freehold, on which was situated the old-fashioned demesne known as Ringinglow Grange, a somewhat dilapidated house on the confines of Yorkshire and Derbyshire, and on the moor edges. It was a bleak, wind-blown, weather-beaten structure, and was known to be haunted, as old Roger Morewood was murdered there in 1757, so the local chronicles relate. No one would take the place on lease, although it had been freely advertised in the Sheffield press. Yet it might be made a very comfortable residence thought Mr Bantam; and so it was that he made up his mind to have the place thoroughly "done up." Having drawn from the partnership at Otterclough Forge, and having received the somewhat unexpected windfall from his late aunt Sabina Bantam heaven rest her!—he had plenty of means; and the thought of having a fine old country seat of his own began to dawn upon him in a most pleasant and attractive light. It was true that the Grange required a great deal of "doing up," for the roomy old house had not been repaired for many years; indeed, it and the garden had been for long neglected.

Now Dandy was not the man to settle down in the midst of chaos; not he. He soon succeeded in transforming the inhospitable-looking place into a very picturesque and comfortable-looking country mansion. Thus it came about that about two months after the death of Connie Millwood, Dandelow Bantam settled down at Ringinglow Grange, and began to take a most proper and praiseworthy pride in "keeping the place up."

He felt himself to be a man of some importance, now that he had got a house of his own to live in, and realised more and more the desirability of lifting himself up to his proper position in society; and perhaps it should be here stated that Mr Bantam "some'oworruther," as he often said, was not well satisfied with his scanty knowledge of the world of letters and other delights of polite society, and being a man possessed of common sense, he argued that it was only right that he, the owner and occupier of Ringinglow Grange, should be conversant with something more than the manners and customs of men who "tang and heft and bull and scrat" for money, and for no ends else.

So it was that he applied himself to literature generally, and bought many books for his library, amongst which was a large dictionary. This was his favourite book indeed, "Webster" became Mr Dandelow Bantam's favourite author.

Also be it here said Mr Bantam "tuk" to the fine arts. He had long ago forgiven Bryan Wolverton for marrying his favourite sister, and they had long since become fast friends. From his brother-in-law Mr Bantam had acquired a love and a smattering of knowledge for oil paintings a taste which later on in life developed into a harmless and innocent hobby, because Dandy never allowed his taste to run riot to any extravagant extent; thus he thought himself lucky when one day he bought two Hobbemas, one Raphael, and a fine Rembrandt for seven guineas! He loved the old masters, and was fond of a bit of "real genuine bonyfidy" work, he said.

'Look here, Bryan,' said he one morning when he was showing off his pictures, 'I've picked up a rare bit; this is an "old Crome."'

'Garrout wid yer' said Bryan, in his playful Irish way.

'Well,' said Dandy, 'I bought it for one anyhow; and what's more, it's a signed picture, and I only gev twenty-three shillin' for it.'

'Dandy, my boy,' said Bryan, clapping him on the back, ' 'tis an excellent bargain you've made. That picture, Dandy, is good enough for the walls of Jericho any day; but faix, my boy, don't be afther givin' so much money for the dhirty ould Saxon rubbish.'

'Bryan!' exclaimed Dandy.

'I mane it,' Bryan nodded.

Dandy changed the subject. He had a strong prejudice against the modern school of painting. He couldn't "abear" it, and he could hardly forgive Bryan for being one of its most promising exponents. Unfortunately, Bryan and he always got to loggerheads about these "old masters." Moreover, Dandy, although he had a very good temper, was apt to get his dandher up at Bryan's Irish "gibberish." He hated "Irish banther wuss nor Cockney drawl." As Dandy's ideas of the world became wider (it is astonishing how soon we can get out of the old narrow ruts if we only try), he began gradually to try and speak after a more cosmopolitan manner; not that he loved the good old Sheffield vernacular one whit the less, not he, but that he thought it more becoming to the Squire of Ringinglow to converse in the language of polite society.

Dandelow Bantam, Esq., had just come down to breakfast. He sat down alone at the head of the table in the large wainscoted dining-room, while on either side of him hung his favourite "old masters." He was seated in front of the old stone-mullioned and latticed window that overlooked Fulwood and the valley of Endcliffe below. It was a charming summer morning, and the soft west wind was lazily carrying the distant inky haze of Sheffield afar off up the unseen valley of the Don. The shadows from the stunted trees that skirted his garden were slowly shortening athwart the well-shaven and velvety lawn, which Mr Bantam's gardener kept most scrupulously tidy and clean.

Dandy, as he sat enjoying his breakfast, felt very happy. It was such a delightful morning! The fresh morning wind that came gently sweeping across the heathery wilds, and that blew through the open lattice, seemed livelier than champagne. Dandy's mind, too, was brimful of pleasant presentiments. He couldn't tell why, so he laughed to himself, and ate his breakfast with the relish of a hungry teetotaller, who, it is well known, has a better appetite than forty hunters.

'Come in,' said he, as someone knocked at the door.

It was his "buttons"—his boy Sam, bringing him a letter on a silver waiter, for the postman had just come. Dandy took the letter in his hand, and looked at it with some feeling of pride. It was addressed 'Dandelow Bantam, Esq., Ringinglow Grange'—nothing more.

He opened the letter and began to read—

"MY DEAR DANDELOW, I am writing to you to say that I accept this, the last of your many kind invitations. Hitherto I have been diffident of availing myself of the opportunity you have from time to time given us of visiting you. It has seemed to me to be too much of an invasion of your hospitality to bring little Bryan, and Gladys, and the baby, with two nurse-maids and myself, to spend a month at Ringinglow Grange; and I cannot but think that in inviting us your generosity has to a large extent over-ridden your discretion. Have you considered how six hungry denizens from Attercliffe will add to the totals of your housekeeper's accounts, and how they will disturb your domestic peace?

"However, we are all coming to-morrow at about mid-day, so may it please you to receive us under your most hospitable roof as weary wayfarers, as glad of your kindness of heart as of the shelter and the food which a true-born Sheffielder knows so well how to provide. I should mention that both the doctor and Mr Lynnacre have influenced my decision in this matter, as they will persist that I should have rest and fresh bracing air, a change of scene, and good jovial company; so let me send you herewith warning, brother Dandelow, that ye all be of good cheer, and of a joyful countenance, when we come to your wind-blown hospice, even as I am fully purposed to try and be happy in your presence, knowing as I do that you live out your simple, cheerful faith as a good craftsman of no mean craft.

"Yours fraternally, etc., etc.
"KENNETH MILLWOOD"

Mr Bantam read the letter over twice—the last time aloud. He then laid it down on the table, and with laconic simplicity exclaimed—

'A'! I *am* glad!'

Again he picked up the letter, and again perused it, so as to be quite sure of the contents.

'Strikes me forcibly,' said he to himself, 'as Kenneth writes a better letter than me; but I'll just ring t' bell and tell Mrs Mottram t' good news.'

Sam, the boy, answered the bell, and Mr Bantam told him that he wished to speak to Mrs Mottram.

By-and-bye she entered the room. She was a sour-looking personage. She had been chosen to act as housekeeper for Mr Bantam by his friend Mrs Stumperlowe, who had, with a well-meaning foresight, thought it advisable to choose a party the least likely to re-kindle the smothered flame which had been luckily extinguished by Miss Barbara Shout's gnattering and nagging ways.

Mrs Rebecca, *alias* Becky Mottram, had been a widow for many years, and no one had ever dared to make advances to her since her good husband perished at Owlerton, in the Sheffield Flood. Her hopes were whelmed in that deluge. She had never smiled since. Two sleek, well-kempt, well-anointed ringlets hung adown either side of her cheeks, that had been unkissed for many years. There was an icy regularity, a precise primness, about her attire as well as her features. As soon as Mr Bantam saw her, nothing daunted, he said—

'Mrs Mottram, we have visitors coming from Attercliffe to-morrow—such a lot! Will you get all the beds well aired? and get in milk, butter, cream and eggs by the cart-load!'

Mr Bantam spoke with aglad excitement in his voice, while Mrs Mottram's face began to lengthen imperceptibly, as an icicle or a stalactite.

'How many are coming, sir?' she half gasped and half sighed, in a melancholic manner, looking them a welcome as cold as sleet in June.

Mr Bantam read aloud to her from the letter—'Little Bryan, Gladys, and a baby— two nursemaids and himself, Mr Millwood, of Attercliffe.'

Becky Mottram emitted a peculiar shivering sort of sigh, something like a snake squirming through lank, withered sword-grass. She also turned up the whites of her eyes as though she were going to be made a martyr without anybody knowing it.

'Are you ill?' he asked in alarm.

'N-n-no, sir, not exactly; but how can a pore widder manage to look after six folks from Attercliffe?

'She laid a peculiarly sad emphasis on "Attercliffe," as though it were far below Owlerton; indeed, as though God had long ago quite forsaken Attercliffe.

'But there are two maids coming too, he explained.

'Yes, sir,' she said tartly; 'but they'll want more attending to than the rest.'

'Rubbish!' said Mr Bantam. 'I'll be bound you'll fall in love with the whole kit of them before they've been here a day.'

'Never, sir, never!' she sighed.

'Oh yes, you will, Mrs Mottram. They're the darlin'est childer; and as for their father he's—'

'But,' she sighed, 'I cannot; I'm only a poor widder, and ever since my William 'Enery perished in the flood—'

'Come, come,' said Mr Bantam, who had heard that tale before; 'that'll do, why, you'd freeze the nose of a brass monkey, you would; and let me tell you I'm a bit nesh myself. This'll never do. Come, come; busk about, honest woman. If you'll only think of others a bit more and yourself a bit less, you'll mayhap forget there's such a person as Becky Mottram, and all her sorrows into the bargain.'

Mrs Mottram left the room with a frigid sort of curtsey and a sanctimonious die-away closing of the eyes. She went back into the spacious old kitchen, and sat down quite overcome.

'Forget my sorrows, indeed! Never!' she gasped.

'What!' she thought, 'shall I desecrate the memory of my long-departed William 'Enery by busking about as a fussy hussif? No, sir; never! Rather will I bury myself in the depths of my sorrows; yea, I will hug them to me as a shroud.'

Such was the tenor of her thoughts, as she sat angrily and fretfully rocking herself to and fro in that kitchen, blind to the fact that her sorrows had degenerated into selfishness into a purblind egoism; whereas the whole being of him against whom she was fretting and nursing her wrath was thrilled with the joy of the lofty altruism—to give a brother a "lift on the way."

Right glad was Mr Bantam to think that at last Ringinglow Grange was going to ring with happy voices. He was quite excited. He went into the stable and gave vent to his joyous feelings to Dan'l the groom. He thwacked his gray mare Luce lovingly under the ribs, in token of the exuberance of his joy. The mare spoke back her thanks with a kind look from her luminous dreamy eyes.

'Fettle her up, Dan'l, lad,' he said to his groom, who was an importation from Ireland, recommended by Mr Bryan

Wolverton, 'fettle her up, and put her into the dogcart, and put your buttons on, Dan'l. I'm going to town, so look smart.'

'Troth an' I will,' said Dan'l, who was flourishing a dandybrush.

'Dan'l,' said Mr Bantam, 'is that young mongrel bitch of yours safe, do you think, eh?'

'As safe as houses, sorr; divil a tush has she. Faix, her teeth's all disthracted wid oud age, glory be to hiv'n,' said he.

'That's all right,' said Mr Bantam, who had a familiar way of talking to his servants; 'because there are some childer coming here to-morrow, Dan'l.'

'Childre, begor!' exclaimed Dan'l; 'troth an' its fairly slain wid their honest prattle you'll be, sorr; but a powher o' good they'll do yer health anyway.'

'What! Do I look ill then?' asked Mr Bantam.

'Divil a bit,' said Dan'l; 'faix, 'tis just dhramin' I am that a long time 'twill be afore *we* throubles the undhertakers anyway. Is it many childres comin', sorr,' he asked with his usual overweening curiosity.

'About a dozen, all told,' said Mr Bantam, with a merry twinkle in his eye, and not wishing to satisfy Dan'l's interrogation.

'More the merrier,' said Dan'l whose mind was beginning to be happily exercised by the thought of the possible galaxy of "swate faymale deludhers that might be a-comin' to look afther the childre."

'Come, look smart, Dan'l,' said Mr Bantam; 'more work and less gibberish, lad, and don't let me catch you red-raddlin' your nose too much in those pewter pots at the Stannidge Pole.'

'Tare an' 'ounds!' exclaimed Dan'l whose dandher was suddenly "ruz"; 'but be aisy wid me, sorr. Faix, 'twas only wance I tuk a thimbleful too much porther inside me weskit.'

'Ay, lad a tailor's thimbleful I reck'n,' said Mr Bantam as he left the stable.

By-and-bye they set off towards Sheffield. Mr Bantam drove, while Dan'l, rigidly erect, spick and span in his green livery, sat behind in the dogcart, looking with an air of true Celtic pride and high disdain upon the "pore misforthunate Saxon blag'ards that happened to be thrampin' on fut in his wake."

Dan'l did not look very happy, as Mr Bantam had again told him to stop his gibberish. This had annoyed him, and thus as he rode to Sheffield he was undergoing that terrible penance to an Irishman, of "smoderin' his anger wid his mouf shut."

'Tundher an' lightenin' be his dhrink!' thought Dan'l; 'an' may the lightenin' be forked to choke him when he swallays.'

But, be it said, Mr Dandelow Bantam had not the remotest idea of being unkind to Dan'l. He only wished to be quiet, so as to digest certain thoughts that forced themselves upon him in stronger array since his interview that morning with Becky Mottram, his housekeeper.

'Yes,' he thought, 'a housekeeper more after my heart would be better; a more permanent institution altogether. In fact, why shouldn't I settle down in life? Why should Dandy wait? There's scores of young ladies would jump at the chance of being mistress of Ringinglow Grange; scores—but ah!' he thought, 'would it be Dandy they were after, or his money?'

The thought pained him somewhat. To think that society was hollow and rotten to the core was not pleasant to him. He knew that he was very plain—almost ugly and he knew that he lacked the polish of a man of the world; and that this same world had ridiculed him ever since he left school. He even remembered how poor Connie (tears came into his eyes when he thought of her, for he had learned to admire her long before she died) had laughed, in her girlish innocence, at his awkward and artless advances to her at that Freemasons' Ball.

Again he thought how Miss Barbara Shout had snubbed him, and what an unfortunate and unhappy affair their engagement had been. Although he knew that Miss Barbara Shout and her brothers had once despised him, yet he now could see how desperately anxious the Shouts were to have the engagement renewed. Money and position had brought about this sudden metamorphosis of feeling.

Yes, money had wrought a wondrous change; and mothers and daughters, in their artless and guileless hearts, had already begun to think of the coming winter season, and had, strange to say, actually included Dandelow Bantam's name in their lists of guests to be invited to their balls, and dinners, and suppers; yea, they had even remembered that he had a weakness for venison pasty and frummaty.

When Mr Bantam arrived in the town, he "put up at" the Stannidge Pole, as was his wont, and in a short time he was busily engaged in marketing, providing for his coming guests in a truly Yorkshire fashion. Your true Sheffielder knows how to make his table groan. Mrs Stumperlowe could not understand whatever was going to happen up at Ringinglow. Her mind was quite agitated. Never had Dandy given her such an order.

Also Gaskell's and Luke's and Porson's were rejoiced to think how their turnover had increased for the day.

Not only did Mr Bantam provide toys and books for little Bryan and Gladys, but he also remembered the two nurse-maids who were coming; and he even did not forget the baby. Furthermore, he went to Kindon's, and bought a pound of old Limerick twist to stop Dan'l's gibberish.

He even remembered Mrs Becky Mottram, the housekeeper, for when he arrived home in the evening about six o'clock, he quite succeeded in mollifying that austere individual's heart by presenting her with an illustrated edition of Fox's *Book of Martyrs*.

After Mr Bantam had enjoyed a good plain dinner, he set off for a quiet stroll towards the moors. He walked in the direction of the homestead of Wild Hatch Farm, a dilapidated farmhouse about two miles distant. He felt impelled to walk thitherward from a spirit of curiosity; also for him there was a something bordering on romance about the place. He had once, and only once, seen a very fair and sweet-faced girl, with long, wavy hair, come out of the old house, that looked so bleak, so desolate, and so drear.

She was clad in a long red riding-hood cloak, which he thought was somewhat too childish a garment for one who was on the verge of womanhood. She was above the average height, and her figure appeared to be of a goodly symmetry. He had seen her face before she was aware that he was near. It was indeed very sweet, but very sad. As soon as she saw him she ran back into the house, and as she did so, he saw that she was quite barefooted.

Mr Bantam's interest was aroused. When he went home to the Grange, he told no one whom he had seen, but he began to make enquiries about the tenants of Wild Hatch Farm, and with no little difficulty he at last found out something about them which tended to deepen his interest in them.

The owner and occupier of the farm was generally known by the nickname of "Old Skelper." Why so, he found out that local tradition was silent. His real name was Dick Starkholmes, and it was said that he had a daughter living with him, named Hetty, who was very rarely seen by anybody except by the few men-servants and women-servants who from time to time were inveigled at some distant "stattis" into accepting service, for which they were never paid.

He further found out that the Starkholmes, together with the Morewoods, had at one time owned nearly all the property thereabouts, and that Dick Starkholmes was the last male descendant of his family. Also he found out that the latter's reputation waned, or rather waxed worse, in the ratio of the enquiries he made. In fact, Mr Starkholmes was now in receipt of the hard-earned wages a—pitiless dole—of a life spent in hard drinking, gambling, and horse-racing. One by one his homesteads and broad acres had been swallowed, gambled away, or lost on the turf. So it came about that Mr Dandelow Bantam's heretofore placid and incurious mind was considerably exercised by the occupiers of Wild Hatch Farm, especially the one in the red riding-hood cloak,— 'bare-footed too!' he thought.

He felt an unspeakable feeling of sympathy that was beginning to be just slightly oppressive. He longed to see that girl again, and often pictured to himself what a sad life was hers, if the bad reports about her father were true. Mr Bantam's sympathies, when once fairly aroused, were not easily allayed. Although he had only seen the girl once, and then only for a second or two, there was secretly upwelling within him a spring of pity for her. Perhaps it was the remembrance of those bare feet, and that sad, sweet face of hers, that had enkindled and enlisted his compassion. Certain it was that as he neared the old homestead he felt something more than an idle feeling of curiosity for one at least of the indwellers.

He walked very slowly past the house, which he had not passed for nearly a week. He could see nobody about. There was, strange to say, not a visible sign or token of life about the place not even the cluck, cluck, cluck of a proud-strutting chanticleer marshalling his dames to roost; nor yet a lean touzie tyke to snarl at his heels as he passed by; not the thick lubric gurgle of a sow lapt in slumberous repose in the slush of her sty; nor yet the twittering of swallows 'neath the jagged eaves of the old tumble-down and straw-thatched barn.

He listened as he stood still by the side of the granary door. The silence was appalling, and yet he heard something, he thought. What was it? He could hardly tell, but it was as the sound of the gnawing or "chavelling" of a rat, laboriously at work trying to get out of that empty granary. 'Poor scranchin' beggar, he's starved out, I'll warrant! Surely the bailiffs have been here,' reflected Mr Bantam and he was right. They had been, and had, so to speak, swept the decks clean. The sheriff's officers had left traces behind them, for on the byre and on the barn door, and on the stone posts at the entrance to the home toft, were the mutilated and tattered remains of big posters which "Old Skelper" had almost effectually scraped off with his old thistle-grubber.

Mr Bantam stood looking at the apparently deserted place for a minute or two, and then he strolled slowly on.

It was a charming evening. Afar off the limestone peaks that frown over Hathersage were afire in the rays of the setting sun. The marvellous weft of colours in the sky seemed to intermingle and change every second as the great orb sank o'er the distant hills.

Through a cleft in the almost parallel bars of soft fleecy cloudlets, the core of the disc shone as molten gold. Gradually the marge of each cloudlet is fringed with tints of crimson and gold, tipped with purest amber. Slowly and imperceptibly the colours intermingle and change again and fade away. The edge of the sun's rim sinks, and dips below the horizon, and suddenly the myriad islets of the dappled sky are bathed and suffused in one wild crimson glow.

'Thank God for that,' said Mr Bantam to himself as he watched the glorious sheen, and sat him down on the flat, lichened coping-stone of a small one-arched bridge which crossed a tinkling moorland streamlet that darkled and danced merrily along its pebbly channel in the direction of Whirlow Bridge, whence it rippled along towards the valley of the Sheaf, to join that tributary of the Don, before its somewhat sluggish and turbulent waters are darkened by the terrible baptism of the smoke of Sheffield.

'Beats old Crone that,' said Mr Bantam, lighting a cigar, and turning his head away from the splendid afterglow to the dreamy shades of the glen below, where the silver-footed stream lapsed and laughed so merrily along.

He sat with his legs dangling on the outside of the stonework of the bridge. He was enchanted with the scene. The sparsely dotted coverts on either side of the stream, and the lowly boskage of gorse and heather seemed so lifeless and so still, save that a grouse whirred by now and then, or a ring-ousel came skimming from some upland wold to seek covert in the sheltered brake, and about half-a-dozen sand-martins busily darted to and fro amongst a swarm of gnats, as night stole on apace.

It was a lovely, peaceful evening, and the enfolding hills seemed lulled and lapt in—

'Please, sir,' whispered a gentle voice close behind Mr Bantam. How he started! It was as if a gas-meter had exploded under that bridge. He slid off the coping-stone as if it had suddenly been converted into an ingot of hot lava; and as he did so, he unluckily fell into a close briar-tangled and multitudinously-spiked blackthorn bush that overhung the stream below, and therein he was safely anchored and suspended, while his hat was carried away in the eddying whirl of the stream.

Mr Bantam felt himself in a particularly awkward and prickly predicament, and almost wished that the kindly earth would chine, or open, and let him in, for lo! to his great astonishment be it said, there up above, just where he had been seated, was the girl in the old red riding-hood cloak— Hetty Starkholmes!

It would appear that she had noiselessly stolen up to him on the soft springy turf, and the very sound of her sweet voice had startled him; just as we ourselves remember to have been startled in the years gone by, when a certain Mr Velveteens[17] put his hand upon our shoulders unawares, and then gently asked us a few very pertinent and proper questions. It was not the questions that startled us; it was the sort of heart-jumping

---

[17] Gamekeepers were known for their wearing of velveteens.

vacuum-brake business suddenly created by that unexpected 'Hello!' of his.

'I am so sorry, sir; can I help you?' she said, looking compassionately over the bridge.

'No, thank you, miss; I can manage very well. I'm only a bit scratched among these 'ere blessed prickedly briars. But, Godfrey Daniells! I can't get out!' he exclaimed.

She jumped over the wall as nimbly as a deer, and helped him to extricate himself from his sorry plight.

'There!' she said; 'you are no longer in a state of suspense. You are on *terra firma* once again; and I beg your pardon, sir, if I startled you. Really, I ought to have known better, and given you fair warning of my approach; but I never gave it a thought. Pray accept my apologies. It was so thoughtless of me. I *do* hope you are not hurt.'

'Not a bit, miss,' said Dandy, whose thought for all veracity was suddenly put to rout by the lissom figure before him.

'Not a bit,' he repeated. 'It's me as orter be ashamed of himself for being startled at the sweet voice of a girl.'

She heeded this compliment with innocent looks, and looking at him with her soft, sad, violet eyes, she said —'Please, sir, are you not Mr Bantam of the Grange?'

'Yes, miss, I am,' said Dandy, feeling constrained to speak as well as he could to one who spoke him so fair.

'I thought so,' she said, 'as I have often seen you pass by Wild Hatch when we lived there.'

'Oh yes,' stammered Dandy; 'that is my usual walk.'

He felt quite pleased at having been noticed, and he quite forgot the innumerable blackthorn spikes that had found their way considerably beyond his raiment.

'My name is Hetty Starkholmes,' she said, looking at him with her sad, dark, violet eyes, and making him a graceful and unaffected bow; 'and I beg to ask you, sir, if you would now do me a great favour.' She spoke with considerable emotion. 'My father is very ill indeed, sir,' she continued; 'he is lying among the long rushes down the glen by the stream-side, and I cannot rouse him.'

'What is the matter with him?' asked Mr Bantam.

'I hardly know, sir, for I can neither wake nor move him; but it may be,' she said, with misty eyes, 'that some of his former friends, the sportsmen on the moors, have been treating him too liberally. They have been shooting since the twelfth, sir, and he has been with them acting as marksman of wounded birds.'

'Let us go at once and see him,' said Mr Bantam, 'as it will be dark in a short while.'

'This way, please,' she said, as she tripped swiftly down the darkening glen. He could hardly keep pace with the lithe and agile figure before him. She knew every inch of the way, and leapt over the stream, from stepping-stone to stepping-stone, in a manner that made Mr Bantam's heart quake to follow her. They hurried along till they came to a clump of stunted birch and willow trees, where the grass and rushes grew rank and long in the moist peaty soil. Here, under the cope of a friendly birch, lay Mr Dick Starkholmes.

Mr Bantam saw at a glance what was the matter. In fact, he could see under the shade of the pendulous boughs a long-necked hock bottle, a large flagon-shaped Steinwein bottle, and a good-sized spirit-flask, all empty, whilst by his side was a cigar-case, nearly empty.

'Been marking wounded birds, eh?' said Mr Bantam, rubbing his stubbly chin in a certain pensive, dubious, and altogether reflective manner.

'Yes, sir. I believe so, but I fear—' she hesitated, sighed, and did not finish her sentence.

'Strikes me forcibly, Miss Starkholmes, 'that he's been marking luncheon hampers too. Look here! Why, here it is under this very tree! And not a sandwich touched, but every bottle gone. A' deary me! Well I never! He's blind dr—'

Mr Bantam here suddenly caught sight of Hetty's face. She was biting her thumb-nail, while her eyes were brimful of tears; and the thought struck him that he had been uncouth, unmannerly, and had said something to wound her feelings. He suddenly felt ashamed of his blindness to filial ties. Ought he not to have thought that love dies very hard, even in a daughter whose midnight vigil had oft been spent in bitterness and tears that words can never tell? He was pained to think that possibly he had hurt sensibilities which were far more refined than his own.

'Shall I try to wake him?' he gently asked.

'No, Mr Bantam; let *me* try first,' she replied, and then in truly loving yet piteous tones she spoke to the prostrate form.

'Father, dear father, awake! we have to take you home.'

But never a sound from the low-lying form.

Home! What a sad hollow sound there was about that word, he thought. How unreal it sounded in his ears! Alas! they were both homeless as wandering Jews outcast on Russian steppes; and for three nights past their respective lodging had been in the byre and on the mouldy fodder in the chinky hay-loft.

Again and again she tried to make him hear, but it was quite in vain. Darkness was coming on apace too. She knelt on the grass by his side and shook him by his arm. He made never a groan. She took hold of his hand. How cold, and flaccid, and clammy it felt! She leaned over him and touched his face with her hand, and then suddenly with a loud shriek she half gasped and half cried, 'He's dead! He's dead!' and fell back into Mr Bantam's arms as a lifeless corpse.

Mr Bantam's nerves were something more than unstrung. He positively shook in every limb. His plain, blunt, matter-of-fact way of facing sudden emergencies quite deserted him. For a moment or two his senses quite forsook him, and he knew not what to do. 'Was she dying?' he thought, or was it only a dead faint?' There was no time to reason about it. He must do something, and do it at once. So he laid her down as quickly and as gently as he on a heathery mound hard by. He ran to the stream, and filled his felt hat full of water, and rushed back to her. He poured it on to her death-white face, but she did not come round at all. He was terribly alarmed. He thought she was dead. He bent down and tried to listen if he could hear her heart beat, but his own was throbbing away as a tilt-hammer, that he could not hear hers. He grew very excited. He called her loudly by her name. He lifted her up. He shook her, but her supple limbs fell loosely back on to the heathery couch.

'Undo them buttons, man!' said a deep bass voice close behind him.

Dandy started as if he had been shot.

He turned round, and saw a big, burly gamekeeper, with a double-barrelled gun under his left arm, and a large black retriever close at his heels.

'Good heavens!' exclaimed Mr Bantam, as though he thought Old Skelper had come back to life again; 'You fairly frightened t' wits out o' me.'

'Don't be scared, sir,' said Mr Velveteens reassuringly, and calmly pointing with the stem of his pipe to the sweet wan face on the ling. 'Undo them buttons, as I said, and loosen that hankychiff, and then she'll come to.'

Mr Bantam did as he was told, while the gamekeeper turned to where the drunken man lay. The retriever sniffed at the feet and trousers of the recumbent form and growled.

The gamekeeper felt "Old Skelper's" hands and forehead, and then listened close to him for the tell-tale sign of life within.

He got up, shook his head, coolly knocked the ashes out of his pipe against his gun-barrels, and exclaimed, 'Poor old Skelper!'

'Is he really dead?' asked Mr Bantam breathlessly and excitedly.

'Dead? Ay, sir, that he be; deader nor a door nail, sez I,' said the stalwart man. 'Poor old Skelper! they'll never dun *him* any more and *he'll* never lay odds agen, I'll warrant. He'll mark no more wounded birds, nor steal good vittles and good liquor, nor poach, nor skelp his servant lasses for axin' for their wages. Never, sir, never. He's gone where they can't catch him, sez I.'

'What's to be done?' exclaimed Mr Bantam.

'Why, just you look arter Miss Hetty, while I signal for a mate or two.'

He pointed the muzzle of his gun towards Whirlow Bridge, and fired. He counted fifteen, and then fired the other barrel. The reports rattled and echoed down the valley, for the air was very elastic.

'Down, Caesar, down!' shouted he, gruffly, to his retriever, that suddenly started and rushed forward to see what his master had shot at.

The noise of the gamekeeper's signal aroused Hetty from her fainting-fit. She opened her eyes and looked up. By the dusky light she saw Mr Bantam watching over her. She lifted her head up and spoke to him. 'Kind sir,' she said in a weak voice, 'is he is he is he really dead? My father, sir?'

'Ay, Miss Hetty,' said the deep, yet pitiful voice of the gamekeeper, who was standing by, 'he'll mark no more wounded birds, he won't; but you? what about you, Miss Hetty? Why of course you had better walk up with Mr Bantam to my cottage o'er the knowe. What, no? Nonsense. I say you must go, Miss Hetty, and my missis'll be a second mother to you, God bless her.'

There was such a kind persuasiveness and an authoritative air about what the gamekeeper said, that the poor terror-stricken girl, pale, weak, and bewildered, got up and walked with Mr Bantam towards the keeper's cottage.

CHAPTER XV

On the following day, soon after the hour of twelve, Mr Bantam's visitors from Attercliffe drove up to the Grange.

Mr Bantam had just come back from a six-mile walk. He had been to the gamekeeper's cottage to do what he could for poor Hetty Starkholmes in her bereavement.

As soon as he saw Kenneth and his family, the sorrowful feelings which had oppressed him since the painful event of the previous evening gave way to those of unbounded joy.

Kenneth, after he had had a good look round, said that he liked Ringinglow Grange very much. He thought it a charming place. It was so far removed from the smoke of Sheffield, and the air was so clear and so bracing to the nerves.

Little Bryan was simply delirious with delight to romp in the garden with Gladys and the nursemaids, who felt as blithe and as hoydenish as the little ones.

After midday dinner was over, it was positively delightful to watch them all playing at the sweetly innocent game of "Stepping up the Green Grass" on the soft velvety turf, and even Mrs Becky Mottram's heart unfroze as she watched them; indeed, it quite melted later on when little Bryan clomb her knees, and lovingly kissed the face that had been unkissed for years, and with a coaxing and childlike simplicity asked her 'O p'ease, dear Mrs Mott'am, do tell me all about de S'effield flood, where poor Mr Mott'am was d'owned. I'm awfully sorry for you, you know, but you'll tell me, won't you? Untle Bantam says you know a great deal about that flood.'

Mrs Mottram soon had one willing auditor to listen with rapt attention and with brimming eyes to her pitiful tale of woe and she was wonderfully surprised to know that such a nice, well-behaved, gentlemanly boy—so sympathetic too!—

came from Attercliffe. She even began to think that, after all, perhaps God had not quite forsaken poor Attercliffe. That night Becky Mottram remembered Attercliffe in her prayers, that it might be "thoroughly purged with hyssop." This, at any rate, was better than giving it over to the arch-enemy of mankind "bag and baggage."

Little Bryan was delighted to be at such a beautiful spot as Ringinglow Grange. He made himself quite at home with everybody about the place, and told Mrs Mottram that he thought 'Linlinlow was nearly as dood as Attertiffe, but not twite.'

He began to entertain feelings of the profoundest admiration and respect for Dan'l the groom. He thought him wonderfully brave to gallop round the paddock on the horse's bare back. Dan'l was a hero in Bryan's eyes. Often would he steal away to the stable-yard to have a peep at Dan'l. One day he came into the stable whilst Dan'l was grooming the mare, Luce. He was struck with the groom's importance as a "fettler" of animals. What an important avocation was Dan'l's, he thought. What a serious aspect he wore! What a marvellous manner he had! What style and flourish! How perfect! What a wonderful sibilous noise he made as he lovingly wisped her shining flanks!

'What for do oo make dat noise wif oor mouf?' asked the child, after a period of dumb surprise.

'Bekase it's de fashion wid grooms, osthlers, an' ryalty, me bhoy' said Dan'l, standing with his arms akimbo, and looking into the boy's sweetly pretty face.

'And what for do oo have a piece of st'aw in oor mouf?'

'Bekase it's de k'rect fashion, *paudeen.*'

'And what is dat in oor hand?'

'A whisp av sthraw. Is it cross-exhaminin' me you are?'

'And whyfor do oo have itta belts lound oor legs?'

'To howld my *dhudeen* in, or what the Saxons calls a baccy pipe.'

'De Saxons?' said Bryan wonderingly. 'Are dey dood peopo'?'

'Arrah, bhoy, no; tis the mischief's own people they are. The Irish is good; the Saxons divil a bit'

'My poor dear mudder was an Iallis lady,' said little Bryan.

'Bless her sowl!' exclaimed Dan'l; 'faix, an' it's meself as thort I was talkin' to a young shlip av a haythen.'

'Did oo know my dear mudder, sir?'

'Troth an' I didn't; more's the pity.'

'She has don to heaven, sir.'

'She's an angel thin,' said Dan'l.

The boy nodded a sweet 'Yes.'

'Are oo glad I tum to Linlinlow?' he asked.

'Overwhellum'd wid jie,' said Dan'l.

'Do oo lub our nurse, sir?'

Dan'l shook his head, as though that would be a most unpardonable offence.

'Av coorse not,' said he, with a sly wink, and laughing down his sleeve.

'What for did oo tiss her so, v'en Mrs Mott'am vent out of de titchen?'

'Tundher an' lightenin'!' exclaimed Dan'1. 'Me characther's at stake? Here, boy; you go an play at throwin' stones at the dhrakes in the duck-pond. Away wid yer, honest soul!' Off went little Bryan.

'Pon me sowl! it's bettre manners that lad must be taught, smart. Faix, 'tis blisther me ears he would, wid his onfathymable cur'os'ty an' honest prattle.'

After Mr. Bantam had shown Kenneth all the charms of Ringinglow Grange, the former began most graphically to relate the incidents of the previous day; and of course he easily succeeded in enlisting much sympathy for poor Hetty Starkholmes, whilst Kenneth could not but observe what a chivalrous spirit had come over the one-time matter-of-fact, prosaic Dandy; and how his heart seemed to glow within him as he told of her pitiful case.

'Let us walk over to Whirlow Bridge,' he said, 'and see if the time for the inquest is fixed. It will be held to-morrow perhaps, and I shall have to be there, you know. I have already arranged for the funeral to take place at Fulwood.'

Accordingly they set off, after bidding kind adieux to the little ones on the lawn, who waved them back many kisses, and shouted, 'Dood-bye, Untle Dandelow,' for he had told them to address him by that name.

After they had gone about half a mile, Kenneth asked, 'Of course you have seen the papers this morning?'

'No indeed, I haven't,' said Dandy, 'I really have been so busy. Any particular news?'

'*Rather!*' exclaimed Mr Millwood. 'There is a remarkable confession of the murder of two men we both knew very well, Captain Underwedge and Mr Humphrey Shout.'

'You don't say so!' exclaimed Mr Bantam, with incredulous amaze. 'It's true enough,' said Kenneth; 'and, what is more remarkable, we both knew the murderers.'

'The deuce we did!' exclaimed Dandy; 'who can they be?'

'My next-door neighbour, Luke Stallybrass, and an Irishman named Sweeney, and a man named Clarkson,' said Kenneth. 'Don't you remember Luke?'

'Remember him!' said Dandy; 'rather! there wasn't a finer-built chap, nor a straight-forrader hand at Otterclough Forge. He was a staunch mester's man. But have they found the bodies?'

'No,' said Kenneth; 'and they never will. They were, so to speak, cremated alive.'

'Cremated? eh? What's that mean?'

'Why, it simply means that they were dashed into Number One Blast Furnace, and of course they would be resolved to ashes in a few minutes.'

'Ay, that they would, said Dandy. 'My hi! wouldn't they frizzle! Ugh! just fancy poor old Shout. I think I see him crozzlin' this minnit. But do you think it's true, Kenneth?'

'Quite so; I see no reason to doubt Luke's confession. The motive seems so clear, too.'

'The motive! What motive, pray?' said Dandy with surprise.

'Well,' said Kenneth, 'the papers make a good deal of it, but to epitomise the whole thing—'

'Eh, what?'

'I mean to put the matter into a nutshell. At that time Luke, Tim Sweeney, and Jukes Clarkson were non-unionists—'

'Yes, blacklegs,' nodded Dandy.

'And some of the members of the Union had threatened to "do for them," as they put it, using other forcible expletives. They had, it appears, received all sorts of threatening letters— the usual sort of thing, you know with death's heads, cross-bones, and coffins on them but Luke and his fellows were not to be coerced by the ruthless terrorism of a despotic Union they still held aloof, despised "Mary Ann's" threats, and bore up against the intimidation and the insults that were hurled at them; but at last they became very nervous and apprehensive as to some of the murderous threats that were secretly levelled at them.

'As the newspapers have it, it would appear that on the night of the mysterious disappearance of Underwedge and Shout, Luke Stallybrass and his mates were working the night-shift at Number One Furnace; and he—Luke—says he saw two men enter by the private door to the works, and then steal stealthily along towards Number Two Furnace, then under repairs. He suspected that they had come on a desperate errand, and kept a sharp look-out from the top of the furnace where he was working. After a while he saw their blackened faces peeping over the parapet of the other furnace, "glowerin' " at him, as he put it. He, thinking to checkmate their murderous designs on him and his mates, stole, unobserved by the strange men, to the bottom of the shaft of the empty furnace, and removed the ladder by which they had mounted up the first scaffolding. He states that, as he and his fellow-workers felt driven to desperation, they were determined to sell their lives very dearly if the two strangers should attack them and that, as the clock struck one, the dark-visaged strangers began to make a move in the direction of the iron bridge between the two furnaces, and then began to walk over it. Luke says that he, Sweeney, and Clarkson then hid themselves in a recess in the ironwork—Sweeney being armed with a short gavlock—waited till they drew near, he previously having opened one of the iron doors of the furnace, so that he could see who their mysterious visitors were. When the strangers got close up to the three iron-workers, the latter could see their blackened faces, but failed to recognise them. As they passed by the open door of the furnace, a sudden impulse to dash them headlong into the furnace seems to have come over Sweeney, for he sprang out of his hiding-place, and knocked them both against the iron door of the furnace; and then there was a terrible scuffle, in which one of the mysterious strangers knocked Clarkson insensible. Then Luke rushed up, and he and Sweeney knocked the dark-visaged visitors right over into the furnace, and banged the door to. They went on with their work as if nothing had happened. They charged the furnace, and never spoke a word about the matter to anybody; and as they left the works, they told the timekeeper that young Clarkson was drunk. In a day or two their mistake dawned upon them, but they were too frightened to speak to anybody as to what they had done. They stayed on at the Forge for a month, and then Sweeney and Clarkson went off to America, but Luke found work as an iron-roller in Attercliffe, and it was not until his recent illness that he divulged the awful secret.'

'Has he given himself up?' interposed Mr Bantam.

'He has,' said Kenneth, 'and is now in the, custody of the police; but Mr Strongitharm, in an able leader on the subject, seems to think that no grand jury would bring in a true bill against him on a capital charge unless the bodies are found.'

'Exactly,' said Mr Bantam; 'young Tear'em knows what he writes about.'

Mr Bantam always pinned his faith to the *Sheffield Daily Standard.* There was no paper so well inspired in the provinces, he thought.

'It always sticks up for the Habeas Corpus Act,' said he; 'but it strikes me forcibly that some folks would have had you —yes, *you*—locked up on suspicion if not hanged, long ago, because you happened to be at the Forge that night, where they had come to ferret out your secret.'

'Yes,' said Kenneth, 'it were hard to forgive some folk for what they have said, but I have done so, although, God knows, the shafts of calumny were very hard to bear; and I know to my cost how they helped to intensify poor Connie's sufferings, and preyed upon her mind; but with regard to Luke's case I am of your opinion, Dandy, that the grand jury would throw out the bill; but if they did not, then no British jury would find a verdict of Guilty, however strong the circumstantial evidence, unless some trace of the bodies was found, and unless the pleas of strong intimidation and the dastardly threats of personal violence were effectually traversed or absolutely quashed.'

'He'll never go for trial,' said Mr Bantam; 'but if he should, then I'll get young Roger Osgathorpe to defend him, blest if I don't! He shall have fair play, for, as old Jerry Diggles once said of squabbling lawyers, "a devil-scrat to a devil-scrat, kale and kale, a fair field and no favour." '

'Of course there can be no trace of the remains,' said Kenneth.

'Well, 'said Mr Bantam, 'you're a bit of a metallurgist and chemist. What do you think, eh?'

'The thing is impossible, of course. Not even platinum could stand the fierce hot blast at times. Doubtless they were as effectually cremated that night as if they had been placed in a crematorium with a hundred horse-power hot blast to play on to them. Only imagine that I was that very night conducting my experiments in the mould-shed of the furnace wherein two of my principals were perhaps being roasted alive.'

'Just fancy, how terrible!' said Dandy. 'Why, they were actually roasted alive by two of their own spies whom they had set on to watch you and your experiments.'

'By-the-bye,' said Mr Bantam, changing the subject, 'how's Schlesinger getting on with your patent?'

'Splendidly, I think,' said Kenneth 'he tells me that he has got the golden medal at the Paris Exhibition with it.'

'The dickens he has!' exclaimed Dandy, 'and a German too! What a pity you sold it!'

'It is,' sighed Kenneth; 'but I get the honour, the fame, you know,' he said, with a half smile.

'How's that?' asked Dandy, with a vacant look of surprise.

'Because it is registered as Millwood's patent,' he replied, with an air of pride.

'Ay,' said Dandy reflectively, 'ay, lad, fame's all right enough so long as there's no kids to keep and no bumbailiffs to baffle.'

This somewhat trite aphorism of Dandy's fell rather flat upon Kenneth's ears, for he still had a genuine love for fame; although his views had not inconsiderably changed since the days wherein his ambition was first fired by his love for Connie.

'But,' continued Dandy, 'wouldn't he resell it to us, don't you think?'

'Hardly,' said Kenneth; 'Schlesinger knows what the invention is worth. He is a shrewd man of business, and would probably now want a long price for his bargain.'

'Well, we shall see him to-morrow maybe,' said Mr Bantam, 'and if you like I will sound him on the subject.'

'No, don't do that,' said Kenneth; 'but ask him straightforwardly if he will resell it to us. He knows why I sold it, so be very straight with him. But who are those ladies coming towards us?'

'Why, bless me, if one of them isn't Miss Starkholmes!' said Mr Bantam, in an undertone of surprise.

As they drew near to them, he politely raised his hat, and crossed over the road to speak to Hetty, whilst Kenneth sauntered slowly along on the turf by the side of the road.

She was clad in black, and wore a thin veil over her face, through which her dark violet eyes shone softly and dreamily sad. She looked pale and careworn, but very sweet. She was the first to speak, whilst her shy companion walked on. She spoke with evident emotion.

'Oh, Mr Bantam, I wish to thank you for all your kindness. It is so good of you to help me so much at this lamentable hour.'

'Oh, pray do not mention it,' said Mr Bantam, with a wave of his strong right arm. 'I shall be well repaid to think I have helped you in any way, Miss Starkholmes. Besides, I am your neighbour, remember; and as such I ought to be considerate, if not kind, at such a time as this is.'

'I know not how to thank you, sir,' she said, with downcast eyes, under which were dark tell-tale lines as of sorrow, that served but to enhance the beauty of her fair complexion. 'But God will bless you, sir, for your goodness,' she said, with misty eyes. 'But pray do not let me keep you from your friend. I am now on my way over the hill to Mrs Rutherford's at Nor' Royds Farm. They have kindly asked me to live with them for awhile. Mr and Mrs and Miss Rutherford will go with me to the funeral on Thursday. That is Miss Rutherford waiting for me, so I must bid you good-bye, as I must be off; but I shall see you to-morrow perhaps.'

She held out her hand. He took it in his.

'Good-bye, Miss Starkholmes,' he said lingeringly; 'but had we not better go with you over the hill?'

'No, thank you, sir,' she replied. 'You will understand,' she said, with a sort of sweet hesitancy, 'that I, at least, need none but my sisterly companion at this most unkind hour—so good-bye, kind sir, good-bye.'

Away she tripped towards her friend, who had just turned up the bridle-path that led to Nor' Royds Farm.

When Mr Bantam turned round he saw that Kenneth was a long way ahead of him, but he hurried along and soon got up to him, and as he did so he said somewhat excitedly—

'Ken, that was Miss Hetty Starkholmes! What do you think of her?'

'Well, Dandy, my boy, you can hardly expect me to give an opinion, as I only saw her face for a few seconds; but she seems comely, sweet, and fair. Her figure is certainly most ladylike. She rather reminds me of our dear old Belle Bantam.'

'Does she?' said Dandy gladly, and suddenly feeling that his ideas of Hefty's beauty were being flattered indeed. 'That's a compliment anyway,' he added.

'Did you not tell me that her father once owned considerable property about here?' asked Kenneth.

'Ay, that he did. Why, he was the freeholder of the three farms and homesteads we can see from this very spot. Nor' Royds, just over the knowe there, South Royds peeping over yon spruce plantation and Wild Hatch on yon windy hillock.'

'And he lost them?' asked Kenneth. 'Aye, he literally pawned them, inch by inch rod by rod.'

'To whom? Do you know?'

'To old Walt Weevil of Castle Folds, probably for a client of his.'

'Ah me! sighed Kenneth; 'it seems very sad to think that she, who perhaps was one time a happy young heiress, a mother's darling, should now be cast penniless upon the cold world.'

'Not while I— Ahem!' Dandy paused a little. Dandy was going too fast. He reined up smart. 'Yes, very sad indeed,' he said, 'especially as she was not brought up to rough it. Her mother was one of the Morewoods of Ringinglow Grange, and I am told that she was a most refined and gentle woman; and until her death she brought up her daughter Hetty as she herself had been brought up. Anybody can tell by Miss Starkholmes' manners, and by the way in which she speaks, that she has been brought up as a perfect lady.'

Mr Bantam's mind was of the progressive order. It was susceptible of being touched by the goodness of things. It was not of the unrevolving, vegetative stamp. It was not content to gravitate towards, nor be propelled along, the narrow groove of caste, with all its inexplicable idiosyncracies. As the world widened more and more in his view, so did his opinions change and widen. Without knowing it, he had become a happy disciple of and believer in the doctrine of a slow but sure evolution from a low and imperfect to a loftier and more perfect state. He was happy in this his undefinable creed, and therefore gladly allowed himself to be influenced and carried away captive by the superior gentleness and loftier ideals of Hetty Starkholmes, and of his friend Kenneth Millwood. As the Squire of Ringinglow, he had before felt conscious of a need for more polish, both in his ways and manner of speech; but now, under the influence of the gentle ground-swell, as of the lisping waves of love, especially when he spoke of Miss Hetty, he seemed to be quite lifted out of himself. He knew not that he was fast becoming a thrall to that delightfullest yet most relentless of teachers and taskmasters—Love.

After Mr Bantam and Mr Millwood had been over to Whirlow Bridge, they returned to the Grange by way of

Whiteley Wood, hard by which they sat down to admire the charming view of the Endcliffe Valley, adown which the stream, known by the infelicitous name of the Porter, shimmers and darkles through sunshine and shade, ere it is dammed up for the uses of those brawny-armed, ochreous-hued sons of toil yclept Sheffield grinders.

'Why don't you leave Attercliffe, Kenneth, and come and live up here? It would pull you together, old man.'

'That might be,' said Kenneth. 'Indeed Mr Lynnacre and I have had some talk about the matter, and it is already decided that I am to leave Attercliffe as soon as possible; but he suggests Bell Hagg or Fulwood, but I prefer Beauchief or Ecclesall. What do *you* think?'

'Well, I think you had better clear out of Attercliffe. Anywhere out of Attercliffe, but the further the better.'

'You don't seem to like your old haunts, Dandy! How is it?'

'Begging your pardon, I have not a word to say against the place, nor its natives either. I'm simply speaking to you from a valetudinarian or hygienic standpoint.'

Kenneth smiled. He wondered from what source Dandy had been embellishing his diction of late. He knew nothing of Dandy's recent literary acquirements, nor guessed he aught of Dandy's favourite author.

After they arrived at the Grange, they spent a very happy evening, and on the morrow, after the inquest was over, they drove over to Mr Otto Schlesinger's at Sharrow Birks.

Mr Dandelow Bantam was not long in introducing the subject of Millwood's patent, for after about a quarter of an hour's chat and exchanging of civilities, etc., he said—

'I was talking to my friend Kenneth here yesterday afternoon about the patent which you bought from him. Are you disposed to sell it? If so, I'm a buyer; and we should work it together, Kenneth and I, you know, if I bought it.'

Mr Schlesinger held up his hands in astonishment.

'Vat for do you want to risk your money, Mr Bantam? A birt in de hant is wort' two in de bush,' said he, as if he had a very bad cold.

'Ay, that's my business,' said Mr Bantam; 'but what's your price, that's all?'

'Vell! Vell! Vell!' said he scratching the top of his head, on which were still three or four hairs, 'dis is a very awkwat question, but I sud fink twenty-five t'ousant pounds was a fair price,' said he, as he stroked his stubbly chin betwixt the tips of his fore-finger and his thumb, while thoughtful wrinkles furrowed and refurrowed on his forehead, and his eyes rolled in a dubious, kaleidoscopic, manner, as though he were about to be "taken in" by the wily Britisher.

'Garrout!' exclaimed Dandy with incredulous amaze, and lapsing once more into the old Sheffield vernacular.

'Yes yes, dat is de price,' said the German; 'in fact I vas offert twenty t'ousant by my frient, Herr Taunitz of Middlesborough.'

'I'll give you a thousand pounds cash down for your bargain—there!' said Dandy.

'Dno, dno, dno; I tould not 'bate von tit or von jottle,' said the Teuton.

Later on in the evening, as Kenneth and Dandelow sat up chatting by the fireside at Ringinglow Grange, the latter observed. 'A'! I *am* mad!'

'Why?'

'Because you sold your patent to that German, Schlesinger. Aren't *you*.'

'Not at all,' replied Kenneth; but, on the contrary, I am delighted to think that someone appreciates and will probably benefit by my invention.'

'Ay, ay, that may be,' said Dandy; 'but it's not comforting, to say the least of it, to find you have sold something for £500 which is worth £25,000.'

'More comforting than finding I had palmed off some trashy invention for £25,000 which was only worth £500.'

'Trew,' said Dandy: 'but folks don't generally seem to think that way—at least not in Sheffield.'

'Perhaps not,' said Kenneth; but I don't suppose that Sheffield differs much from other towns in this respect; for even the sanctimonious Scot has been known to accept "saxtie gowden guineas" for a lineal descendant of Tam O' Shanter's grey mare Meg that had been condemned to the knackers; but with regard to the selling of my patent to Schlesinger, of course I cannot but feel sorry for my children's sake. They may now never have the advantage of a first-class education, whereas formerly I had hoped to he most liberal in this respect.'

'Ay, Ken, I know you would do what's fair by the youngsters, and if you'll take my advice you'd do well to go into partnership with Locksley Lynnacre. He's jannock, I'll warrant, if anybody is.

'But he has not even hinted at the possibility of a future partnership. Why do you say this?'

'Ken,' said Dandy gravely, 'Lynnacre's a man that means to forge ahead in the world. He is *not* a man overflush of capital. Now, supposing I were to find a thousand or two, don't you think that he would be only too glad to take you in as a partner, eh?'

'Dandy, my dear boy' said Kenneth putting his hand on the former's shoulder, 'your idea springs from a kind heart, and I am almost persuaded to accept your benevolent offer, but—'

'But what?' said Dandy, jumping up in surprise; 'surely you don't hesitate?'

'No, I do not hesitate, Dandy,' said Kenneth calmly; 'but you do not quite understand my principles. I have set my face dead against borrowing ever since I left my mother's roof, and I must confess that I feel too proud to begin now. Perhaps my pride is blameworthy, and it may have a terrible fall; but this one thing I can plainly see, that borrowers, for the most part, are a most thriftless class of men, prodigal of others' savings, extravagant, full of fond delusive hopes, and ready to curse the lender when he demands back principle and interest. I will tell you a secret, Dandy, which I have told to none, excepting to poor Connie. Just before I came of age, I had a thousand pounds offered to me if I would go out to the Cape. Whom do you think offered it to me?'

'I haven't the remotest idea,' said Dandy.

'It was my stepfather, the Rev. Theodore Millwood,' said Kenneth.

'You don't say so!' exclaimed Dandy. 'Deary me I thought he was as poor as a church mouse—but I thought he was your *own* father.'

'No, thank my stars!' said Kenneth. 'He knew what he was doing when he married my poor mother, but, as I have said, he offered to lend me a thousand pounds to go out to the Cape with.'

'And of course you were foolish enough to refuse it?' interposed Dandy.

'Exactly,' said Kenneth 'and I will tell you why. At first I was almost inclined to accept the offer, and had it not been for my secret love for Connie, I should have done so; but it happened that one day my mind was made up for me by my overhearing a conversation in our garden at Patmos Lodge between Mr Walt Weevil the lawyer and my stepfather. They were smoking and drinking Madeira underneath my bedroom window one Saturday afternoon in the summer, and I was lazily reading over and polishing up a love-sonnet to the ideal of my love in the room above them, with the window wide open. I distinctly remember Mr Weevil saying, 'If you want to get rid of a friend, either lend him some money or settle some old jerry-built cottages on him—that's my advice; and if you lend this lad of yours say a thousand pounds you'll, ten to one, get rid of him altogether. If he succeeds, well and good; you are rid of an incubus, and you have done a charitable act. If he fritters away the money, which is infinitely more likely, well and good, he will be ashamed to come back and confess that he has lost it; and supposing he were to write you a whining letter for more money, as young dogs will, then I might write him on your behalf a letter that would keep him quiet. What if I were to tell him you were not his father, eh?

‘ "For heaven's sake don't do that!" ' exclaimed my stepfather.

‘ "All right, Theodore; perhaps that's the ace of trumps, which we can play later on; but my advice now is, lend him the money. Its a trump card, and a clencher nine cases out of ten."

‘ "But what if he persists in refusing the money, and will not go to the Cape?" ' asked my stepfather.

‘ "Well, then, we must devise other means, said the lawyer."

‘ "What means?" said my stepfather.

‘ "Well, if you won't be shocked at what I say," ' said the limb of the law, ‘ "your next best plan is to rein him in so tight with bridle and bit, and so goad him with religious maxims—"

‘ "Come, Walt! Walt! I can't stand this; you forget I'm a minister! You are going too far," ' said my stepfather, with an air of annoy.

‘ "Ha! ha!" laughed the lawyer; "you needn't be so squeamish. Didn't you yourself first suggest to me the desirability of your marrying the widow Matilda when her son was only five months old, and before you knew for certain whether his father was dead or alive? Have you forgotten the Roche Abbey? Didn't you induce her to sign that deed of alienation, and induce me to swear to her all manner of lies? Come, come, Milly; this won't do, old boy; you should surely have counted the cost before you put your hand to the plough. It is now too late to go back."

‘ "Well, well, well,' said my stepfather; 'I will try him on again to-morrow after chapel; but it's a sorry job. My conscience smites me, Walt. It does really. Do you know that I feel as if I was drifting hell-ward."

' "No wonder!" said the lawyer, with a sneer, but cheer up old man. A few charitable bequests'll set thee sailing to the right port. Remember, Theodore, that you will have the means of doing incalculable good if all turns out right. What charitable bequests you can make! Good may come out of evil at times, you know."

'I did not hear any more of the conversation, as someone called for my stepfather, and he had to go away. I thought I must have been dreaming, but, as sure as fate, next morning after chapel he asked me whether I had reconsidered his offer to find me a thousand pounds to start me in business at the Cape.'

' "Yes, father," said I, addressing him as father for the last time, "I have considered it, and have come to the conclusion that I will never borrow a penny from anybody after I am loosed from my apprenticeship. I should not like to think I was under any obligation to anybody not even to *you*." I emphasized the word you. I shall earn my own living in a few weeks' time, when I shall be of age; and for certain reasons I had rather stay in Sheffield to be near my *dear mother*, I said with emphasis." He stared at me and looked annoyed, and then told me he thought I was "wayward, headstrong, and foolish," to refuse such a generous offer.

' "Some day you will be glad to borrow a shilling or two," he said, with a sort of sneer.

' "No, sir; never!" said I, as I left him to have a walk towards St Osyth's Cottage, thinking to myself: "Ah, I have discovered your secret! Now I know why you have kept me in with bridle and bit, and goaded me with religious maxims, and drowned the voice of every godlike cheer."

'That, Dandy, is the chief reason why I do not borrow. Old Weevil's sinister advice sank deep into my heart. He was right. Alas! have not I proved it to my cost, in the matter of that acceptance which I once foolishly signed? My friend has never troubled me since, not he.'

'Well, Kenneth,' said Dandy, 'you tell me a strange story, lad; and I admire your independent spirit, for I know it's been a closish shave with you many a time.'

'Yes, but I have weathered the storm so far,' said Kenneth, 'and I think I shall do so still. Mr Lynnacre is a kind man, and a just. In his hands I feel happy. He is now paying me four pounds a week, and I can manage to live in a little cottage for that, and be comfortable. What do you think of my taking St Osyth's Cottage, Dandy?'

'Why, I should think it would suit you to a T; but wouldn't it awaken within you many sad memories to live there?'

'No, Dandy, my boy; memory is my kindest friend. I have but few sad memories. They are mostly very happy ones. But before we go to bed let me tell you that I thank you as a good brother for your magnanimous offer, and I shall take the will for the deed, which surely shall not be forgotten in that sweet dawn of the eternal spring wherein all true fellow-craftsmen shall surely find rest.'

'Ay, Kenneth; that's a good thought to go to sleep on. Let's away to bed, lad.'

The two Masons went upstairs, and sweet and light was their sleep that night. Very sweet is the sleep of the upright and the just.

CHAPTER XVI

A CHANGE OF SCENE

Yellower than gold shone his glittering eyes, and his face too; and even the shiny top of his bald head was of golden hue. His few stray locks were white as snow. His cheeks were shrunken and hollow. His hands were bony and thin, and looked knotty, like whipcord beneath guinea-fowl skin, the swollen veins being in no measure concealed by the all-pervading saffron-yellow tinge.

He had a dry, short cough, which seemed to cause him considerable pain, as he sat with his legs almost inside the fender, close to the fire of his rather dingy little room, the bay window of which overlooked the shimmering sheen of Llandudno Bay, towards the Great Orme's Head. His legs were very much swollen, and he wore large roomy shoes made of soft cloth, padded with softer wool, and soled with thin leather.

In his skinny left hand he held a somewhat formidable-looking document, whilst in his right he held golden pencil, which ever and anon he used as twere to revise or excise something, or to jot down a new idea. At the back of the document, which was nothing less than the draft of the will of the Rev. Theodore Millwood, was an abbreviated summary of all his bequests that had been jotted down with the golden pencil, aforesaid.

He turned to this summary, and read to himself in a sort of hollow feverish whisper—

'The Millwood Memorial Chapel, £27,000; the W.M.S. £25,000, Home for Inebriates £7,000; W. Cent. F. £10,000; Society for the P.G.A.H., "£10,000; Beck't and D'k'n Ins., £5000: Royal Inf., £10,000; B. & F. B., £10,000; Kenneth M.

£2000; Mary Sturrock, £150; my Cook, £50; Walt Weevil, £5000, and residuary legatee.'

After he had totalled up his numerous bequests, he pulled out his watch, and saw that it was time to take his medicine. He reached it from a little table that was close to his chair. He got the phial in his left and the medicine-bottle in his right hand, and measured out the dose. His hands trembled as he poured out the draught. The Rev. Theodore was excited. The bare recapitulation of his immense riches had over-powered him.

In his nervous excitement he forgot that his medicine had been altered, and so he measured out the old dose of two tablespoonsful instead of one dessert-spoonful, as marked on the bottle in his hand. He drank off the dose at a gulp, put the phial down, and making a horrid grimace, said, 'Ugh! 'tis beastly stuff this ugh!' he shuddered, ' 'tis like essence of Harrogate water with the chill off.'

But as he reclined back in his arm-chair he felt a pleasant soothing sensation steal over him.

His pain seemed to be suddenly alleviated, whilst a delightful warmth seemed to glow within him.

Tremulously holding the document in his hand, he again began, as it were, to gloze upon those amazing figures; but somehow his eyes grew hazy. He rubbed them, but it was useless he really couldn't see the grand total. His hands fell upon his knees. What pleasant dreamy thoughts came over him!

'Fame! Fame! fame! Yes, I shall have fame,' he dreamily soliloquised 'yes, fame, when I—am —dead,' he dreamt.

He fell fast asleep.

The draft deed slid from his hand. It fell inside the old brass fender. There it lay awhile.

How he slept!

A pyritic nodule in the coal exploded. What superstitious folk call a "coffin" flew out. It fell upon the paper and ignited it, and before many seconds the draft was burnt to a thin white film of ashes.

How he dreamed!

He heard not his housekeeper's knock at the door. She had brought him a letter from Weevil of Sheffield. 'He is asleep,' she said softly; 'I will not wake him.'

As noiselessly as was possible, she swept up the ashes in the fire-place and fender, brushed the fire-grate bars, and left the room.

How deep was his sleep!

How he dreamed!

He dreamt that he was going nearer and nearer and nearer to a white dazzling light. ' 'Tis heaven,' someone whispered in his ear. He felt terribly alarmed. Never had he had such a shock.

His heart sank within him. He began to try and repeat a well-known prayer, but, strange, his lips were holden as of death. They were fast sealed, dumb. Not a prayer could he mutter. Brighter and brighter glowed the dazzling light; and then he heard a strange sound as of multitudinous wings flitting by him, but his eyes could not bear the fierce glare, so that he could not see anyone. Suddenly all was still as death. Blind with light, he stood alone. The silence was oppressive; but hark! he hears the far-off sound as of an angelus bell tinkling among Alpine dells; clear and silvern it rang through the startled air. Someone touched him, and took him by the hand. He started in an agony of terror. 'Open thine eyes,' whispered the voice of someone close by his side. He opened them, and saw millions of faces that he seemed to know and yet not to know.

'Thy sheaves? thy sheaves? thy sheaves? What bringest thou hither' cried out millions of voices.

He tremblingly held forth his right hand, in which was the draft deed of all his charitable bequests. He gave it to a bright, swift-winged messenger who bore it to the innumerable hosts, that seemed to be near, yet distant as the stars.

Erelong he heard tumultuous sounds as of millions of voices crying—

'A forgery! a spurious title-deed, unstamped of the King's signet! Away with him!'

Suddenly all grows dark, and someone comes up to him, and takes him by the hand again, and whispers exactly with the voice of his old school-master, the Quaker—

'Go thou and do one little deed of love, unknown to man. God's children on earth may haply be an-hungered and athirst. Go.'

How dark it became! He was falling, falling, falling to immeasured depths, as darker, darker, and darker it became, until, as it were, he came to the bottom of a terrible abyss. Blind with darkness, alone he stood. The darkness was most oppressive. He could feel it. Someone touched him and said, 'Don't start! Welcome to thine everlasting home, good brother!'

He opened his eyes, and there immediately before him saw a most hideous, loathsome beast, which came up to him and sang to him in a hoarse, croaking voice—

'I am thyself, whom thou hast wrought in Time,
Now deathless grown, untouched of age's rime;
Here thou mayst bide in these grim halls of death,
Nor list again to what the Daystar saith;
Bid soothfastness farewell and welcome guile;
Absence from good should make the sinner smile.'

A deep hoarse laugh of applause uprose as from millions of parched, unslaked throats. The laugh seemed to re-echo, and then to die away in the vaults of hell. So loud it was that it woke the dreamer.

'Good heavens!' he gasped, and beads of sweat stood out on his yellow brow, for the extra dose had done its work well. 'Where am I? Ah! 'twas but a dream, thank God; a dream—only a dream, "the baseless fabric of a vision." Oh, but how I tremble! How terrible! how terrible! oh, how terrible! Ah!' he gasped, 'I felt unfit, unfit yes, unfit for either he gasped, place. Mary! Mary!' he shouted as he violently rang the bell. She soon made her appearance. 'Mary,' he said in a breathless manner, 'why didn't you wake me before? You know that the doctor said I was not to be allowed to sleep after meals.'

'Yes, sir, but I couldn't wake you; you slept so very heavily. Lor', how you moaned, sir! I was nigh fetchin' the doctor, sir.'

'Mary, let me have a drop of brandy. I am faint—so faint. I think my heart will stop.'

He shook as an aspen leaf.

'Now,' said Mary, looking dubiously and somewhat severely at him, 'you know the doctor said it was slow poison.'

'Ay, ay, Mary; but this is a special case, you know. Give it me, and I'll remember you in my will, Mary. I'll remember you.'

She did as she was told, and gave him a small glassful. He felt better for it, he said, and then looked nervously around him as if he had lost something.

'Mary,' he half wheezed and half gasped, 'have you seen that paper?'

'What paper?'

'Why, that large lawyer's draft which came this morning?'

'No, I haven't seen no paper, sir.'

'Are you positive?'

'Postif certin, sir; but there's a letter come for you seemin'ly.'

'Eh? What letter?' he asked eagerly.

She handed it to him. It was from Walt Weevil of Sheffield. He opened it, and began to read, whilst Mrs Mary Sturrock, the housekeeper, left the room.

'MY DEAR THEODORE,—When you have perused and approved of the draft of will which I sent you last night, please return it, and I will have it engrossed at once.

'You will hardly be grieved to hear that Dick Starkholmes is dead and buried, and therefore, thanks to my diplomacy, the properties of Nor' and Sou' Royds and Wild Hatch virtually become yours (I will not say ours) for the price of an old song, so to speak. So much for the bottle!

'You will be pleased to hear that Sir Charles Brumfit & Co., Limited, have agreed to the terms I offered them for the minerals under old Anthony Bantam's properties at Conisbro' and at Swinton. The royalty which they agree to pay is £235 per acre, and a minimum rental of £5700 per annum.

'So much for black diamonds! This news should gladden your drooping spirits and make you feel young again in spite of the "jaunders," as your housekeeper calls it; but I hope you are getting better, and that we shall yet live to crack a few score bottles of champagne together, especially after this lucky bargain, which is as much resulting from my diplomacy as from the boom in the iron and coal trades.

'By-the-bye, old Jowitt, the mining engineer, assures me that the coal-field is as full of faults or "throws" as hell is full of devils. If this be so, we have made an excellent bargain with Brumfit's. *Caveat emptor!* That's their affair. So much for diplomacy. You ask me about K. M. I don't see why you should bother about him. He is still at Attercliffe. Certainly the confession of Luke Stallybrass somewhat alters the case with regard to K. M.; but this confession is probably a trumped-up affair. They are neighbours at Attercliffe (*arcades ambo*, so to speak).

'The patent which you ask about is K. M.'s. I think the *S. D. Standard* makes an altogether unnecessary fuss about this young upstart's crude and new-fangled idea. But why do you make a trouble about him? You have nothing to fear. The money and property at Conisbro', Swinton, and Mexbro' were absolutely settled on your wife four months before her husband, Mr Anthony Bantam, died. Doubtless he, being on a sea-voyage to Australia, was not aware of her condition when he made that will; but the fact remains he did make it, and there is no question about the validity of your late wife's settlement (which I made myself) of everything in a perfectly legal way upon yourself. Surely your conscience isn't pricking you about this?

'Old Stanilaus Bantam was cousin, and not brother, to Anthony Bantam of Conisbro'. Is your memory getting befogged? There is no other heir but K. M., and should you die intestate, of course the property will revert to him, which *will* never do.

'It is certainly somewhat unfortunate that you should have registered him as your son, Kenneth Bantam Millwood. The strangest and most unaccountable thing is that he, knowing you are not his father, and that his own father's property has been alienated by you, should have kept quiet so long. This caps my comprehension. It may be as you say, that he is too proud a man to ask a farthing at your hands; but my motto is, "Let sleeping dogs lie."

As you suggest, it might not be altogether impolitic to increase your legacy to him, seeing that you will soon be receiving an unearned increment (as the Rads. have it) of £5700 per annum from the unexpected source of coal royalties. He may not be the undeserving dog I take him to be; but if he is, give him another bone to pick to keep him quiet, in case anything awkward should turn up.

—With kindest regards and best wishes for your health, and hoping to be with you in a day or two, I am, my dear Theodore,

'Yours faithfully, 'WALT. WEEVIL."

'P.S.—After perusal, please burn this informal letter, which I have purposely marked private.'

Mr Millwood laid the letter on his knee. He looked positively alarmed. His face turned most ghastly. 'Five thousand seven hundred pounds!' he exclaimed; 'and all extra. An unearned increment indeed! It is appalling! positively appalling! I will not touch a penny of it—the cursed gold! I will wire old Jowitt to whisper to Sir Charles that the coal-field is full of faults and "throws" as— but O what a horrid expression!'

He sank back sighing all the breath out of himself at one deep sigh, and completely collapsed into his armchair with his head sinking low upon his chest. But his yellow glittering eyes opened, as he lifted up his head again, and inhaled a long, deep breath to make up for the long, deep sigh. He turned his head with a timid movement, toward the table by his side, just as a snake does ere it begins to uncoil and crawl towards its prey. His eyes glistened brighter, and became rivetted on the brandy decanter, which his worldly-wise housekeeper had purposely left out, thinking that as delay was the thief of time, it might also be the thief of a possible legacy; and she rightly argued to herself that the shortest cut to an early demise was *via* l'eau-de-vie. He helped himself liberally, and with trembling hands he uplifted the glass to his lips, the bottom one of which suddenly seemed to shelve out, like that of a rhinoceros waiting to catch buns at the Zoological Gardens. He drank eagerly. The Rev. Theodore had not forgotten that unpleasant habit of smacking his lips. But he was alone, and there was no one to feel annoyed.

'Ah!' he said, that does me good; braces my nerves that!'
Again he sipped.
'Ah! one has need of cast-steel nerves to bear such a shock without a shudder. Fancy! five thousand seven hundred extra!'

he soliloquised; 'and I have one foot two ay, two feet maybe in the grave! Terrible news! terrible news!' He sighed and gasped for breath, as he lifted the glass up to his lips again.

After a few minutes' meditation he again began to talk in a feverish, low breath to himself—

'And that Walt Weevil is my residuary legatee—calls me his good friend—going to crack scores of bottles with me—says, "Give Kenneth another bone." Calls him a sleeping dog—an undeserving dog—asks me to burn his letter, forsooth!' The old man laughed to himself in a sort of cachinnatory wheeze; 'Not I. "Unfortunate," he says, eh? "Unfortunate" that I should have had him christened as my son, my very son. Who says unfortunate? Ay, who says it?' He put his skinny hand up to his yellow, wizened, wrinkled forehead, and began, as it were, to think. Unfortunate? Is it unfortunate? Who says so? Ay, who says so?'

'The devil and his imps!' he exclaimed, as he thumped the table with his empty glass. 'Ay, ay, ay; I know him to my cost *now*,' he said, filling up his glass again, and again rivetting his eyes on the letter in a sort of vacant stare. 'And so Starkholmes is dead,' he continued, talking to himself, 'and old Weevil thinks I'm pleased; but would to God that he were living to kick old Weevil down the—; but stop! ah!' he said to correct himself, 'I am becoming uncharitable, positively uncharitable,' he reiterated, as though charity had not been dried up in his heart by greed of gold long, long years ago. 'But,' he harked back as a huntsman off trail, 'why shouldn't this poor dog *have* a bone? this undeserving dog! He never snarled nor snapped at me no, not when I turned him out of his mother's kennel. He never came cringing and whining, as I cringed and whined when I wooed Matilda. He never barked at my shadow when I stole his heritage, and told his mother hecatombs of lies. Did he ever flash a tush or fang at me, when I smote his flanks as a puppy? Did he skulk or growl when I sent him to bed supperless? No, no, no. He ever came up smiling when I cuffed and thwacked him. He never flinched at the gun. He stuck to his game, he did! But I? I? I? what have I done?' he sighed.

'Ha!' He started as if he saw that hideous form before him again.

'Ha! what did that terrible voice say?—

"Bid soothfastness farewell, and welcome guile."

'O that horrid dream! 'Twas terrible! too terrible!'

His head sank down upon his chest again. He closed his eyes, but only to see that hellish form which said to him, 'I am thyself.'

His thoughts were unspeakable. Fear seized upon him. He reached out his trembling hand for the bell on the table by his side. He clutched the handle and rang it violently. His housekeeper came up to his room in a great hurry, as if she thought something had happened.

'Mary!' he gasped, 'I'm ill very ill! I've had bad news about my money affairs, and I've had a horrid dream. Mary, I'm going to repent. Yes, repent,' he nodded.

'Don't,' she said in great alarm, 'pray, don't sir! O don't leave me penniless, sir!'

'I'm going to repent I say, *repent*; not cut you off with nothing, woman. Fetch me a lawyer, and I will make your portion ten times as big as I intended.'

'O lor'!' she exclaimed; 'how can I thank you sir? That comes of giving him his whack,' she thought; 'but where shall I find a lawyer, sir?'

'Next door,' he said. 'Go and ask if Mr Osgathorpe of Sheffield is in, and if so, ask him to come in at once—this very minute.'

'Yes, I'll strike while the iron's hot. I'll do one little deed of justice, if not of love,' he said to himself. In less than five minutes, as luck would have it, Mr Osgathorpe came in. He, it would appear, had taken a house at Llandudno for the season, and Mr Millwood had noticed the fact in the local papers.

'Sit down, Mr Osgathorpe,' said Mr Millwood, after the scant preliminaries of introduction between lawyer and client had been gone through.

Mr Osgathorpe sat down very carefully, for, being a massive man and a weighty, he eyed with considerable mistrust the ricketty cane-bottomed chairs which the Rev. Theodore had thought good enough to provide for any guests that might chance to call upon him.

'Mary,' said the old man, 'open the top drawer of my bureau there, and feel in the left-hand corner for some of my old sermon papers.'

Mary soon found them, and brought them to him, and left the room.

'Now, Mr Osgathorpe.' said Mr Millwood, 'I want you to make my will at once. I want to do one act of reparation before I die, and to prevent a certain old rascal getting hold of half my property. Make it as short as you can. Begin in the usual way.' The lawyer began to do his work in right good earliest, although he thought it no joke to be called from his lawn tennis to earn a few shillings from an apparently poor and jaundiced old man with the dropsy, living in a frowsy room without ventilation.

'The legatee's full name and address, please?' he asked, as he scribbled away.

'Kenneth Bantam Millwood, known as Kenneth Millwood, son of the late Anthony Bantam of Conisbro.' He was christened at Pontefract.'

'Never mind the christening,' said the lawyer hastily.

'But I do mind it,' said the old man peevishly; 'put it down, please.'

'All right,' said the lawyer, 'but it's unusual, that's all. His occupation?'

'Steel melter,' said Mr Millwood. 'His address?'

'Bessemer Street, Attercliffe, Sheffield.'

'An unconditional and absolute bequest?' asked the lawyer, who pricked up his ears at the name of Sheffield.

'Yes, all my real and personal estate, whatsoever and wheresoever situate.'

The lawyer smiled to himself, and thought, 'A rum old stick this, I'll warrant.'

'Excepting a sum to be invested in the Three per Cents. as an annuity for my housekeeper, Mrs Mary Sturrock, and a smaller sum for my cook Eunice.

'What sums, sir?' asked Mr Osgathorpe, putting the feather tip of the pen into his mouth, and looking out of the dirty window with a lackadaisical air.

'Say five thousand pounds,' said the poor old man.

'Eh? What?' asked the lawyer, opening his eyes and mouth a little wider, and staring at his queer old client as though he thought he was a lunatic.

'Five thousand pounds,' he repeated but stop,' he said reflectively, 'you might well make it ten for Mary and five for Eunice.'

'Oh, certainly,' said Mr Osgathorpe, laughing to himself, and now feeling certain that the old minister was off his head. 'Anything else?' he asked smilingly.

'Yes, I'd like to be buried in little Saint Tudno Churchyard. Five pounds will do for that. Non-consecrated ground is cheap, and there will be no mourners nor mutes, and no cards wanted, and no illuminated lies on a marble slab.'

'Nothing else?' asked the lawyer again.

'No,' said Mr Millwood; 'but it requires signing and witnessing. Is it written out all right?'

'Perfectly,' said Mr Osgathorpe. 'Are there two disinterested parties in the house who would sign as witnesses?'

'I'm afraid not,' said Mr Millwood; 'what's to be done?'

'Why,' said Mr Osgathorpe, 'there are two friends of mine playing lawn tennis in the garden below. Shall I ask them to come up?'

'Ay, that will do,' said he. 'Shout to them out of the window, if you can open it.'

Mr Osgathorpe, after breaking the rusty hasp and the rotten cords, succeeded in opening the window, and called to his friends.

In a few minutes the two lawn-tennis players appeared in the little parlour, and the lawyer told them what they were wanted for.

'Read it. It's my will,' said the yellow-faced decrepit old man.

Mr Osgathorpe gave a solemn wink to his friends, and began to read the document, while an incredulous smile lit up his jocund face. When he had finished reading, the testator signed it— "Theodore Millwood" and then Mr Osgathorpe's two friends witnessed the signature, signing 'Bryan Wolverton, Artist,' and 'Miles Bousfield, Sculptor.'

The feeble old minister looked at the wet signatures, and then looking up with his yellow glittering eyes, exclaimed with surprise, 'Bryan Wolverton! I should know that name, What! aren't you Kenneth's brother-in-law?'

'Mr Kenneth Millwood of Sheffield married my sister, if that's what you mean,' said Bryan.

'And are you good friends?' asked the sere old man.

'Rather!' he exclaimed; 'if I had only one plack or a *thrauneen* I'd share it with Kenneth, more power to him.'

'Then can I trust you with this?' said the old man, pulling Weevil's letter out of his pocket.

'You may trust me with all *you* have,' said Bryan; 'but if that letter has any legal bearing upon this your extraordinary will, then I think you might safely entrust it to the keeping of my sworn friend and lawyer, Mr Osgathorpe of Sheffield.'

The minister gave the letter to the lawyer, and observed—

'Remember, if there should be any squabbling over this my will, then this letter will quieten one at least of the litigants; but I implore you to deal kindly with him. Old Walt Weevil is bad enough, but I have made him what he is.'

He paid Mr Osgathorpe his fee, and then the latter, with Bryan and his sculptor friend, left the old man in his armchair, and went to the garden below; but somehow they forgot lawn tennis altogether, and began to be absorbed in all kinds of conjectures as to what the old man might be worth, and Bryan said 'The old man's sane enough, and it strikes me that old Ken'll come into some considerable property before long,'

'Yes,' said Mr Osgathorpe, laughing; if the old man can afford to settle £10,000 on his housekeeper, and £5000 on his cook, his son-in-law, the chief legatee, should come in for something handsome.'

Soon after they had left the old man the daylight began to wane, and the fisher folk began to anchor, one by one, their craft under the lee of the headland, while the wide stretch of sands became more deserted and more dreary every minute, and the shimmering sheen of the sea gradually changed into leaden hue. The old minister sat gazing out of the window on the dull expanse of the wide waste of waves. Drearier and darker it grew, and a big storm-cloud came looming o'er the headland. A few drops of rain were dashed on the dirty window-panes. The wind upsprang, and the few lingerers on the promenade hurried home. The rain began to fall in torrents. He could not see the headland any more, it was so dark; and yet the poor old man's heart felt more at rest, more peaceful, and happier, as he sat alone in that quiet room. He reached his hand-bell and rang it, as he wanted a light and some more coal on the fire. Mrs Sturrock came and lit the gas, and pulled down the shabby old blinds.

'Mary, I have repented. 'You will be well off when I am gone. Leave me alone for awhile. I will ring when I want my supper.'

And then the poor old man, warped and wizened, sat alone, gazing into the fire. The storm-wind beat heavily on the panes. Hark! he could hear the long resilient swish of waves; and suddenly he felt as if he was as a lost mariner, chartless on life's wild sea, and the tears fulfilled the old man's eyes as he lifted them up aloft and sighed—

'Thou, God, knowest that I sold my chart for gold. Thou knowest that I am a wreck, "drifting away," yes, "drifting away." '

Surely Kenneth's Muse inspired him prophetically when he wrote those lines—

> *'And seaward my dim eyes ope,*
>   *While the light in the lift grows drear,*
> *And behind me the wings are of hope,*
>   *Ringed round by rocks that are sheer.*
> *Lo! the landmarks of love seem shifting,*
>   *As the tide of my being cloth set*
> *To the bars where my soul is a-drifting*
>   *To leaward—unanchored as yet.'*

He looked at the document in his hand; the hazy eyes caught sight of some writing at the back of the will. It was part of the trial sermon he had preached at his chapel ere things corruptible had eaten deeply into his very soul. He began to read it.

"O my brethren, how rarely is the spiritual race an earnest one! Few there are that enter the field who ever dream of winning. Do they ever train? No. They never even hope to make one last spurt for a fourth-rate place. Borne on the lullaby waves of the sentimental gush of a Dead-Sea faith, they lapse along; yet their faith is never heartened to run the race that is set before them, as men and women fulfilled of the love of Christ. Their faith is not quick, nor does it earn wages in the gates of love.

"Brethren, I remember when I was a boy at school once saying to my master, just before our annual athletic sports, that '*I* wasn't going to train—not *I*; but that I would take my pot-luck in the Consolation Scramble.'

"The schoolmaster, who was a good old Quaker, said to me very gravely—

" 'Theodore, thy name ill befits a laggard in life's race.'

"I was puzzled. I was abashed. I slunk away as the meaning dawned upon me. I did not even dare to enter the Consolation Scramble. I was heartily ashamed of myself.

"Are there not some among you young men in this house of prayer who are going to take pot-luck in the Great Consolation Scramble?"

He had read to the bottom of the page. There was nothing more to read. He sighed as he laid the paper on his knee, and said, 'Would to God that I had kept the faith, the living faith —the faith that earneth wages in the gates of love! This is what I have lost.'

He then nervously reached his medicine and his medicine glass close to him; and as one error prepares the way for another, so he again took the wrong dose as before. He sank back in his chair. The same delightful warm glow stole over him. Soon he fell asleep. Again he began to dream. He thought that he was a boy at school again. Yes, it was Old Campo Lane. It was the day of the athletic sports. It was the last race—the Consolation Scramble for all unsuccessful competitors. The pistol fired. How he ran! He was winning, winning, winning; but no, someone outstripped him, and another, and another. He was exhausted. He could run no further; but his school-fellows came howling behind him, "lamming" into him, and shouting. "Go it, Milly; well run, Milly.' He came in a very bad fourth. He was "clean pumped," and fell into young Walt Weevil's arms in a dead faint.

The Rev. Theodore Millwood never awoke from that dream. The last over-dose had been too much for his weak heart.

Mary Sturrock came upstairs with his supper. She thought he was sleeping. She went to the window and pulled aside the blinds. She looked out. It was still pouring in torrents.

'How it siles!' she said, as she turned to her master. But he made no sound. She poked the fire, and the blaze shot up, lighting up his face. She started back.

'O master!' she cried, as she rushed to the door and shouted to the cook—

'Eunice! Eunice! Fetch the doctor! Your master's dead!'

CHAPTER XVII

A FEW YEARS AFTER.

The Millwood Steel & Iron Co. of Sheffield was the style of a firm possessing the newest and best laid-out works in that town. The firm was composed of five partners Mr Kenneth Bantam, Mr Dandelow Bantam, Mr Locksley Lynnacre, and Mr Otto Schlesinger, and Mr Roger Osgathorpe. The capital was £200,000, of which Kenneth had found half out of the personalty left to him under the will of the late Rev. Theodore Millwood. This will, when proved, had caused indescribable consternation in the hearts of some of the worshippers who had one time "sat under" the Rev. Theodore. What annoyed them beyond measure was the fact that he had always concealed from them his great wealth, and how he had obtained it. They boiled over with indignation at the thought of having furnished his house, and pensioned him off on his retirement, when at that very time he was possessed of at least £60,000, invested in the Three per Cents. Of course the scoffers made the most of it and rejoiced in the fact.

'Diddled his own flock!' they jeered.

'Left not a cent. to charities, the old scrat!' they laughed.

'Deceived his poor wife, the miser!' said others, in scorn.

Old Walt Weevil was wild with vexation, and threatened to upset the will; but Mr Osgathorpe's artillery had only to flash once, and the old lawyer sheathed his sword and bit his lips, and laughed a faint metallic sort of laugh, which subsided into an ironic grin.

But to revert to Kenneth. His heart and soul were in his work. Of course he need not have done another stroke, but he was a man who felt himself to be a trustee of large means, which ought to be used in the production of real wealth, namely, goods that are a joy to the maker and to the user. And besides this, he loved to work, and thought that the true philanthropy and benevolence consisted rather in finding his fellow-men work than in endowing eleemosynary institutions, however beneficent, albeit he was no niggard in this respect, as indeed some of the noblest institutions in Sheffield and Rotherham knew to their joy, and, so to speak, counted upon certain cheques coming in on New Year's Day almost to the very minutes. As a man of business, he was most punctual. Every morning, wet or fine, a carriage drawn by a pair of handsome greys left his house at Beauchief Holt at eight by the clock. He always drove himself; and laggard schoolboys and other way faring folk knew what time it was when they saw Mr Kenneth Bantam's carriage pass by. He was as punctual in payments; indeed, it was his pride not to allow an account to remain unchecked and unpaid in his office for more than twenty-four hours. His firm did not bank with any of the local banks but with the Bank of England. Some folks said that Mr Kenneth Bantam refused to bank with local institutions out of sheer spite, because one of them had ruthlessly sold him up in the days gone by; but this was not the reason. He was not the man to bear ill-will. He simply believed in stability and strength, and in having an unimpeachable credit. His firm made no bad debts.

'We cannot afford to do so,' he once said to a fussy buyer of one of the largest shipping houses in London, who wanted to pay by a three months' draft; 'we sell money's worth for money and not for paper.' Millwood's, as it was generally known in Sheffield, became a most prosperous concern, much to the envy of the partners at Ottcrclough Forge. "Safer than the bank" was a common saying with regard to their stability.

Mr Dandelow Bantam's and Mr Locksley Lynnacre's practical knowledge was an invaluable adjunct to the firm, whilst Mr Otto Schlesinger, who was an excellent linguist and a far-sighted diplomatist, succeeded in getting orders from almost every European Government for "Millwood's Patent" steel.

Mr Roger Osgathorpe, although he did not render any valuable assistance in the practical carrying on of the business, became nevertheless a most desirable partner, inasmuch as his legal opinion was not infrequently sought for at the works, and moreover, be it said, he was so exceedingly urbane and jovial that no monthly meeting of the partners seemed complete without Roger's jocund face. Kenneth Bantam in a moment of dry pleasantry ordered a special chair for him at Mannywell's; for, in all good sooth, Roger was a portly gentleman; and being unlike the Scotchman who "jok'd with deeficultie," he occasionally needed a buttress or strut to his chair what time he exploded with laughter at the phases of Dandelow's courtship, for that gentleman, be it known, was occasionally of too confiding a nature, not only about his love-affairs, but also about the fine arts, concerning which his opinions were undergoing a gradual change, and were becoming more and more at one with those of his brother-in-law, Mr Bryan Wolverton.

And with regard to Bryan, step by step he rose in his profession, and took a charming old-fashioned house on Hampstead Heath, whereabouts many of his brother artists resided. Soon after he had been elected an Associate of the Royal Academy his wife was presented at Court by Lady Jocelyn Fanshawe.

Bryan saw his wife as she started for the Drawing-Room, and thought he had never seen her look lovelier and sweeter before.

As he kissed her, he could not resist his old "bantherin" way.

'Adheelish, me jewil! troth an' it's like a dafy-downdilly rowled out av a bed of shamrock you are this minnit! Faix, 'tis fairly bewildhered the Horse Dragoons'll be at the sight av yer.'

As her carriage rattled along through Hyde Park, an old Sheffield acquaintance recognised her.

'Don't yer kno' that lady?' asked a shabby, seedy-looking fellow of his companion, as they were walking between Marble Arch and Hyde Park corner. They were spending a week in London with the view of avoiding certain writs from old Walt Weevil, who was pressing them for a client of his.

'No, Tom, I don't,' replied Robert Underwedge, whose nose vied with his friend Tom Shout's in point of colouring.

'Why, man, it's Mrs Wolverton!'

'Who?' said Robert, who spoke very thickly.

'Belle Bantam that was, as sure as heggs is heggs!'

'Oh,' growled Robert indifferently, 'let's be out o' this 'ere uncivallized place; I'm sick o' London. We're nobodies here, Tom, but we are somebodies at Diggles'.'

'Ay, lad,' said Tom; 'an' I've got a drouth on me like a helephant's, an' there isn't respectable bar parlour within miles, I'll warrant.'

Away they went, arm in arm, on the great downward trend.

In the course of time Kenneth Bantam Millwood, or Kenneth Bantam as he was generally named, became one of Sheffield's chiefest and wealthiest citizens, and was appointed a magistrate, which office he filled with striking ability.

It was a matter of considerable surprise that he did not marry again; indeed it may be safely said that it was one of the deepest concerns in the hearts of certain well-to-do and good-looking young spinsters, who never missed attending he church where he read the lessons every Sunday morning.

He was beloved by the menfolk and the womenfolk whom he employed on his model farm, and in his house at Beauchief Holt. He was kind and gentle to them, and by his good example provoked them to do good works, and never

magnified their frailties with a microscopic lens whensoever
their ancient feasts and welldressings called kith and kin
together, and when perchance certain village customs began to
verge somewhat upon the worship of Bacchus, when, it might
be, that discretion was occasionally put to rout.

It so happened that Jowitt's opinion of the coalfield which
Kenneth's father had with great foresight bought some forty
years before proved quite erroneous, as four large collieries
had thereon successfully worked and were working the great
Barnsley bed of coal which probably stretches as far as the
German Ocean.

This brought a large revenue to Mr Kenneth Bantam's
exchequer, which moneys he used to further developing the
industries of his native town; but when it chanced, in the
course of time, that a prolonged and deep depression came
over the fortunes of the coal industries, and "Best Hards" and
"Best Softs" became unsaleable save at unremunerative
process, then it was that Mr Bantam met his impoverished
lessees at Beauchief Holt and arranged a *modus vivendi* with
them, whereby the amount of royalty per acre was made
dependent on the average selling price of coal, an arrangement
which worked out satisfactorily, and which even some of the
most unbending and unflinching of landlords were, owing to
stress of circumstances, soon obliged to fall in with.

It was in the slack tide after this long wave of depression
that the old firm of Bantam, Underwedge & Shout came to
grief. Two of the partners had speculated in Glasgow
warrants, and had got heavily worsted. The old place came to
the hammer, and Mr Joe Troutbeck, the auctioneer, knocked it
down to Kenneth Bantam's bidding, who bought it with the
view of helping his kinsmen recoup themselves for the loss
which they had sustained through Mr Thomas Shout's and Mr
Robert Underwedge's ill-fated speculations, and thriftless, idle
and dissipated habits; and furthermore, Kenneth was proud of

the name of Bantam, and secretly resolved that none of the Bantams of Sheffield should suffer through others' reckless trading.

Kenneth's children, Bryan and Gladys, are at school yet, as is their foster-brother, Basil, whom they have been taught to love as their brother.

Young Bryan, whom his uncle calls a "broth of a bhoy," has not forgotten the story which Luke Stallybrass once unguardedly told him about those two poor men who fell into that big furnace at Otterclough Forge, and he now understands why the old ironworker suddenly became so disagreeably and inexplicably reticent about that tale.

Luke never went for trial, although his story was generally accepted as true. Some thought him mad. Others, wiser and more compassionate, thought it would be real kindness to assist him to emigrate. So it was that a good private subscription was raised for him and the last thing heard about Luke was that he was leading a most exemplary life as a foreman at some ironworks in Pennsylvania, and that he was "addlin' good money."

Billy Benskin still survives his mate Mike Callaghan, who died two years ago after he was turned out from Otterclough Forge. "Old Billy" is now living in retirement at St Osyth's Cottage, which is still lit warm with love, for a deep and forever enduring love has slid into his heart. Mr Kenneth Bantam is very kind to him, and treats him as an old friend. Every Sunday the old man hobbles to the chapel where he worships, and there often his thin, tremulous voice is to be heard as his heart is uplifted to the Allfather, who lives to love the aged pilgrims of the earth as the wee toddling feet that peep as briar-rose buds o'er "life's untrodden brink."

Honours are at last falling thick and fast upon Dandlelow Bantam, the Squire of Ringinglow. Not only is he W.M. of his

Lodge, but he is also Master Cutler—the veritable Prince of Hallamshire.

He deems it befitting the dignity of his new office to patronise the modern school of painters in oils and in water-colours; and *mirabile dictu*[18], his rather questionable old Crome, and a few more of some of his somewhat doubtful favourites, have been relegated to the walls of his second-best spare bedroom, while his one-time favourite author has not only been removed from its coign of vantage in his library, but has had to give way to other favourites, such as Speeches of Famous Men, The Art of Rhetoric, The Stones of Venice, Men who have Risen, Shakespeare, Don Quixote, and a goodly array of others; but above all, be it said respectfully, Mr Dandelow Bantam prefers the volume of The Scared Law, wherefrom, night and morning, at family prayers, he reads to all the members of his household the language of the soul.

'Sheffield's a werry nice place when you gets to be Master Cutler,' observed our friend the tramp from the sunny south to a bandy-legged groom, who had his shirt-sleeves tucked up, and a besom over his shoulder, and a short "dhudeen" sticking upside down out of his jowl.

'Begorra, 'tis thruth yer've spok wanst in yer life anyway,' said Dan'l, who was just getting over the effects of Mr Dandelow Bantam's first ball on his election to the Mastership of the Cutlers' Company. ' 'Tis rare ructions we had last night, an' it's a splittin' sconce I've got this marnin'—glory be to hiv'n!'

'Ay, ay,' said the old tramp, with a merry twinkle in his eye; 'it strikes me his riverence'll talk to you about the other place when you next goes on yer marrer-bones, Paddy.'

'Gerrout wid yer tamfoolerie!' says Dan'l. ' 'Tis a dhrop o' the ould craythur his riverence likes hisself, mebbe; but what are you prowlin' about here for, eh, honest man?'

---

[18] Wonderful to relate

'Prowlin'!' says the tramp, with disdain. 'By'r Lady! beggin yer pardin; but seein'; as the provincial press makes so much fuss about your master's generosity, I've jest walked up to Ringinglow to try and borrer a tanner or two from him. Is he purty generous?'

'Troth, he's the mischief's own hand at it and what's more, a nod's as good as a wink to him any day. But faix, the master's fairly worrited hisself intho a lather to-day, so beware, me bhoy, if he doesn't put the toe av his fut among the swally tails av yer coath by way of divarshun.'

'For what, young man?' asks the tramp.

'Bekase he's therribly excited to-day seemin'ly. Troth, he's as peevish as a hen wid a hundhred t'owsan' chickens, all drakes, begor'.'

'It's his liver's out of order mebbe, Pat?' says the tramp.

'Divil a bit,' says Dan'l; 'he's too fond av the wather-butt for that; but, to spayke thruth for wanst; 'tis an invasion av Saxon infanthry he's expectin' ivvery minnit.'

'What do you mean, Paddy? Are you tryin' to have the laugh agen me?'

'Faix, no' says Dan'l, 'it's an invasion of one, more or less —of Saxon childre, I mane. Don't yer undherstan'? Troth, man, the missus has tuk to her bed. What! Can't yer see wood for threes, yer ignorant *omadhaun!* But, tundher an' lightenin'! here he comes hisself, tearin' away at us. Look out for squhalls, me bhoy. Prepare to recave cavalhry; and hitch up the tatthered acreed av thouserin' beyant yet.'

'Hi! Dan'l, hi!' shouted Mr Dandelow Bantam, in a "mighty fluster"; 'put on your jacket at once, and run off to the telegraph office with these telegrams.'

'Troth an' I will, sorr; an' beggin' yer pardon, might I be so bowld as to ax whether it's another bhoy?'

'No, it's a girl this time,' said Mr Dandelow, smiling.

'Hiv'n be praised!' said Dan'l, 'it's a brace av all sorts yer've got now, sorr. Tare an' hounds! I'm off like lightenin'! Good news shall thravel quick for wanst anyway, regardliss av expinse.'

Away went Dan'l running towards Fulwood as fast as he could go.

The old tramp then went up to Mr Bantam, and reverently doffing his hat, and showing his thin white locks, said, 'By'r Lady! sir, have pity on these hairs.'

Dandelow eyed him for a second or two, and seemed to recognise the poor, old fellow', and, putting his hand into his pocket, pulled out the only coin he had in it—a sovereign. As his heart just then over-brimmed with thankfulness to heaven, he slipped the coin into the old tramp's hand. 'Here, take this,' says he; 'you are getting older every year I see you.'

'God bless you wid your childer, sir,' said the tramp; 'but do you remember me, sir?'

'Ay, man; didn't I once go bail for you after Rotherham Statutes?'

'Good heavens! I thought no one remembered that. But you must have altered since then, sir!'

'Yes, things have altered with me since I was a hair-brained 'prentice lad out for a lark, and I'm getting older and a bit wiser now.'

'And I am, sir,' said the tramp; 'and these old limbs'll hardly carry me to Froggatt Edge, which is a werry nice place when you've been to Sheff—'

But Mr Bantam could not stop to hear what the prosy old man had to say. He hurried away to see how his wife Hetty was getting on.

The aged tramp looked at the golden coin. How his eyes sparkled again! He breathed on it for luck, laughed to himself; and put it back into his pocket, uttering a benediction on the giver, and after carefully notching his old ashen stick so as to score that birthday more deeply on the fleshy tablets of his heart and mind, he fared towards the sunny south beyond Wild Hatch and Nor' Royds Farms, then over the moors towards Fox House, past Longshawe Bottom. Away he trudged till the sunbright locks of defeated day were tangled among jagged mountain peaks, while the tree-tops on the distant hills seemed fused and welded to the very sky. Then all was hushed and still, and the world seemed bathed in the mellowing afterglow of even; and erelong, as the ebon wings of night stole on apace, the aged tramp crept 'neath some dry, withered bracken fronds in the corner of a wood-man's hut in a copse at the foot of Longshawe Moss.

By-and-bye, as the jewels of that belted knight Orion sparkled and burned through immeasurable space, the out-worn and out-wearied pilgrim of earth, muttering something about 'Sheffield being a werry nice place when you gets to Froggatt Ed—,' fell asleep.

THE END

Dear reader

If you enjoyed reading *The Bantams of Sheffield*, I'd really appreciate it (and I'm sure Mr Balguy would have too) if you'd write a review on Amazon or Goodreads or whichever online sites you use: just a line or two would be great. It would be nice to see it being read again. I have no marketing department to provide support: reviews are all I have to promote this endeavour. I do it for a hobby just because I like to see classics back in print. It would take a lot of sales to even pay the minimum wage in terms of the time spent formatting this and making this as clean a read as possible. Thanks!

My website www.1889books.co.uk contains information on my first novel *The Evergreen in red and white* about the first Romani gypsy to play for England: Rab Howell. Set in Sheffield in 1897-98, it follows Rab through his last turbulent year in the city as he struggles to do the right thing having fallen in love with another woman. You can get in touch via facebook.com/SteveK1889, Twitter.com/SteveK1889 or e-mail me at stevek1889@gmail.com

Amongst other things, I have published three other forgotten classics: *The Skipper's Wooing* by W W Jacobs, *Spirit of Old Essex*, a collection of works by Arthur Morrison and *Put Yourself in his Place* by Charles Reade. *Historical Football Stories*, is a collection of the oldest football (soccer) stories in the world, and *Joe Stepped off the Train*, is a collection of short stories from which all author royalties go to the charity *War Child*.

Thanks.